A White Call

Serena M. Y. Rose

ISBN: 978-1-326-64023-1

PublishNation, London
www.publishnation.co.uk

Acknowledgements

I started writing (word processing) this book in 2007. That was when my spiritual journey began. Much as I was distressed with what was going on in the outer world, I found occasional moments of total bliss in my own inner world. My ideas flowed from there towards creating this work of fiction.

I express my immense gratitude to God for blessing me with deep insights, dreams, ideas and imagination that motivated me to write this book.

I would also like to thank all these people from the bottom of my heart: my beloved parents for encouraging me to probe for deeper meaning of life through the paths of serenity, spirituality and mindfulness, they believed in me and thought the world of me; Kareen Rahman for proofreading and editing the first chapter of the novel and for her thoughtful comments on subsequent chapters that enabled me to make significant changes to the story; for her useful tips on novel-writing and thought-provoking ideas that came up during our small talk; Sarfaraz Rahman for helping me to embark on vivid mental journeys to Cambodia and Japan, especially to the awe-inspiring Mount Fuji; for familiarizing me with Japan and its culture and for Japanese words and phrases, and also, Eri Uchimura for kindly doing some Japanese translation; Dr Angela Debnath for inviting me to Rome and for her insightful comments and ideas that surfaced during our endless conversations on various riveting topics; Joseph Rochlitz and Ida Bollito for tirelessly translating and ensuring accuracy of Italian words and phrases; Matthew Chalmers for keeping me informed about local and world events, and technological advances; Jonathan Tabizel for proofreading the novel, this assisted me in doing the final proofreading and editing; Nadia Lodhi Wahhab, Dr Karishma De and Tariq Sheik for ensuring accuracy of Hindi words and phrases and for suggesting their suitable spellings in English.

I wrote some poems and phrases myself in languages other than English. However, I had to turn to the experts for doing Italian and Japanese translation. I trust that they did their best based on the information provided.

I thank Mr C. Srinivasan, the Project Director of IGS (Indian Green Service) who kindly communicated information about the eco-friendly project currently implemented in Vellore in Tamil Nadu, India.

I am truly grateful to my teachers, trainers and mentors Mahmuder Rahman, Les Benney and Louis de Souza for teaching me, inspiring me and instilling in me the message: *You can do it*. Their high expectations of me helped me to rise above my abilities. Their sage and insightful words kindled my imagination and ideas.

I am forever grateful to my sisters Mrs Mani Debnath and Mrs Sajeda Malek, who are also my guides and pathfinders, for their words of wisdom, encouragement and vivid accounts of events in the world.

My mother was a short-story author and my father was a novelist, a poet and a playwright. Their literary work has inspired me and has given me an impetus to try my hand at writing a novel. I am also inspired by the literary work of great poets and authors: Tagore, Tennyson and Mark Twain.

I draw inspiration from the intriguing findings of the researchers and scientists Dr Rupert Sheldrake and Dr Masaru Emoto and from the work of the modern-day spiritual master Anandmurti Gurumaa. I have referred to their teachings and findings without which my work would have been incomplete. Therefore, I am eternally grateful to them.

I thank Enid Passmore, Flora Alam, Huma Rizvi, Mary Chaib, Anne Rowe, my children, my godchildren, my siblings including my dear sister and author Nazneen Rahman, my nieces and nephews, my cousins, my neighbour Rose, my friends and colleagues, my students and scores of well-wishers for their continued support and encouragement.

I must mention my adorable young friends Serafina, Isabella, Jesse, Daria and Neal whose inquisitiveness and imagination steered me towards looking inside children's minds.

I am indebted to Google and Youtube for providing a reservoir of knowledge and information that I needed for the story.

Last but not least, my heartfelt thanks go to my publishers, David and Gwen Morrison and their dedicated team for their patience and kind assistance in printing and marketing the book. They literally walked me through the procedure with great care and attention.

Readers do not have to agree with my views and ideas but, in line with what one of the characters in the novel says, I will be more than happy if only one reader gets inspired by this book!

Chapter 1

'WHERE ARE ALL THE BIRDS?'

Grace directs the question more to herself than her husband, sitting on the concrete seat in the open space in Trafalgar Square in London, tilting her head demurely towards Paul who is absorbed in his pocket book. His reading glasses are perched snugly half way along his nose.

On the last day of 1999, Grace inhales a lungful of not-yet-polluted morning air and muses over scanty pigeons that were once notable features in the open square. The grey-white clouds that match the shade of her hair are floating against the backdrop of wispy blankets of white clouds. The sky behind the clouds is blue. The sun has gifted the city with a fresh morning. Scattered pigeons dive onto the ground of the square in search of food.

'Paul...remember...the pigeons used to flock around us? It wasn't too long ago.'

'Yeah, but they'll have to go. They are apparently seen as health hazard,' Paul informs Grace. He briefly looks at the pigeons before turning his attention back to his book. Frenzied, food-seeking birds circle courageously around Paul and Grace as if to compensate for their fellow endangered species. Some of the other birds cautiously check the vicinity before pecking on carelessly littered food crumbs.

'What about robins and sparrows? Are they going to disappear too? They rarely visit our garden these days.'

✿

Amidst the pigeons and the crowd, two members of a TV crew walk towards Grace and Paul with the intention of asking them questions about their hopes and expectations for the New Year, the New Millennium. They seem to have appeared out of thin air in the middle of the square. One of them, a lanky fellow, is assessing the public's willingness to participate in the impromptu show and asking them questions; the other, his go-getting female colleague, is video-recording. They have been here since daybreak; now morning is slowly but surely creeping into midday. The weather is relatively mild in London at this time of the year; it is Friday - the beginning of a long weekend with the prospect of a public holiday on Monday, the third of January 2000.

The crowd has not fully built up yet.

✧

Earlier on, with his wireless microphone, the broadcast journalist paced towards a woman. In tune with the fair weather, she was wearing a black and white knee-length double-fronted check coat; its knee line rested on her patterned black tights that complemented her low-heeled, tall black leather boots. She was standing by one of the gushing fountains in the square, talking to her Chinese female friend.

'Got a moment?' the journalist asked. Without waiting for a reply from the woman, he continued, 'We're from Community TV.' The woman flung her crinkled black wrap around her shoulder. Slightly lifting her black woollen hat, she glanced inquisitively at the enquirer. The journalist was a little surprised when he properly looked at her,

'Look who's here!' He coughed a little and fired a question at her, 'Hello Anne…good to see you…erm…what are your hopes and expectations for the fast approaching new Millennium?'

Anne looked smartly at the camera and replied,

'Hello, I'm Anne Wilson,' her eyes wandered in search of a fitting answer to his question. She said,

'Well, I'd like to see more peace and harmony in the world.' She paused for a moment and reflected on what she has just said. Her fleeting thought about people coming out of their shelters on New Year's Day and hugging each other to start the peace process made her grin. However, the beginning of such a process had to start someday, somewhere – she reasoned in her mind.

'What about you, ma'am?' without repeating the question he shifted the microphone towards Anne's friend. She responded animatedly,

'Hi, I'm Sue Li…erm…I'd like the warring countries to call a truce or to stop the wars, at least, for a year.'

A passing group of youths overheard her statement; they smirked at her comment as if to say:

A year without wars? You must be crazy!

2

They then strode sideways to shy away from the camera and proceeded towards the wide steps leading to the National Portrait Gallery behind the square. Some people were sitting on the steps; they were just chatting and having a good time in the pleasant ambience.

At the top of the steps, a man stood behind a wheelchair in which his thirteen-year-old son, Jamie, was sitting restfully. They were looking down at the leisurely view of the square: the crowd, the fountains, the scattered pigeons, the statues of Nelson's Column and the four lions, distant cars and London buses. Jamie broke the silence and said,

'I wonder what mum's doing right now,' the image of his forever busy mother came into his mind.

'We're giving her a break, son.'

'Good for her,' Jamie sighed. The man steered him away from the steps and headed towards the ramp for wheelchair users. Today he took time off for a day out together!

○

Down the steps, Sue glanced sideways at the sniggering crowd of youths and continued, disregarding their attitude,

'If we really have faith in a holy God who has created all things, we will never hurt another being because that will be the same as hurting ourselves.'

'Thanks Sue,' there was a trace of amusement in the journalist's voice; he shifted the microphone towards Anne who appeared keen to add more to the discussion.

'I personally think that not everyone wants the same thing at the same time, be it peace or war,' Anne says. She then whispered to Sue, 'Wish Millie was here.'

The man catches her hushed remark. 'Who's Millie?' he asks.

'She's a friend. She'll be here any moment.'

'So Anne, you're into working in documentary films. Any project in the pipeline?'

'Yes, there is. Some consider it controversial, that's all I can say for now.'

'Interesting! And Sue, what do you do for a living?'

'Well, I'm her assistant. Joined the team recently.'

The video camera panned slowly across the scene, vertically filming the 52-metre statue of Nelson's Column standing tall atop a six-metre granite pedestal in the square with its four guarding lion statues at its base.

☼

Images of shops, people, streets, cars, buses and distant advertising boards behind the column come into view on the camera monitor once again; it then displays the fountains and the concrete seating area on the edge of the square where Grace and Paul are resting and speculating about the disappearance of the usual flock of pigeons. They have come here countless times. They love coming here; the place never loses its appeal. Trafalgar Square, surrounded by many interesting features, has ceaseless charm to attract tourists and natives alike throughout the year, come rain or shine, especially today: the end of the year, the end of the Millennium.

On hearing the Millennium question Grace comments,

'I think I'd love to see everyone being nice to each other, as they already are, but we need more of that.'

Paul differs in that for him *everyone-being-nice-to-each-other* exists only in an ideal world, adding that this could only be brought about if enough people are empowered with more knowledge and understanding in critical areas of their lives. They will then need to use this perception to experience their lives differently.

'And how's that possible, sir? The camera now zooms in on Paul.

'This is possible through a specific shift towards collective consciousness. Otherwise just like the *invincible* ship, the Titanic, in slow motion heading directly towards the tip of the iceberg, the most precious *earthly ship* could come to a halt, destroying its beauty, strength and its legacy along with the dreams, morale and faith of its people.'

'My hope is', Paul continues, 'that the much-needed shift in our collective awareness is already taking place and will gain enough momentum maybe during our lifetime or during the lifetime of the next generation towards building a more loving and peaceful world.'

'How do we know that this is already happening?' the journalist asks.

Paul raises his eyebrows and says, 'Look at what you're doing right now, for instance. You have ventured to ask us thought-provoking questions. Besides...,' he pauses to take a deep breath, 'When things like that happen, you just know it.'

The reporter thanks them for their comments and before leaving, asks what they do for a living.

'We're both retired teachers.'

'Was this the surprise Lillie was talking about?' Grace whispers to Paul.

'Maybe. We're staying here for a while, we'll see what else is in store,' Paul sounds enigmatic.

The couple arrived here early in the morning. Their daughter Lillie told them that a pleasant surprise would be awaiting them in the square.

'What's the surprise?' Grace asked.

'It wouldn't be a surprise anymore if I told you,' Lillie laughed. Paul chuckled. He had some idea about what it was going to be as he had browsed through the events section in the newspaper earlier on.

✿

The TV crew move to a different location in the square. It's time to record the next important segment of the show. The popular entertainer must have arrived here by now. It is not difficult to spot him in the crowd.

✿ ✿ ✿

Chapter 2

WHEN YOU ARE READY, CLOSE YOUR EYES...
Take a deep breath... gather your anxious thoughts as you inhale.
Exhale, let go of your thoughts and just r-e-l-a-x...
Relax your head, neck and shoulders.
Again, inhale deeply...exhale fully.
Relaxation is flowing through every cell in your body.
You will soon take an awesome journey to a place of your imagination.
You can go to amazing places in your imagination.

Maya closes her eyes – an influx of calmness gradually overcomes her. A soft-spoken female voice echoes into her ears through the headphone. Soothing Tibetan singing bowl music is playing in the background. Its sound frequencies, featured by multiple harmonics, spread blissfully into her veins. Gentle rubs of a wooden mallet along the rims of varying sized bronze bowls are producing the gong-music that blends in harmoniously with the sounds of raindrops presently falling outside the block of flats. Maya's flat is on the third floor.

✿

Millie - Maya's daughter - bought some self-help books and meditation compact discs. She left them in the flat in a disorderly manner; her sole intention in doing this was for Maya to notice them. Millie was certain that her tidy-freak mother would put them away or invent a place for them, and she might read one of the books or listen to a disc out of curiosity. Millie read the books herself; some of them were uplifting, others were somewhat mystical and complicated. She also made an attempt to do the guided meditation; this did not have much impact on her fidgety mind, but she thought that this may help Maya. Millie deemed it a possible solution to the grief that had befallen them.

✿

Today, Maya picked up a meditation compact disc, checked its cover from all angles and found the caption on it quite interesting:

Relax your mind and body. Be in the realm of bliss.

She decided to try it out. She somehow felt the urge to do this after briefly sighting that woman in her garden plot from her lounge window. It happened just before the rain! The woman was staring admiringly at the enormous sunflowers in the garden. She was wearing a glossy golden outfit and a golden scarf; not a hair was out of place in her carefully set chignon. She was tall and slim and looked graceful and fashionable. Was she a friend of Barry's, one of the residents in the block, who was building a nature reserve for frogs, toads and newts a while ago with his little girl Sylvia or was she a trespasser? Maya wondered. The woman looked familiar. Maya racked her brain but could not recall where she had seen her.

While Maya was contemplating on calling Mr Baker, the concierge, the woman noticed her. She broadened her smile; there was compassion in it. Maya was trying to have a better view of her from behind the curtains. Then she reached out for the phone handset to call Mr Baker. Within a second, the woman was gone. Instead of feeling alarmed, Maya felt peaceful. She abandoned the idea of calling Mr Baker; she rather yearned to do something fitting to hold the calm feeling. It was then that she spotted the meditation disc.

✧

After that initial pleasant experience of meditation, Maya feels a constricted feeling around her shoulders. This makes it hard for her mind to focus on the calming exercise. Her mind wanders off. Deep breathing, as communicated by the voice in the guided meditation, helps her to relax.

The female guide then asks her to count her breaths:

...in and out, in and out...

The guide instructs her to listen to imaginary birds singing and water splashing. The unreal becomes real in Maya's imagination aided by the sounds of nature. In her imagination, she finds herself

7

on a canoe, smoothly gliding along a stream. She well-nigh perceives the motion of the boat.

The guide continues:

You will shortly arrive at the riverbank.

*You are nearing the bank....(*Maya hears the splashing sound of the waves while the boat makes its way through the water).

You are now safely mooring the boat...(the imaginary manoeuvring of the boat comes to a halt).

In her mind's eye, she disembarks and makes her way through a marshland. She hears her own footsteps:

...squelch, squelch, squelch.

Maya is enjoying the experience in her visualization. She has never felt so calm and relaxed before.

The voice now asks her to visualize a route through a dense green forest that meets a mountain path; she hears the swish of the cool mist coming from a nearby waterfall. The mention of the *green forest* triggers her mind into thinking about something that goes back to her distant past or rather someone else's distant past!

Her prattling mind becomes alive once more in an attempt to find a link between the image of the green forest and her stored-up memories; then her thoughts return to the earlier scene of her own garden plot where she grows flowers and vegetables. The weather has not been very hospitable to the soil this year; besides, she did not toil hard enough in the garden the way she did in her aunt and uncle's garden. There were not many bees around to aid pollination, but her sunflowers have done well this year. The thought of the sunflowers reminds her of the mysterious lady!

If your mind wanders, focus on your breathing.

The voice announces this as if it is aware of Maya's wandering mind. Maya has missed parts of the guided meditation because of her lack of concentration. The voice continues,

Look closely at the city. It's an ancient city that has remained flawless for years.

Maya cannot figure out exactly what city the guide is referring to as she has missed some parts of the instructions. Nevertheless, she tries to create a vague image of a city in her mind; the conjured up image of the city does not bear any semblance of an ancient city. The street layout, buildings and pedestrians represent a familiar scene of today's world. A dim image of a building with a pastel green dome becomes visible in her mind's eye; a pulsating life exists within. She can hear echoes of footsteps and sweet and sharp clinking and rattling of cutlery on plates. People are doing different things in different parts of the building. Maya labours within the dark confinement of her closed eyes to create more detailed images. She cannot. It is akin to a dreamlike state in which one strives to do something or catch a better view of something, but it does not come to pass or it is delayed, prolonged or lost into nothingness.

She stops trying.

She lets it go.

A sense of calmness now envelops her. She suddenly wakes up from the reverie - what an amazing experience it was even with the intrusion of her random thoughts! She hopes to pay more attention next time!

Millie must have done the guided meditation herself since the disc belongs to her, but she has never mentioned any outlandish experiences! Then again, Millie does not tell her everything! Maya is careful not to encroach on her privacy. What she considers as normal parental concern or curiosity has often been misconstrued as her being unnecessarily inquisitive and patronising.

✧

Maya looks out of the window. The rain has subsided now with its last slow, tuneful drops. The dark grey clouds are still hanging around; and across their span, there is an enthralling expanse of dense, milky clouds trimmed with shades of saffron red and gold.

Within seconds, the backdrop changes and blue splodges of the sky peek through the clouds. It is not going to rain again as the birds are flying high, heralding the good news of imminent pleasant weather!

Maya yearns to share her new experience with someone - Millie is the right person. She could also tell Radiant Rosie.

☼ ☼ ☼

Chapter 3

FROM HIGH UP AGAINST ONE OF THE LION STATUES IN Trafalgar square, a Rastafarian, wearing a quilted brown hooded jacket and faded blue jeans, has been inspecting the filming. He has some idea about what is going on down there; he wants to get a better view of it. He jumps down, walks a few steps towards the place but takes a detour and ends up where Marcos is. Marcos is a popular country singer who is currently roaming about with his guitar in search of a suitable spot. He finds one, a few yards away from the fountain to the east of the square; he opens his portable seat and sits down on it.

Community TV commissioned Marcos to come to the square on the last day of the Millennium and sing to the public.

'What should I sing?' he asked them.

'Just sing what comes to your mind,' came the reply.

☼

Marcos starts strumming his guitar and humming along. Like bees to flowers, the TV crew march towards him. The Rastafarian squats hesitantly near Marcos, his eyes are aglow with amazement; he is bewitched by the singer's melodious voice. Marcos briefly grins at him and busies himself in plucking the guitar strings and his voice in singing a song of praise - the song that came to his mind:

You are God of ailing hearts,
You are God of fallen stars,
You are God of the wanderers
You are God of the new world
You are my father, my shepherd.
My heart sings in awe:
Hallelujah, Hallelujah, Hallelujah.

Those who instantly recognise the long-haired, jolly-faced Marcos gather around him. They are amused to see the Rastafarian who promptly participates in the act with his own made-up words:

Oh yeah, you are one God, one love, one hope.
You are my father, my shepherd.
You live through me, walk through me and talk through me.
Oh yeah, you are one God, one love, one hope.

He then sings along with Marcos as if he has sung the song before. The spontaneous act goes on for some time, pulling in more audience. Marcos apparently takes pleasure in singing with the uninvited singer who seems to have good vocal skills.

Both of them are now singing the finale:

My heart sings in awe: Hallelujah, Hallelujah, Hallelujah.

Some spectators join in. Their collective melody fills the space with enchanting echoes. The scene reminds the broadcast journalist of Paul's reference to *collective consciousness.* The words become meaningful through the crowd's mass participation.

The song ends with a hum and the last phase of the strumming of the guitar. Marcos gets up from his seat and embraces his singing companion.

'Hey man, you sing very well. What's your name?'

'Ruben'.

'Hello Ruben, I'm Marcos. It was nice singing with you.'

'Praise di Lord,' Ruben nods coyly.

The camerawoman continues to record the natural flow of their conversation. Marcos waves at the camera. He then asks Ruben,

'Are you trying to make the most in God's world?'

'Not just tryin', makin' di most in God's world, man. And God's people are doin' di same right now. Praise di Lord.'

'Who are God's people?'

'You, me, dem… everybody widin and beyond our perception.'

Not quite catching what he has said, Marcos rejoins, 'So Ruben, when shall we see you again?' a hint of hurriedness in his voice implies that he needs to continue with the one-man show.

'Tis not to our liking to come back here but when we hear a *new world* emergin', we'll turn up...Praise di Lord.'

Ruben disappears into the crowd as fast as he appeared, humming the lines from the song. Marcos carries on singing; the viewers are still growing in number.

The pleasant winter sun with its warmth and glory is well on its way towards the afternoon. After recording a few of Marcos's songs, the reporter and his assistant leave him alone with the audience and meander around the square where people from varied backgrounds constitute isolated circles.

✿

On the camera monitor, a woman's anxious countenance is now visible. She is expressing her opinion about what she wants to see in the new millennium,

'I want to see an end to abuse to women.'

'You mean, women in specific parts of the world?'

'Women all over the world...some mistakenly believe that this only happens in certain places. Well, more often than not, this is the case *everywhere*,' she stresses the last word.

✿

The reporter occupies a corner of the square with busy London scene behind him. He wraps the show up by saying:

'We've been listening to people's views and comments about their hopes and expectations of what they want to see happening in the fast approaching new Millennium. Their comments, by and large, were about their expectations of more peace and harmony in the world, of the end of wars, poverty and abuse to women, and of raising human consciousness - the process of which has already started as claimed by one.

People are gathering here to embrace the new Millennium and to say 'goodbye' to the old one. In a few hours' time, the crowd will grow bigger. Right now, a crowd is also building up around the newly erected London Eye, the Ferris wheel, by the bank of the River Thames. Our evening footage will also cover the area. We will be back later in the evening to countdown to the New Year – the new Millennium.

This is Mike Callaghan from Community TV at Trafalgar Square.'

The team pack up for now.

✿

'I forgot to mention to the reporter, dear,' Grace gets up from the concrete seat and says, '...that if only we could learn to hold the joy longer, you know, during the celebrations of the New Year, Christmas...,'

'And what about the Olympic games? They connect the whole world for a month or so,' Paul installs himself next to Grace.

'Yes, they do, but things like that are short-lived, they leave us feeling lethargic,' Grace says.

'Who knows, there may be simpler ways to prolong the joy; we ought to look elsewhere.'

'Where?'

'Well, for now, let's go over there. Marcos, our singing star - our surprise - has already arrived.'

The two mingle with the crowd.

✿ ✿ ✿

Chapter 4

IT IS MONDAY, THE 5TH OF JUNE 2000.

The morning sun with all its glory adorns Victoria in London. Its warm rays roll softly onto buildings and on the sprouting green vegetation around them. Nature has woken up from a good night's sleep; it is gurgling, buzzing, chirping and swishing across the region, imbued with fresh, unpolluted morning air.

The pastel green dome of a notable building in Victoria shines with renewed vigour. A food hall right under the dome of the building with a neat arrangement of round, wooden tables and chairs offers English and continental breakfast in the morning followed by a selection of appetizing food for lunch and dinner. Specially brewed coffee tickles the nostrils of coffee lovers. The mixed whiff of cooked breakfast, eggs and sausages, awakens famished customers' morning taste buds.

Leon Tyler often attends office meetings in this building; the conference room in the building is hired for this purpose. The head office, his base, is in London Bridge – a booming spot for business and culture by the River Thames.

Leon came to the Victoria venue early today to flip through the article on environmental issues in the departmental newsletter. The contents of the article will be examined in today's meeting. It is calm and quiet up here around this time of the day. The early morning brawl he ran into on the train is now behind him. The tranquil setting inside the building is a total contrast to what he had experienced inside the carriage of the underground train this morning.

✿

This morning, he left his modern studio flat and walked towards St. John's Wood underground station to travel to Victoria. He bought a newspaper from a kiosk nearby and got on the train. The train was packed as usual. The rush hour had begun; fortunately, he found a seat to himself on the train. He sat down, smiled casually at an elderly gentleman sitting next to him, opened the newspaper and quickly cruised through the headlines:

No tears – just a silent squeal for a daddy lost in the massacre;
Betrayed by the man who sold his soul for a banana;
The old warhorse may yet be back for a last leg of the journey;
Let's put an end to the waste of words.

And then there was a piece of good news:

The UK flu rates are at an unparalleled low.

The debilitating infection had cost the life of his dear grandmother. It had been affecting scores of people every winter for years and, this time around, it was at an all-time low. Against other pieces of news, it was good news indeed. The gentleman cast his eyes on some of the headlines inquisitively and chuckled; Leon smiled back and jiggled the paper to have a better and wider view of the rest of the news. He soon became unmindful of the surroundings.

Suddenly a big brawl broke his oblivion. Two men inside the carriage, sitting near the exit door, were hissing and cursing each other for only God knew why. One was sixty plus and grumpy, the other was in his early forties and aggressive. Their words were punctuated by frequent malediction.

'You **** go to hell,' the younger man yelled.

'You **** bet I will…from my tummy cancer…in three months,' the older man shouted back. The younger man calmed down a bit and, although still at the top of his voice, he informed the older man that he lost his mother last year from the same terminal illness. The common topic of death seemed to have restored some peace and calm in the carriage. The tension around them subsided and the older man got off at Bond Street, shouting, 'Nice day.'

'You too,' the younger man said in a slightly apologetic tone. Leon silently breathed a sigh of relief.

✧

In the spacious lobby on the ground floor of that building in Victoria, tall vertically grooved pillars meet the ceiling; their bases stand on the beige and grey marble mosaic floor. The wall-mounted large paintings exhibit the vibrant colours and inimitable tastes of the artists who fashioned them to match the aura of the place. Exquisite clothes and food shops occupy this floor. The public library is on the first floor and the conference room and offices are on the second floor. The food hall is on the third floor under the green dome.

People come here for various reasons – for business or for pleasure. The sounds of their footsteps, occasional coughing and inaudible murmurs echo on the elegant walls and high ceilings of the building. Workers present their identity cards and sign in at reception before gaining entry to their respective offices and shops. Others come here to take advantage of the facilities on the ground floor and in the food hall; they also need to show some form of identification to enter the building. The place is for those who really want to be there.

✧

With his morning coffee, Leon settles himself down near a large French window in the food hall. The window overlooks the bustling main road and tree-lined avenues. He runs his fingers through his middle-parted, short, blond hair and browses through the newsletter. He would prefer to be in the library on the first floor, but it has not opened yet. Leon loves reading books and the distinct paper smell of their pages. Reading gives him a break away from the computer screen. This has an affiliation with his weekly visits to the local library with his mother, Mabel, and his younger sister, Gemma, during school holidays. He often dwells on his fond memories of those trips.

There was a book reading competition for children in the library with rewards in the form of book or game vouchers. Leon entered the competition for the vouchers while Gemma did so for the pleasure of reading. He used his vouchers to buy computer games and Gemma used hers to buy more books. Reading was not his passion, it was Gemma's. Getting him to join the competition was Mabel's clever way of coaxing him into reading. The attractive reward eventually got him hooked onto reading that finally developed around the biographical genre.

✧

The sound of approaching footsteps breaks the silence. Leon puts the newsletter down and looks for the source of the sound.

'I knew I would just find you here,' Millie says with a half-amused smile.

'Hey, you're here so early?' Leon asks. It is more of a statement than a question. He corrects his sitting posture and beckons Millie to sit opposite him. Millie sits on the chair and says, 'I just wanted to catch you before the meeting.'

'What's up, Miss Morgan?' Leon banters. Millie is in need of some reassurance before entering what she considers to be a dreaded meeting. She carefully looks around to weigh up the degree of privacy in the hall. Some early birds have arrived here to have breakfast. Her slender physique is slightly restless.

'R-e-l-a-x Mill! We've got plenty of time. It's only 8:30.'

Catching a habitual glimpse of his watch, Leon peeks at the array of steaming, hot breakfast that is visible from where they are. He produces a book from his briefcase and pushes it towards Millie as if to help her with the process of calming down.

✿

Leon stopped by the library yesterday just before closing time. Mr Dempsey called out from behind the information desk. The charismatic librarian stared from above his thick, black-framed glasses. Leon strode towards the desk. The computer was down so Mr Dempsey wrote down on a piece of paper the title of the book that he thought Leon would enjoy reading as well as its corresponding number on the bookshelf. He carefully folded it and gave it to Leon.

'The book Millie ordered is here too. You can use your own library card, if you want, to borrow it for her,' Mr Dempsey said, lightly tapping on the book in front of him. Leon was engaged in mouthing the title on the piece of paper Mr Dempsey had given him.

Long Walk to Freedom: The Autobiography of Nelson Mandela

He then looked at the book Millie had ordered. Its title was unusual.

✿

Millie's playful eyes fall on her favourite book on the table; she vividly reminisces about the pictures inside the book. They are so real as if each of them has a story that links it with the intricate

18

lifesaving substance on Earth: water. She saw the advertisement for the book with enlarged pictures of frozen water molecules on a poster in a bookshop; the captivating photos spoke volumes. Millie felt inspired and bought a copy of the book for herself. It was an interesting and enjoyable read; she thought it may also interest Leon, but she played it safe by ordering a copy of the book from the library.

Some fascinating facts in the book run through Millie's mind: physicists have been examining the notion that everything is energy including thoughts, words and actions with their own vibrational frequencies that can affect their immediate environment – water is one of the major constituents of the environment. By taking photographs of frozen water molecules after having them exposed to positive or negative words or phrases, one can get astonishing images and information about them!

'Emoto also claims that serious crimes take place in most areas where people curse frequently, so recurrent negative words attract negative events,' Millie says.

'Pardon?' Leon gives her a puzzled look.

'Oh, I was just thinking out loud. I was talking about what's in the book. It has changed my whole outlook on life,' she says. She now has a better understanding of the reason that caused a rift between her mother, Maya, and herself after her father, Jonathan, had passed away.

'In what way?' Leon asks.

'I'll tell you someday,' Millie says; she rests her hand on the title cover that says: *The Message from Water* - Masaru Emoto. She picks it up and searches for specific pages.

'Here. Look at these.' She shows Leon photos of water molecules that were exposed to positive messages just before crystallization, like *thank you* and *I love you,* and negative messages like *you fool* and *I hate you* in English, Japanese, German and other languages. The photographs of the crystallised water molecules matched the warm-heartedness or malice of the messages. The ones that were exposed to positive words produced beautiful symmetrical shapes and the ones exposed to negative words formed distorted, formless images. Leon is fascinated by the photos.

'Very nice! If you know so much about the book why do you want it?' Leon asks.

'Who says I want it? I want you to read it,' Millie thrusts the book into his hand without further ado.

☼

The food hall is now fairly full. A good many of the visitors are employees and there are also some early morning shoppers who have come here to grab a bite to eat before heading for the summer bargains in the shops downstairs. The shops will open soon. The clanking of cutlery and plates and the collective inaudible murmur now fill up the room.

Millie scans the place. Within her visual span, the ceiling right under the green dome, the windows, the food counter and the customers are visible.

'Let's get some breakfast, shall we?' Leon gets up and walks towards the food counter. Millie joins him reluctantly.

Leon gathers a couple of trays and offers one to Millie; her gesture implies that she does not need one. He goes for steaming yellow, soft buttery lumps of scrambled eggs, seasoned with freshly ground coarse black pepper and sea salt. Millie picks up a tea cup still warm from the dishwashing and presses it against the downward nozzle of the drinks machine to collect hot water. There are some dark chocolate bars with orange and green words on the cocoa coloured cover. They are neatly arranged in a tray next to the drinks machine. She picks one up. It is a bar of dark chocolate with chilli and ground coffee flavours. She draws it close enough to her nose to smell it. It has a mild aroma of coffee with subtle spicy flavour. She gets a couple of bars for Maya.

☼

Maureen, Jonathan's ex-wife, attended his funeral. Maya thought it wise to invite her although that was not what she really wanted. Maureen was apparently shocked and devastated by her ex's sudden death. When it was her turn to bid farewell to Jonathan, she could not contain herself; she broke down in tears and said between sobs, 'Goodbye darling. In my heart of hearts, I know how much you meant to me and I to you, darling, I'm your very own Mo.'

Maya's mind was miles away; she felt completely numbed. Maureen's lamenting got her back to reality. She threw a chafed look at her and muttered under her breath,

'You may have his money, Maureen, but he left a piece of his heart with me, with his very own Venus, his *goddess of love.*'

A tall and slim woman softly tapped Maya on the shoulder as if to comfort her and help her to rise above any resentment that she may hold against Maureen. The woman was wearing a glossy black dress and a black scarf, a strand of hair from her chignon was resting gently around her neck. Maya did not know who she was, nor did she want to know; she suddenly felt peaceful. A small voice echoed in her mind:

Let go of your hurt, seek peace within.

Jonathan fell ill with a rare heart condition. Within a week, he was no more. It was a sudden blow for Maya and Millie; they were at a loss not knowing how to move on in their day-to-day lives without him. It took ages for Maya to come to terms with her grief at losing him; the grief that had caused a rift between Maya and Millie, the mother and daughter.

Radiant Rosie, the supervisor at the café where Maya worked as a chef, gave her time off. Rosie took on a temporary chef to assist her in the running of the café. Her empathy and compassion helped Maya to pull herself together. Millie, conversely, under the guise of opposing emotional pulls, immersed herself in office work. Their stored-up emotions created a distance between them day by day and some days they just lived as strangers under the same roof.

Millie unearthed ways to mend the rift by looking into self-help books and compact discs. Gemma, who she met a couple of times, also helped her with the process. She said to her, 'Try to make peace with your mother now; if you don't, you may regret it later.' Her advice kept echoing as a soft murmur in Millie's thoughts and dreams.

Despite the impasse, Maya wanted Millie to continue to live with her but Millie was ready to fly the nest. After living with her friends for a short while, Millie moved to West End where London was at its best: interesting and lively all day and night with theatres, shops and museums. She found a bedsit right in the middle of Oxford Circus. It was not far from where she worked.

✧

'Earl Grey?' Leon swings a tea bag within Millie's smelling range.

'Yes, please,' Millie receives the tea bag with her nimble fingers and dips it in the boiling water she has just collected. The tea bag floats on the water before slowly sinking. The exotic beverage goes well with her love of fine tea; a long sniff of the subtle spicy tea revitalises and calms her body. Leon gets a glass of freshly squeezed orange juice and a stack of toasts and butter to go with his scrambled eggs. He has a proper breakfast when he has the luxury of time.

After paying for the food and drink, they settle back down in a sunny spot next to the window. Their former seats are now occupied by a mother and her son. The little boy is singing *Old MacDonald had a farm* in his cute little voice.

'Are you singing karaoke at the summer fair?' Leon asks while putting a melted buttery blob of cooked eggs with a crunchy piece of toast into his mouth.

'You mean the one I told you about? You must be joking. What makes you say that?' Millie takes a sip of the aromatic tea.

'Oh, just idle curiosity,' Leon discreetly looks at the boy who is still singing away at the top of his voice.

Leon tells her that the last time he was in Tokyo, he sang karaoke in a restaurant with his work colleagues. He felt that this Japanese guy also wanted to have a go, but he felt shy.

'I told him in Japanese words that meant: *If you don't sing today, you'll regret it tomorrow*. The man said *O-mae wa ii otoko da ne.*'

'Meaning?' Millie asks.

'You are a really good man,' Leon interprets.

The sound of their fragmented conversation melds with the scattered noise in the hall with Millie doing most of the talking and Leon listening, sometimes uttering a few words here and there and sometimes nodding with a mouthful of food.

Millie now engages in small talk about Gemma.

'Yeah, she needs to be away from London,' Leon's sardonic smile escapes Millie's attention. Her mind is now back on the imminent staff meeting – each meeting is different with new ventures and challenges. The next milestone in her thinking links with a piece of news she has picked up regarding Isaac's special project. She hurriedly briefs Leon about this and adds,

'I don't know who he is going to assign it to.'

'I won't mind if he offers this to you and me,' Leon's wide-set eyes wink at her. Millie throws a furtive glance at him. She then becomes aware of something or someone in the vicinity; an odd sensation overcomes her, she feels the presence of a third person, but she can only see the surveillance camera skilfully installed on the corner of the ceiling.

'Are you expecting Sayed?' Leon asks.

'No, I thought someone else was watching us,' a meditative image of Maya pops up in her mind!

'Anyway, Sayed will join us any moment,' Millie says.

✧

Sayed and Leon first met Millie in an entertainment event. It was a brief encounter; it was not so convivial!

✧✧✧

Chapter 5

ALEENA LIVES NEXT TO THE PANTHEON THAT STANDS IN the heart of Rome. The Pantheon in all its glory is a well-preserved building in Rome that was completed during the reign of the Roman emperor Hadrian. It has been an emblem of awe and magnificence since then. Cool shade and light sinuously enter the porch of the building with eight tall granite columns at the front and two sets of four columns behind. The porch leads to the rotunda – the globular floor plan – enclosed by a dome with an oculus, the median opening to the sky. The place emits an implicit message to modern-day visitors:

Step inside the Pantheon and experience the abiding legacy of ancient times.

Aleena is having a summer break from the primary school where she works as a deputy headteacher. It is a break for her from the school but not from her work. She is running a summer school at the school premises; she wanted Gemma to come to Rome and assist her in teaching a group of eager children (or rather children of eager parents) English, Italian and Maths in order for them to remain up to date with their studies during the long summer holiday. Gemma gladly accepted the offer. She can teach English and Maths, if not Italian.

Gemma is attracted to Rome like a moth to a flame. Her passion for the city made her past visits memorable and interesting. In Rome, there are countless things to do and places to go to throughout the day; there are piazzas – open squares with hard surfaces, shops, open stalls, restaurants and museums; no one seems to get weary of places of interest or events that are taking place on every corner. Her perception of life in Rome resonates with that of Aleena's.

✿

Gemma is hardly in contact with Leon these days; however, she sent him a mobile text message before coming to Rome at short notice. Not that she cared about it; she thought she would tell him anyway. Leon has always been cynical about acting on impulse. He seems well disposed towards weighing up pros and cons before committing himself to anything. Gemma, on the other hand, considers this as seeing things in black and white.

'Life isn't all black and white, you know, you're so deluded,' Gemma once said to Leon.

'Am I? It's not all grey either,' Leon argued.

'Why don't you paint a picture together in black, white and grey with blobs of red, blue, green and yellow?' Mabel jokingly tried to mediate between the two.

✿

Gemma intends to look for a job in Rome while working in the summer school. All she requires is the national health services number as a prerequisite to search or apply for a job. Aleena became an Italian citizen years ago so she was not informed about the current official requirement for someone who wished to live and work in Rome. Gemma was unaware about this during her previous visits to Rome. It only came to light when she went from one government office to the other in search of proper information. Finally, a kind gentleman directed her to the right department where she learnt about obtaining the number. It was time she went back to London so she thought she would give it a shot during her next visit to the city. Now that she is in Rome again, she can pursue the matter further although she is not sure if that is what she really wants.

'I'll never get that number,' Gemma validates her indecisiveness by being negative.

'Think positive. Thoughts and words have power, you know,' Aleena says.

✿

Standing inside the Pantheon surrounded by piazzas, Gemma absorbs rays of the midday sun that pour in through the oculus. She visited the temple many times and each time it revealed new aspects, new stories and new sets of questions:

What was it like during those days?
What were the people like?

Who visited this place?
What was it used for?

She admires Roman architects and planners for their clever construction of the Pantheon with amazing precision especially in the positioning of the oculus in the centre of the dome that allows sunbeams to enter through it at intended angles and shine on different parts of the colossal interior at different times of the day. She is unmindful of the murmurs of visitors in mystical darkness inside the Pantheon. She moves towards the shifting sunbeam to take in its warmth. Outside, it is broad daylight.

Within the museum walls, Gemma could almost hear the echoes of the footsteps of Emperor Hadrian. She closes her eyes - there he is in her imagination, the emperor himself standing in the shadow, away from the beam with a piercing gaze that holds stories of sadness and happiness, cruelty and kindness, failure and triumph. The thought of Hadrian compels her to think of a specific person, Brian who, in her eyes, was a shrewd, articulate opportunity-seeker.

✿

'There you are, I was looking for you in the piazza,' Aleena says in her melodious giggly voice; her hazel eyes wince with laughter. Gemma's daydreaming-self comes back to her present conscious-self like trillions of subatomic particles forming back into their solid existence. She walks away from the shaft of light towards her friend. They come out of the Pantheon and step into Piazza Della Rotonda. Hotels, scores of restaurants and cafés blend in seamlessly along the piazza. The algae-smell wafts across from nearby fountains.

They approach the enchanting fountains made up of primeval sculptures. Water is gushing out from many facets of the sculptures, forming a moss-green pool underneath. Tourists, as well as natives, throng around the place. Some are simply enjoying the view, sitting or standing; some are taking photos, others are having a beer or two.

Street sellers are selling single stemmed roses to the tourists.

✿

In her workplace in London, Gemma had been repetitively cited in the office newsletter for her achievement of weekly targets, but she did not want to continue to work for a tedious recruitment agency all her life. She left the job.

'What the hell does that daughter of yours want to do?' Brian, her step-father, barked at Mabel. Gemma heard it through the flimsy walls. She did not see her mother's face; she could only feel her pain. Leon was not on the scene; he was miles away.

Gemma finally left home to live with Sheila, Mabel's octogenarian mother. Sheila received her with open arms. Gemma felt at home in the welcome abode – she ate whatever she liked, slept and went to places whenever she liked – no questions were asked. Sheila soon succumbed to a chest infection.

Many odd jobs later Gemma wanted to be away from London, at least, for a while. Aleena's door was always open for her.

Aleena is two years older than Gemma; they went to the same school. She is not only Gemma's best friend, she is also like a sister, a guide and a pathfinder.

✿

'Hungry?' Aleena asks.

'A little bit,' Gemma says. The Pantheon is visible from here. The dome is giving off waves of sweltering heat; it felt much cooler inside.

They start walking towards the stalls and cafes that are lined along the piazza.

'Shall we eat something light now? I'll make something special for dinner from Mama's Recipe.'

'Your mama?'

'No. It's a cookbook called Mama's Recipe,' Aleena replies once her chortle trails into a smile. She makes a mental note of the dish she is going to cook that evening – succulent boneless turkey garnished with maple cured bacon that is stuffed with coarsely chopped Italian chestnuts and seasonal sausage meat. She has been preparing the bacon for the past five days.

They go into a café. The glass counter inside the café displays an array of Italian cheeses in all shapes, colours and sizes with accessories of black and green olives, freshly shredded red onions, juicy and crunchy lettuce leaves, thick chunks of fleshy, red tomatoes, pickled onions in vinegar, thin cucumber slices and a myriad of other delectable choices. Behind the counter in a woven basket, there are thin elongated loaves of freshly baked bread with their inviting smell coming from small and big pores inside them.

Aleena selects a mozzarella cheese sandwich with black olives, red onions and tomatoes. Gemma has the one with grated Pecorino Romano cheese with layers of sliced cremini mushrooms and green arugula (long leaves used in salads and sandwiches) drizzled with olive oil.

☼

For Aleena, food and drink are not only for consumption; they are also for her aesthetic pleasure through all her five senses. Seeing, touching, smelling and tasting bread transport her to the land where its main ingredient, wheat, was grown beside the waterways under the bright sun. She was not present there physically, but the crop travelled all the way with the nutrients it absorbed through the soil of the land; all of which would later be assimilated into her body.

Swirling, smelling, and tasting wine take her to the vineyard where it originated; where the roots of grapes drank the sap of every inch of the earth to make their produce juicy, ripe and right for the drink. Her preparation and consumption of food and drink are inspired by the thought of the chain of events behind the scenes. Her love of food is infused with the natural flow of life in Rome with its populace, architecture and scenic beauty where there is always something to see, something to do and something to admire.

Her parents did not quite understand her penchant for studying Italian that later inspired her to move to the historic city of Rome.

☼

Aleena and Gemma are back by the fountains. They locate a spot nearby and sit down to enjoy their designer sandwiches. They gaze around with great curiosity as if they are seeing everything for the first time!

'It's as if we are essentially woven into…,' Gemma pauses to think of a suitable word.

'…a tapestry?' Aleena suggests. The summer breeze strokes her brown, curly tresses.

Gemma nods. 'Yeah. We are inside the tapestry and things are moving and changing within it.'

'Nothing was born,
Nothing will die,
All things will change,' Aleena recounts thoughtfully.

'That's Tennyson, but in another poem, he says just the opposite:

All things were born.
Ye will come never more,
For all things must die,' Gemma says.

'He perhaps saw the polarity of things, as in life and death, light and darkness,' Aleena points out.

Gemma finishes the last bit of her sandwich. Mabel used to say:

Don't waste food. Don't make leaving food on the plate appear part of social etiquette. Remember, your crumbs could be someone else's dinner.

A small bread crust from the sandwich bag drops near her feet. She picks it up and tosses it towards a bird. The bird flutters its wings and scampers off; it hesitantly comes back to the crust and pecks on it.

✧

The afternoon sun and shade dance hand in hand on the streets, on rooftops and domes of ancient buildings in Rome. The uniqueness of the city becomes lively and vivid once more! Aleena and Gemma are ready to go home.

'Rose for the lady?' a young man apparently of Asian origin offers a single stemmed rose to Gemma.

'It's beautiful. Where is it from?' Gemma asks.

'From India,' the man replies, keeping his arm outstretched.

'Really?' Gemma is amazed.

'You mean you are from India, right?' Aleena wants to clarify. The man nods.

Gemma stoops over and draws in a deep breath to absorb the sweet scent of the flower. She is almost instantly consumed by its splendour and fragrance; she momentarily slips into a distant realm of beauty and bliss. Gemma's passionate admiration for the flower inspires Aleena to get the rose for her. Gemma accepts the gift from her friend with a hug and a smile.

Before walking on, Gemma asks the seller if he can speak Italian.

'A little bit,' he replies with great enthusiasm, 'Come stai? Di dove sei?' he halts and tries to remember something, then utters, *'L'uomo saggio.'*

Aleena says, 'Yes, *L'uomo saggio - the wise man*, nice one.'

While walking back home, Aleena says that most of these people come here for studies or better career opportunities. Some of them come with a student visa and they supplement the cost of living by selling stuff or working in bars or restaurants.

✿

Aleena opens the huge entrance door leading to the front yard behind which stand six blocks of converted flats; one of which belongs to her.

'I've got your ticket for the yoga show tomorrow.'

'Fantastic. Thanks,' Gemma says.

They proceed towards the flat through the yard. The scorching heat mellows into the cooler ambience of the yard and the sudden croon of crispy, dry leaves announces that there are things to look forward to in the days to come.

✿ ✿ ✿

Chapter 6

'GOOD MORNING.'

Isaac Monyesa's deep voice echoes around the walls of the air-conditioned conference room. He has occupied a seat at the far end of the wine coloured oval table. Millie and Sayed are sitting next to each other opposite Leon and Jacob Newman.

Isaac is a burly man in his late fifties. He is a man of no-nonsense and, as a team leader, he initiates discussions and expects contribution towards them from his team members. His eyes are deep brown against faintly cloudy whites; they emit expressions that intuitively weigh up people and the surroundings. He starts the meeting slightly earlier than scheduled as all members of staff are already present in the much sought after venue.

The stylish blend of the wooden furniture and built-in ceiling lights exude a semi-dark atmosphere in the room. The room is at the end of the gallery area on the second floor of the listed building in Victoria. Upper sashes of three large windows are open for fresh air. Venetian blinds over the windows are pulled down with open settings to avoid direct sunlight. Ceiling lights are just enough for the mood and needs of the current users of the room. They sit around the table with Miss Phyllis, the personal assistant to Isaac. She is sitting slightly away from the group and keying in the notes of meeting on the laptop computer that she has carefully placed on the table.

Millie is anxiously awaiting news of the special project Isaac has in mind. Although this is too early to happen at this stage of the forum, she is eager to know if she is going to be a part of it. She does not exactly know what the project entails; this could well involve travelling overseas that she would have otherwise welcomed had she not had plans of her own. By virtue of her work commitment, she cannot refuse to undertake such an assignment if she is selected for it unless she has good reasons. She discreetly starts breathing deeply to let go of her concerns.

After the morning greeting, Isaac informs his team that the environmental issues call for more attention now than before and that the Department of Environment and its partner, Climate Change Governance, are negotiating courses of action to instil more awareness of the issues among the public.

'As part of an added initiative, the allocation of low emission zones in some rural areas is under consideration. As you know, a traffic pollution charge scheme will be operative within these zones with a view to controlling the emission from commercial vehicles. This project is going to be one of the major additions to the cost.' Isaac continues, 'However, the implementation of the scheme in urban areas may not be feasible in the near future.'

'Any comments?' Isaac raises his grey-black bushy eyebrows and tosses the question supposedly towards Leon.

✪

Isaac Monyesa, a self-made man from Mzuzu village in Lilongwe, Malawi, grew up with the adage:

Hard work is the gateway to success.

In his childhood, he had to work doubly hard in an orphanage that largely depended on donations of money from their sponsors from around the world. His sponsor, a gracious wealthy French lady, continued paying for his education even after he had finished studying at the village high school. This helped him gain a place at University College London, a leading London university, where he embarked on combined studies in Economics and Geography. He studied during the daytime and moonlighted as a waiter in a restaurant some nights and as a bartender in a local pub other nights to keep up with the day-to-day living costs in the city.

During his days in the orphanage, he secretly wrote to the lady in broken French, asking for a gift he longed for. The orphanage supervisor was furious when he found out about this; this was considered inappropriate at the orphanage. 'How dare you ask for something like that? What if the sponsor decided to discontinue the donation?' Isaac received a strong reprimand from the supervisor.

The lady was kind enough to send him his most desired gift in a box by ship mail that arrived four months later. He plonked the box on the unsteady table, the only other piece of furniture he had in his room beside his single bed, and stared disbelievingly at its contents for as long as his eyes could cope. Out of sheer ecstasy, he was unable to choose between a laugh and a cry.

✿

Leon knows he has to give a satisfactory answer to Isaac's question – the answer that already exists within Isaac's knowledge but he wants to hear it from Leon.

'Well, setting up low emission zones in cities may not be imminent, but, as you know, congestion charges in certain key areas in London will be enforced. Once this happens, the volume of traffic in those areas will be reduced considerably, thereby reducing congestion and pollution in the city,' Leon says.

'Yes but the plan is only at its initial stage. Sayed, you have been quiet today,' Isaac's inquisitive eyes now fall on Sayed.

'Oh yes, erm…cycling routes will be extended, and in two years' time there will be more,' Sayed replies.

Millie adds that to encourage people to walk, the department's website has incorporated information about suitable routes. 'This will be useful for walkers in different parts of London who regularly like to walk,' she informs.

'Good. And you, Jacob?

'I was looking into the department's plan for the construction of more one-way routes. This is also in the pipeline to encourage people to make more use of public transport and car lift sharing,' Jacob briefs.

✿

Jacob Newman left his job in advertising where he worked for more than eighteen years and joined Isaac's team. The opportunity arose in a chance meeting with Millie at a New Year's Eve party. He had a slight limp and walked with the help of two walking sticks. He held the door open for Millie at the entrance of the venue with one hand, balancing on his sticks with the other hand. His courteous gesture conveyed the message:

There is no need to feel pity for me. My visible physical disabilities have empowered me to think that I am no lesser being

33

*than other able-bodied fellows, therefore, I can hold the door open
for you just like any gentleman.*

Millie found Jacob charismatic. In their animated conversation, she told him about the need for another member in Isaac's team. The work the team undertook seemed varied, interesting and challenging to Jacob. He felt it was time he changed his career direction and took up the position in the team although he was not sure about leaving the comfort of his position in advertising which was equally good. When he met Isaac for an initial interview, it felt right for him to take the plunge.

✿

The distinctive building in Victoria is now busy. Shoppers are assembling in the designer clothes and furniture shops decked with inviting decors and exclusive items, some of which are on sale. People are dispersed in the seemingly limitless hallway on the ground floor. Lifts and stairs behind the electric sliding door lead to other floors. Offices have now become busy.

The library on the first floor is now open; it is quieter than other parts of the building. On the top floor, the restaurant is selling a variety of food with hot and cold beverages whose outreaching flavours attract both the in-house staff and passers-by.

✿

Up in the conference room, Miss Phyllis' nimble fingers are busy keying in the notes of the meeting. She occasionally pauses to decide what to include and what to leave out from the notes. She has become adept at doing this.

The sun is now beaming through the Venetian blinds creating jagged lines of light and shade across the table. The shade wavers faintly prompted by the slight movement of the window blinds. The occupants of the room are oblivious of the outside world, of other workers and shoppers elsewhere in the building.

Isaac expects to hear more from Leon. Leon discreetly checks on everyone in the room before presenting his own thoughts in words. He says, 'The latest statistics, drawn up by the experts, show that it is not a matter of decades but merely years before the issues in question go from bad to worse. The amount of carbon dioxide in the atmosphere has reached its highest level in human history, faster than it did during the second half of the last century.'

'Well, there are all kinds of speculations and predictions,' Isaac intervenes, 'We aren't sure yet about their degree of accuracy.'

'Yeah…but we can't deny the impact of such issues…we need to educate a large number people to go green!

'How?'

'By doing something NEW!' The words uncharacteristically spill out from Leon.

Isaac observes him from underneath his bushy eyebrows. Leon is more shocked than anyone else by what he has just suggested. He really does not know what motivated him to say that; it is unlike him to advocate something like that on the spur of the moment. He knows that only tried and tested methods, as opposed to some abstract concepts, are preferred by the members of the team and certainly by the decision-makers.

His mind is searching for an answer to what he meant by *doing something new.* He mentally distances himself from the conversation, allowing the rest of the team to continue talking. He tries to retrieve a piece of information from his memory. A picture of a coke bottle floats into his imagination.

Realising that Leon needs more time to shed more light on what he has suggested, Sayed says that mass advertising is the means to educate the public about green issues, the downside is this type of advertisement may prove costly.

'Yes… that's it,' Leon exclaims in a eureka-tone, 'The costs of advertising can be kept down with reduced but effective words and visual presentations.'

He tells them the story about the new coke advert that lasted for 30 seconds during the intermission at a cinema. The sale of coke went up by 20% that evening, so people tend to respond more to fewer effective words and corresponding visual images. The same principle can be applied to still images on roadside advertising boards and to other advertising media.

'Similar tactics may not be feasible here,' Isaac comments. 'Besides, almost everyone loves coke anyway,' a shade of disappointment is evident in his voice.

Millie and Sayed exchange discreet *I-told-you-so* glances.

'But the idea behind this is to gradually educate people to go green,' Leon argues. Jacob agrees. He says that adverts with powerful messages are the ones that leave a visual imprint in the mind; he refers to one of the most successful examples - McDonald's logo - it is everywhere.

'Oh yes, the other day I saw an internet pop-up of the big yellow M-logo. It made me want to eat McDonald's right away although I'm not a big fan of it,' Millie agrees.

'So, more effective visual images with selective words,' Isaac summarizes their observation, 'Adverts are usually based on these tactics anyway. We are looking at being more innovative here.'

☼

Isaac Monyesa can see the benefit of the use of visual images from his team's perspective. Industrial science was not as advanced in the 1950s as it is today. When he was growing up in the Mzuzu village in the fifties, there was no television, no cinema, no mass advertising, but after he had seen a picture of a pair of blue classic Samba trainers on a crumpled leaflet carelessly thrown away on the wayside, he hankered after them. That was when he wrote to his French sponsor, asking her to send him a pair of Samba trainers and when he received them, he gazed at them without blinking, forgetting the supervisor's sharp rebuke, forgetting to try them out on his brittle-skinned, muck-encrusted bare feet!

☼

Isaac is pleased by his team's overall input that was in agreement with the points raised in the article in the newsletter. He is well-informed about Jacob's contact with the media and asks Millie and Jacob to oversee the advertising campaign, pointing out that roadside advertising companies are not doing very well at the moment. Mille argues that this is essentially the right time for the venture because these advertising companies are not getting enough customers so they will probably offer their services at reduced prices. She cautiously looks around to weigh up the effect of her proposition. Her eyes briefly fall on Leon's.

Isaac informs his team that in the next staff meeting, sustainable building designs and eco-friendly houses, and four UK universities that are in the process of coining new ideas and options for eco-friendly architectural designs will be looked at. Everyone now expects to hear about the new assignment. A sudden silence becomes prevalent.

'Some Japanese car manufacturers are prepared to export car parts for the assembling of environment-friendly cars, but our regional assemblers are not so sure about the market response,' Jacob breaks the silence.

'Yes, I know,' Isaac halts for a moment and then he announces. 'In line with what Jacob has said, I've got this assignment for you,' he focuses his gaze first on Sayed and then on Leon so it becomes clear to all as to who he meant by *you*. He briefly sheds light on the imminent tasks and fixes a further meeting at the London Bridge office when instructions relating to the assignment will be given.

Knowing that the meeting is drawing to a close, Millie drifts off to a mental preview of her trip to Delhi, India, with Maya. She has not been to Delhi for a long time. She kept putting the trip off because of her workload. Now that Isaac has not included her in the project, she can put her heart and soul into planning the trip. She wants to renew her acquaintance with Delhi and with her roots in Muzaffarabad, the capital city of Azad Kashmir that was once a part of the undivided India.

The day now develops into late morning, just before noon, and the meeting ends with the team members reviewing their respective future tasks. Miss Phyllis stops typing, heaving a secret sigh of relief. Everyone thanks her. She nods with a smile.

✧✧✧

Chapter 7

MAYA PULLS THE CURTAINS TOGETHER TO BLOCK THE intense sunlight pouring through the lounge window and walks towards the sofa. She plunges herself into its soft seat. Summer afternoon stumbles in swiftly with daylight sneaking around the rims of the curtains. Her spacious sitting-cum-dining room in her one-bedroom flat in South Croydon, in the southern part of London, is sombre in semi-darkness. The beige wall is in contrast to the dark green sofa and the green rubber plant on the corner; the beech coloured wooden low bed next to the wall very nearly passes for a piece of seating furniture. Millie loves to sleep in this bed when she visits her. She will come home today to give Maya her flight ticket to Delhi – it is going to be a gift from Millie to Maya for her fifty-second birthday.

Maya has oven-baked rainbow trout - Millie's favourite - with a dash of lemon juice, herbs and seasonings, crushed cloves of garlic, a drizzle of olive oil and potato slices, all cooked in the fish juice; this will be served with garden salad.

Maya bides her time.

She points her remote control at the TV and presses the *on* button. A scene from a film springs out on the screen; the scene is somewhere in a desert. Under the blazing sun, a barefoot boy, aged 10 or 11, wearing an over-sized dirty shirt and torn shorts, is running wild in what appears to be a battle zone. Both warring groups are baffled; they do not know whose side the boy belongs to. No one knows where he came from or why and where he is running towards. The boy slowly draws something out of his loose shirt sleeve.

Everyone aims their guns at him while he draws out a white make-shift flag tied on a fallen twig. He holds it up high, it flutters in the wind caused by the speed of his running; in the middle of the desert, he is an emblem of truce. Confused fighters from behind the hide-outs shout crudely at him in their local dialect and ask him to scram away. The boy stops running and remains obstinate with the flag held up high. There is a magnificent oasis in the distance with palm trees and a dazzling pond. The scene is a strange mixture of beauty and battle, of harmony and strife. The message in it is implicit:

You can have bliss or misery – it's your choice.

Maya turns the television off; she is unwilling to see what is in store for the boy although it is only a fiction. She reaches out for the TV guide to read about the film.

✿

The scene was a grim reminder of the tale about Maya's grandparents' altered life situation. Her grandparents, Pavitra and Randitya Suri, were residents in Muzaffarabad in undivided Kashmir in the north-west part of India, where they led a deluxe life with their two daughters, Rani and Archana. They lived in a stately home in the centre of the city and had servants at their beck and call. Grandfather Randitya Suri held a prominent position in the then civil service of the Indian government under the British rule. The house, with its grand facilities, was available because of his status in the service.

After prolonged unrest, bloodshed, and opposition from the natives, the British bequeathed their colony, India, its independence in August 1947 and had it divided into two countries based on the majority religious faiths in different regions: India for the followers of Hinduism and Pakistan for Muslims, leaving Kashmir in chaos with a never-resolved territorial dispute. Part of it fell to Pakistan and part of it fell to India. Muzaffarabad fell to the part of Kashmir that belonged to Pakistan.

The consequence of such unresolved issues resulted in on-going outbreaks of violence among the partisans and Indian and Pakistani troops. To make the matter worse, frequent riots would often break out between Hindus and Muslims that spanned from Muzaffarabad to Kupwara, Kathai to Baramula, Rawala Kot to Punch and New Mirpur to Naushahra – these were places on either side of the divided Kashmir. Ripple effects of these riots would engulf the newly born countries that once existed on the map as undivided India.

It was at this juncture when Randitya, a follower of Hinduism, decided to leave everything behind and emigrate to Delhi in India with his family as he was worried about their safety in Muzaffarabad, the Muslim-dominated region. Azmat Khan, his Muslim friend, urged them to stay; he promised he would do everything within his power to protect them from any possible danger. Randitya, on the other hand, did not want to jeopardise his friend's own safety. The story of their struggle began from here.

☼

Maya browses through the pages in the TV guide. The title of the film she was watching a moment ago was *A White Call* - a call for all in the land to return to peace, love and harmony. The film was based on a true story - a story about long-drawn-out fights between the oppressors and the oppressed of the land. The whole family of the boy in the story were killed. He helplessly heard his mother's plea to God before she perished:

Our Lord, please save us from the oppressors in this town and send us from You the one who will protect and send us from You the one who will help.

The boy was distraught with anguish and vengeance; he felt the compulsion to join other vengeful youths of the land to retaliate against the tyrants but his mother's plea prevented him from doing this - it kept echoing in his heart and soul. He eventually became *the one who protected and the one who helped.*

A father figure who took the boy under his wing and his young daughter, the would-be love of the boy, showed him how to resolve the problem without attacking the enemies and defenceless people who happened to belong to the enemies. He did this by forming a vigilant group that protected scores of families from the tyrants. The group became larger and stronger day by day; their defensive actions and negotiations with the enemies towards conflict resolution eventually restored peace in the land.

Before releasing their captives, the group firmly implanted three questions into their minds to which all gave the same replies!

☼

Maya gives her mind a break from the intensity of the story and the painful memories of her family's past by doing guided meditation. She tries to concentrate on the exercise; she does not want to miss any part of it as she did before.

The pleasing voice puffs into her ears once more through the headphone.

Close your eyes .....

Take a deep breath... imagine you are gathering your anxious thoughts as you inhale...hold it.

Exhale, let go of your thoughts and just r-e-l-a-x...

You will soon take an awesome journey to a place of your imagination.

You can go to amazing places in your imagination.

Maya breathes in and out slowly and deeply, relaxation flows through her body; it becomes easier for her to progressively relax her mind and body. The soft, whispery voice numbs her limbs; the peaceful sensation diffuses into every cell in her body. She is now more heedful of her imaginary boat journey than before; she arrives at a river bank and anchors the boat.

The voice continues to guide her:

You are ascending your way up the path with ease.

You come to a flat terrain and discover the archaic city from close proximity.

She envisions gliding through the path with a body that is lighter than a feather, landing onto a flat surface.

The guide continues:

It is a city of peace and prosperity.

Take the opportunity to look into the city from a distance.

What are the shapes of the buildings like?

What sort of people lived there?

What were they like?

The guide now speaks about the city:

It's a primeval city that has remained flawless for years.
Explore the city's many mysteries.
When you look at it, how do you feel?
Do you feel the sensation of peace, harmony and prosperity just like
the city itself?

Peace... harmony... and ... prosperity, the words kept echoing in her ears in the comfort of her own room. The familiar city she saw vaguely in her last sitting - the green dome or the hustle and bustle inside it - is no longer there. Instead, there is a dim image of another place within the darkness of her closed eyelids. The nebulous outline of the occupants in this esoteric city emanate feelings of love and amity. The city certainly does not appear to be primeval as repeatedly suggested by the guide; it rather looks very advanced. This is a city of love, peace and harmony. This seems far removed from the real world where many exist as doleful individuals. In her trance-like state, Maya hopes to remain in this sacrosanct space forever.

After a long pause the voice asks:

Do you see any changes?
What did the people of the city do to bring about the changes?

She spots some apple trees, vaguely hears trailed laughter of children and then the scene disappears - the curtain of darkness drops down.

There is an abrupt surge in her blurred visualization; she is now moving farther away from the scene. Her novel insight gradually discloses a tranquil sanctuary with a cool misty spray of her own expanded consciousness that fills up the space. She is the only appeased spectator of this imaginary place; she can still faintly hear the background gong sound of the singing vessels as if it is coming from a far-away land.

Maya opens her eyes on hearing the distinct door-unlocking sound. Millie is here.

✿ ✿ ✿

42

Chapter 8

'PREGO, PROVA QUESTO GUSTO DI GELATO È ESOTICO.'

An Afro-Caribbean woman inside the auditorium for the yoga show, wearing a pink dress and a broad pink-lipped grin, is calling out in Italian and offering free samples of ice cream in small paper cups to her potential customers. The language is not a barrier when food is offered; Gemma's elementary knowledge of Italian tells her that *gelato è esotico* means exotic ice cream. The woman then demonstrates how to make the ice cream by tossing some chopped up cabbage leaves and carrots with lumps of strawberry ice cream in a food processor and giving them a swift twirl.

Gemma collects a sample. She tilts her head backwards and drops the content into her mouth in one go. It tastes like strawberry ice cream with no detectable taste of vegetables that went in it; it is perhaps healthy ice cream if there is such a thing!

The hall for the yoga show is spacious with the expansive high ceiling supported by metal structures, the single unit of which looks like the inside mechanism of an open umbrella. Gemma tries to roughly assess the vastness of the hall; she is dwarfed by its enormity. There are many stalls inside the hall.

The auditorium stands on Via Tunisi in Rome. The show is for three days. Today is the second day.

✿

The morning was warm and crisp. Gemma was queuing up a while ago in front of the main entrance. The crowd was diverse – people from all races and ages were rhapsodizing in a wide range of languages. '*Good!*' she thought – she was not the only non-Italian speaker here! She fanned her face with the computer-printed entry ticket. The heat of the day was upon her!

The English words, *The Yoga Show*, tightly knitted in red, blue, green and yellow tiny light bulbs, were mounted on the top panel of the tall, closed wooden entrance door. The lights would emit their brightness more in the evening.

'But why have they kept the English name *The Yoga Show*?'
Gemma asked Aleena when she saw her ticket.

'Because they usually keep the foreign words that are pretty
familiar to all,' Aleena explained. She was not coming with Gemma
to the show as she had other things to do. Besides, she thought
Gemma needed the time and space to herself.

When the entrance door to the hall opened, Gemma got in with
the others. She picked up a bag of goodies from the large square
table covered with a white tablecloth; the table was positioned right
after the colossal entrance and the bags were meant for everyone that
joined the show. Each bag contained the programme booklet,
leaflets about yoga and meditation courses offered at different places
in Italy, a white rubber bracelet with the words *Om Shanti – pace per
tutti* in red on it and a nutritious mixed seed bar.

Gemma wore the bracelet on her wrist. She took a deep breath
and repeated the words on the bracelet, 'Om Shanti, *pace per tutti*,
hmm, *peace for all.*'

☼

After tasting the *healthy* ice cream, Gemma walks towards a stall
where freshly squeezed fruit juice is sold. This is apparently a stall
run by English-speaking volunteers; the names of the drinks are
displayed in English with colourful pictures along with luscious
displays of hand-picked fruits: *Big banana, Very Berry, Lemon Aid,
Green Bang, Big Five.* She gets herself a small glass of Lemon Aid
and takes a sip of the refreshing citric drink; it tastes deliciously
tangy.

There are free and paid yoga and meditation classes and shows in
the auditorium. One has to proceed through many stalls before
reaching these classes and shows. In addition to food stalls, there are
other stalls that are exhibiting their unique commodities: creative
earth singing bowls of varied shapes and sizes, miniature wooden
models of glittering elephants and household decorations,
embroidered shawls and garments of eastern styles and traditions,
herbal skin care products and scores of other things that once
glimpsed cannot but enchant the eyes of the beholders!

Gemma tries her hand at playing the singing bowls with round
ended wooden sticks. The tune from the bowls could be equated

with the sound of music produced from contrasting-sized water-filled containers; the difference is that the tune from the bowls has more melodious depth and it lingers on in the air even after it dies down. Its sound waves generate a gentle surge of tranquillity in the body and mind. Gemma thinks that it will be even more enchanting if the singing bowls were played by a professional. She moves towards a stall of lamps that resemble big glowing mushrooms inside a dense forest.

'Parla italiano?'

The seller wants to know if she can speak Italian.

'Un po,' she says. She can speak a bit of the language.

'Queste lampade sono di sale,' the friendly man lightly pats a salty lamp with his index finger. He then licks it and from his facial expression and the slapping of his tongue, one can tell that the lamp is made from salt and that is what he meant in his speech. Gemma mimics him. Salty lamps! She has never seen or heard about them before. She imagines their inevitable dissolvability in the water! She then locates multi-coloured tiny balls of coarse bath salt in large jars next to the lamps.

Gemma thanks and leaves the eager seller behind her. She is like Alice in wonderland, stumbling upon fascinating things and people!

✧

A sudden rush in the gathering of people jolts her forward.

Feeling a little peckish, she reaches out for the mixed seed bar in the bag she got for free. In each bite, she can taste a mixture of pistachio, pumpkin and sunflower seeds in solidified layers of honey with a subtle scent of rosewater!

Gemma now arrives at an open space in front of a makeshift tent. The programme booklet says that a mini-meditation exercise will be offered inside the tent. Volunteers, wearing white clothes and red scarves or ties, are giving away leaflets on various meditation and yoga courses held elsewhere in Rome. Divine meditational music and the smell of rose and cinnamon incense burners generate a lulling sensation in and around the place. She hesitantly asks a one-word question to a volunteer at the entrance to make sure she is at the right place.

'Meditazione?'

'Si, signora. Venga e pratichi momenti di silenzio.'

Gemma gets the essence of the speech by interpreting fragments of it – *enjoy moments of silence*. She can tell from his way of speaking that he is inviting her to join in.

'Grazie,' she thanks him. With no further ado, she steps inside. A soothing Eastern flute music fills up the place. She silently installs herself on a chair in the back row near the opening; if she does not like the exercise, she can always slip out of the seat without disturbing others.

The speaker is wearing a white shirt, white trousers and a red tie. He gives a short speech in Italian and demonstrates how to focus on the *third eye* between the eyebrows and how to breathe deeply in preparation for the meditation. He then leisurely says:

'*Chiudete gli occhi.*'

Upon hearing the instruction, everyone closes their eyes. Gemma follows suit; however, with the noise outside the tent, she is not being able to focus on her third eye. *How on earth can one meditate in this clamorous environment?* She thinks.

☼

Gemma's eyes are still closed; she must have reached some degree of the relaxed state of mind during the exercise; she has not come to realize that the practice has already ended. After a while, she opens her eyes wide. The next group of meditators are pouring in. She leaves the tent at once, she has no intention of repeating the session as she wants to move on and participate in other practices on offer.

In an open space further down, there is a drop-down screen. A show which evidently started a while ago, is being projected on the screen. There are scattered sturdy white plastic chairs in front of the screen, some of which are occupied by spectators. She finds an empty chair and sits down on it. She shuffles backwards to gently rest her spine on the back panel of the chair. A man called Alfredo is interviewing Roy Avery. Both of them are speaking in English with Italian subtitles. Gemma has heard about Roy Avery - he is an inspirational speaker and author. He is now talking about his next book that will soon be published. He appears happy, content and talkative. His eyes sparkle as he speaks.

'Yes, my next book is about my experience with three pigeons, a fly and a butterfly…I regard them as my gurus.'

'Interesting!' Can you tell us more?' Alfredo asks.

The author reports that while he was relaxing in his garden one sunny afternoon, writing in his notebook, three pigeons appeared. He had left birdseed and water out for them on the corner of the garden earlier on. He was alert and still. He tried not to be noticed by the birds as even his slightest movement could frighten them! Roy secretly observed the birds; they were in constant fear, frequently checking around before pecking on the seeds. Suddenly, his notebook fell on the ground - the commotion scared the birds away. Their perception of the world around them did not allow them to understand that he did not mean any harm to them. They anticipated fear, they dwelt on fear, and they lived in fear-based situations, guided by their survival instinct. Roy continues,

'Erm…it occurred to me that, in a way, we are like those birds – we live in constant fear. Fear has only one outcome - that which is feared. If, for example, you fear that tomorrow, pouring rain will play havoc with your normal life, then you have only one outcome that you may bring into your experience and that is *pouring rain*.'

'But we're looking here at an almost accurate, high-tech prediction of the weather,' Alfredo points out.

'Ah yes, but fear is an energy, and all our collective fears can affect our physical environment in negative ways. Remember, *energy flows where your attention goes*? Where are you frequently putting your attention to? Where do you think the majority of people in a community, in a nation, in a country, are putting their attention to?

'So where your attention is mainly focused on becomes your reality,' Alfredo re-phrases Roy's statement.

'Exactly.' Roy continues passionately, 'The other day, a fly flew into my kitchen. It shot past me a few times and tried to hop on things to see if it can feed on them. I tried to guide it towards the open window, it frantically flew past me; the more I tried to help it to find its way out, the more it headed erratically in another direction. You know, we tend to behave in a similar fashion. Driven by fright or hopelessness, we deviate from our goals.'

'And how does this analogy translate into deviating from our goals?' Alfredo asks.

47

'Well, let me give you another example to answer your question. This butterfly flew into my bedroom one morning.'

'You seem to get lots of creepy crawlies in your house!' Alfredo jokingly interrupts him.

'Well, yes. You see, we have quite a big garden and my wife is an avid gardener,' Roy rejoins in a modest tone. He says that the butterfly kept banging its whole delicate body onto the polished glass window assuming it was the way out; the wide open part of the window was right next to it. The clear glass window was just an illusion. 'But then, everything is illusion except love,' Roy says. He carries on,

'We're trapped in illusion, but there is always an open door right next to it. Love and optimism constitute that door, and through our collective focus on it, we can impact our world in positive ways. How good is that? Again coming back to the example of the weather,' Roy continues,

'Many possible outcomes of our positive expectations can be a light drizzle, a little rain without any real disruption, a cloudy day with some rain, a cloudy day with no rain, a part cloudy and part sunny day or a glorious sunny day. How many outcomes are possible from positive expectations unlike the single expectation of *pouring rain?* Bear in mind that I'm happy and grateful for whatever weather I get.'

'So, you're saying that we should trade fear with love, optimism or positive expectations.'

'No, you don't trade fear with anything. The more you try to do so the more you invite it into your experience.'

'Isn't that what you are suggesting?'

'Okay then, if I tell you, *don't think about a pink elephant,* what picture can you see in your head, right now?'

'*A pink elephant!*'

'Exactly. So if I tell you: *don't focus on fear or don't trade fear with love,* what will you be focusing on?'

'*Fear.* So what do you do?'

'You just give your attention to love; fear will then subside - *energy flows where your attention goes.*'

✿

The words *love and fear* prompt Gemma into thinking about her own relationship with her family and about the reason why she had drifted away from Leon. Gemma's constant resistance and indifference towards Mabel led Leon to think that she was only adding to Mabel's misery.

From a very young age, Gemma was sensitive to her parents' unhappy marriage and later to Mabel's incessant need for seeking advice and comfort from her friend and neighbour Brian, ten years her junior! Gemma was utterly repulsed when she overheard someone referring to Brian as Mabel's *toy boy*. Although Leon was not affected in the same way as her, he physically distanced himself from the family. He lived away from home on account of his studies and grabbed every opportunity to move farther away.

Gemma did not think Brian was the man for Mabel; she thought he was just taking advantage of the situation. Hatred towards the whole episode brewed up within her along with her fear of losing her mother to Brian. Mabel's marriage to David finally broke down; she ended up with Brian. *'From the frying pan to the fire'*, Gemma mouthed the words under her breath when this happened. She could never accept Brian as an acquaintance, let alone as a step-father. By that time, Leon had achieved his university degree and had gone to Japan; Gemma, not sure about what to do with her life, left home and moved in with Grandma Sheila. She stayed with her until her final days. Grandma died of a chest infection.

✿

Familiar words bring Gemma back to the present moment.

Alfredo is currently saying, '…it goes like this - *La casa è dove si trova il cuore, e dentro al cuore esiste l'uomo saggio* – home is where the heart is and inside the heart, there is the wise man. Am I right?'

Gemma is amazed to hear the specific words - *l'uomo saggio*'– she had heard the phrase somewhere… yes, that Indian guy who sold roses in the piazza had said this. Aleena interpreted the words as *the wise man*; and now Alfredo is suggesting the same.

'You're right there…it's fascinating. And once we feel the presence of *l'uomo saggio* - the *wise man* or the *wise being* - in our hearts, love will flourish,' Roy Avery concludes.

'Love will flourish,' Gemma repeats the words in her mind.

☼

'I did not sign on for this,' an exasperated Mabel blurted out one day. 'I'm not just a mother, who eats, sleeps, poops, wees and looks after her family.'

'I bloody well know that,' Gemma shouted back and slammed her door shut. This was during the time when she came back to stay with Mabel and Brian after grandma had passed away.

The only time they patched up their differences was when Christmas was around - they cherished their time together. Mabel took great care to make the event special. She would cook delicious festive food, leave gifts under the Christmas tree and, when Leon came round, the siblings would fight over who would open the gifts first.

Before the festive season last time, Mabel went to the Whitgift shopping Centre in central Croydon to do Christmas shopping. Leon had just come back from Japan. He settled down in a different part of the city but promised to come home at Christmas. Gemma's wish list for Christmas included a coffee maker and a durable but fashionable umbrella that is frequently needed in the drizzly British weather. Leon, on the other hand, was sensitive to the noisy, ticking clock so he needed one that silently revealed time. His gloves were tattered, he needed a new pair.

Magical Christmas lights were hung loosely on trees, and glittery festive images and patterns festooned street lamps in the precinct. Mabel went inside the centre and visited many shops, not only to buy gifts but to savour the Christmas spirit around her. She went upstairs and leaned against one of the tinsel decorated railings that overlooked the bustling life inside the mall. The place below her was packed with a sea of enthusiastic, chattering shoppers who were moving about in all directions. Pearl drops of neon-light strings, hanging down from the high ceiling, were rocking gently in the still air. A cave-like opening to an enchanting white tunnel led towards the fat-bellied, white-bearded and rosy-cheeked Father Christmas who was in there to provide a paid service to happy, unsuspecting children; they were ardently waiting in a long queue in front of the tunnel with accompanying adults. Two lifelike models of white, sparkly reindeer with a white sleigh were standing outside the tunnel as if they were ready to take off. Christmas carols, the sound of non-stop music and the perfumed whiff from nearby shops further heightened the magical spirit of the place.

Mabel took one last look at the busy mall below her and stepped into the indoor lift; escalators were a pain for her aching knees. She came out of the mall into the open space and sat herself down on a seat deployed for public use. There was some litter around the seat; she wondered why it was there despite the presence of a dustbin nearby. She picked the litter up, threw it into the bin and came back to her seat. She suddenly felt exhausted, her left leg felt weak. Her face was weary and jaded, and her mind was scanning every nook and cranny of her memories.

A street musician was playing George Michael's Careless Whisper on his saxophone. Cascading bursts of the jazzy music captivated her imagination; in a way, the lyrics mimicked some aspects of her life. Snowflakes began to fall in slow motion with the music when the lyrics reached the part that said:

...so I'm never gonna dance again, the way I danced with you, oh. You're gone!'

In the morning, Mabel was found lifeless on the bench covered with snow – brain haemorrhage was the coroner's verdict. In her reusable sturdy shopping bag that her stiff, frozen hand was still strongly clutching, there was a pair of men's gloves with fleece lining, a silent table digital clock, a frilly umbrella with pink rose patterns and a coffee maker!

☼

'Will you be my *yoga buddy*?' A sweet voice disrupts Gemma's thoughts. A slim woman in her early thirties, of the same height as herself, is eagerly waiting for a reply.

☼ ☼ ☼

Chapter 9

'HOW NICE!'

Millie marvels at an imitation necklace in a jewellery stall in the open street market in Chandni Chowk in Delhi, India. The place is teeming chaotically with vendors and their many exhibits; they are calling out from their stalls in an out-of-tune yet friendly tone of voice to entice customers into buying their products. The ground surface is uneven, reddish and muddy with patches of sun-burnt grass. Concrete pathways run alongside it. Savitri recommended a western style shopping mall, but Millie had her heart set on the traditional one - the open street market in Chandni Chowk - authentic and typical.

It is quite hot today especially for Maya and Millie who are accustomed to cold and wet weather. However hot and humid it is going to be in Delhi, Millie intends to make the most of her visit.

Sayed and Leon are now in Tokyo. Sending them to the green conference in Tokyo was at the top of Isaac's agenda; the annual conference is witnessing visitors from quite a few countries. In Isaac's opinion, this event is too good to miss. Sayed will stop over in Delhi on his way back to London to meet up with Millie, this is the plan thus far. This way she will not have to wait until she returns to London to discover how things went in Japan. She is expecting a phone call from him so she has set the volume on her mobile phone high. She knows that Leon will not return home immediately after the conference. He has other plans.

✿

'Let's go over there,' Maya begins to gently pull Millie away from the jewellery stall. Dreading the loss of a potential buyer the vendor insists, 'Eh, didi, ye pachaas Rupee mein ley lijiye.'

'What's he saying?' Millie asks.

Maya says that he is willing to reduce the price of the necklace to fifty Rupee - it is simply a bargaining ploy to cajole customers into buying things. She is no longer in contact with the art of haggling over prices of goods; the natives are generally well versed in this.

They usually accompany their touring friends or families to the shops. They know the traders' selling tactics well and guide their unwary companions away from the trap of overpayment.

Maya leads Millie to the pottery stall where Savitri will meet them. Savitri said she would drop Ranjit at school and come to the meeting place by the stall. Savitri is Maya's second cousin's daughter. In a country where the majority of people live with their extended families or are in contact with them on a regular basis, cousins and second cousins are looked upon as family members. Being born and brought up in another culture, Millie finds the sentiment incomprehensible; she is beginning to take delight in the company of these people all the same.

The busy market at the heart of Delhi with all its commodities and hustle and bustle is overwhelming. There are mazes of closely-knit open stalls. Traders are selling traditional garments, hand-woven rugs, bags, jewellery, novelty shoes, ceramic and clay pots, household items, regional food and so much more. There are also organised blocks of shops, the bulk of which are clothes shops.

Delhi is an amazing city with its new and old regions and systems. There are contrasting features of old and modern buildings and of modes of transport, some of which are power-driven, some others are driven by domestic animals. One needs to cautiously get around either on foot or by available conveyance through a seemingly endless flow of people and chaotic road traffic.

'There you are, you gorgeous ladies!' Savitri emerges from behind the pottery stall. She is wearing classy earrings and a red and yellow salwar-kameez suit with glass-embedded embroideries with a rich and diverse variety of colours under the front neckline but less intense elsewhere in the suit. Her attire and sunny disposition blend in well with the bright summer day. She hugs them with warm greetings.

The threesome begin their shopping venture by looking at the handmade potteries that come in all shapes and sizes; some of them are flawed, but this makes them more special and authentic. Millie gets some cute little painted pots as souvenirs for her friends and colleagues: Anne and Sue will surely love them.

Savitri tells her not to get carried away by them as there is more to see and buy during their stay in Delhi. Maya who left her homeland years ago, and Millie, a visitor in her mother's country, are all ears to Savitri's advice and recommendations.

'Mum, I'm hungry,' Millie sounds edgy what with the scorching heat and hunger. She adjusts her stylish sun hat in an attempt to feel cooler.

'Me too. Let's go to the food stalls. You will be spoilt for choice, I tell you,' Savitri is ready to lead them to their favoured destination. These stalls stand along the street not far from where they are.

They stroll towards arrays of food enticingly set out, where there is evidently more variety than one can imagine. The sizzling, spicy smoke from freshly cooked regional cuisine diffuses into the air. Among many types of food, there is chicken tikka in thick home-made curried sauce, caramelised onions and yoghurt, served with clay-oven-baked soft fluffy Nan bread that melts in the mouth. In a special clay pot there is lamb Rogan Josh, an aromatic spicy lamb curry; it comes with rosewater and saffron flavoured pilau rice and salad. Vegetarian options include chopped baby cucumbers with crispy lettuce, tomatoes and chick peas, sprinkled with coarsely ground black pepper and chaat masala - a special spice mix; and lightly cooked, crunchy mixed vegetables in a thick bed of moderately spiced onion sauce with pancake-type unleavened bread, roti, holding the lot. Food is served in a boat-shaped dish made from plaited banana leaves with a wooden fork.

Millie goes for vegetables and roti while Savitri tucks into chicken tikka wrap. Maya settles for juicy baby cucumbers, tomatoes, crispy lettuce and chickpeas. On Aunt Rani's insistence, Maya had full breakfast in the morning so she is not that hungry. She usually has two meals a day – breakfast and late lunch. She skips dinner, a habit she had developed during her childhood when she would often go to bed without food.

✿

'Auntyji, have you ever noticed that in a crowd, individuals often wander around singly or in small groups? They are hardly mindful of what's going on around them,' Savitri says musingly while walking away from food stalls.

Maya relates Savitri's observation to her own past experience; she tells her that when Millie was a year old she took her to a local mother and toddlers' club. Other mothers in the club laughed and joked among themselves - they never even said *hello* to Maya. Later she came to know that those mothers gave birth to their babies around the same time in the same hospital so they knew each other very well – that was the reason why they kept to themselves.

'Well, they should've at least said *hello* or smiled at you. Smiling doesn't cost anything, you know. I always smile at people anyway,' Savitri airs her own opinion.

'I'd be suspicious if a stranger smiled at me. I'd rather they didn't. I think we are all hung up on talking or smiling at people that we don't know,' Millie says.

For Millie, smiling is acceptable but a very friendly stranger, more often than not, may arouse suspicion. However, she thinks that Savitri is right in that acknowledging someone with a short greeting or a smile does not cost anything.

✧

In her childhood, Maya would often picture huge, transparent plastic bubbles in her imagination, floating and gliding up and down through space, close to Earth. Each bubble contained individuals or groups of people. There was Mrs Dayal, a wealthy neighbour, in one of the bubbles, having her afternoon nap while her dog lay leisurely underneath her four-poster bed; inside another bubble, there were dirty children playing in the street, dodging around street cars, rickshaws and bullock carts; in another one, there was a high-rise packed shopping mall with exquisite items; there was also her mother, Archana, in one of them, doing her usual chores and dreaming the undreamable! Sometimes Maya was with Archana inside the same bubble.

In Maya's imagination, the bubbles co-existed as parallel worlds, not touching each other, only barely crossing each other's paths. No one in them was aware of others' existence; no one ever noticed others' sorrow, joy, pain or pleasure, they were blissfully oblivious of the world around them - everyone was immersed in their own little, bubbled worlds. Sometimes, Maya would travel from her bubble to Mrs Dayal's.

In reality, when Mrs Dayal needed a head or a foot massage, she would send for Maya. Maya would always welcome this as this gave her a chance to look at Mrs Dayal's tinted glass showcase that held delicate show pieces from around the world. Mrs Dayal would often give Maya pretty things from her collection afterwards as a thank-you gift for her service. Once she gave her a miniature red and blue glass dolphin. Maya tied it around her neck with a string like a necklace for a long time. She was careful not to break it!

Many a time Maya wondered what it would be like to prick those bubbles with a big, sharp needle and make the barriers disappear! She has been in search of that needle ever since!

✿

'Unless, of course, a scene is created. Just watch,' Savitri says with regard to people's apparent indifference towards others. She walks away from the group to give a demonstration of what she meant. She enacts tripping over with a big, painful *ouch* sound. A passer-by quickly steps forward and extends his helping hand towards her, 'Aap thik toh hona, bahen-ji?' (Are you alright, sister?). A few others quicken the pace to her aid. Savitri picks herself up and brushes off the dust she willingly brought upon herself. She thanks her potential helpers and keeps up a pretence of limping. Millie and Maya soon join her. This is amusing for Maya. Savitri has managed to momentarily pierce *the bubble*.

'At least, you've got friends in need!' Millie jokes. They crack up as they walk on.

The three women leave the marketplace and carefully cross the main road. They need to catch an auto-rickshaw, a three-wheeled power driven vehicle, from this side of the road because of the one-way traffic system. It is less crowded here. The slabs in the pavement are giving off heat they have absorbed throughout the day. The shops on the other side of the road are still busy. Although the journey back home is not that long, Savitri thinks that it would be wiser for them to travel together. It is usually difficult to hail an auto-rickshaw that will take three passengers as the seat inside it is wide enough for two. The driver's willingness to take an extra passenger on board depends on how convincing passengers are and how fat the tip is going to be.

Savitri looks for a cooler place where they can wait and, at the same time, keep an eye on the road to track down a vehicle. She spots a rough-and-ready hut with an awning above its front door and ushers Maya and Millie towards it. A hand-written message in

56

Hindi, stuck on the door of the hut, draws Savitiri's attention; she interprets this into English:

Come inside for Baba Sattyaram's sage words.

'Mum, if there is really a holy man inside this spooky hut, tell him about your meditative experiences,' Millie suggests. She knows that India is a land of sages and hermits; she will be delighted to meet one today. She starts inspecting the front of the hut and its entrance door that look somewhat timeworn. Maya is not so sure if there is a real sage inside the hut; there are also con people around. She asks for Savitri's opinion.

'You are right auntyji but there are genuine ones too. *Sadhus* and sages generally help people with spiritual awakening,' Savitri says.

A rather skinny boy in his late teens spots them from inside the hut. He comes out and beckons them in, using whatever knowledge of English he has, 'Mera naam Nimu hai. This way come.' He introduces himself as Nimu and leads them into the hut.

✪

The tour in the Delhi market was in total contrast to their brief visit into the hut; it was as if they had slipped through an unguarded black hole into a surreal existence for a few moments. After a fascinating experience inside the hut, Savitri's native ways of persuasion convinces an auto rickshaw driver to take them on and drive them to the house in Aram Bagh Road.

Once squeezed inside the vehicle, Savitri requests the driver, 'Bhai saab, thora jaldi chalaiyena, please.' Shruti, the housekeeper, must have picked up Ranjit from school, bathed and fed him and Naaniji must have finished her afternoon rituals of prayers. Compelled by her sense of responsibility for their wellbeing, Savitri asks the driver to go a bit faster. The traffic is appallingly slow at this time of day. The driver assures her in a tiresome voice that he is doing his best.

Inside the auto, Millie mulls over the brief encounter they have had with an Indian sage in the hut.

✪

'Do we have to wait long?' Maya asked Nimu haltingly for his comprehension.

'No waiting, no waiting,' he assured her, 'Baba (father) is ready.'

'He sounds as if he knew we were coming,' Millie commented.

The small empty front room inside the hut had a door at the rear that led to another room through a long, uneven open alleyway with muddy puddles; there was a dank smell in the air of wet soil. It had rained yesterday. They carefully stepped on dry patches of the path to reach their destination – the journey felt endless; the time stood still. They finally found their way into the room.

Inside the room, a man in his early forties was sitting on a bamboo mat, wearing orange, cotton *dhoti* trousers and a long, brown bead necklace that rested on his bare chest. His yoga-toned body was lean and flexible; he was sitting with his legs crossed. He had a curled moustache; his beard was tucked in under his chin. Strips of white holy paint shone across his forehead. His eyes were half closed. An oil lamp was flickering in front of him, creating a mystical aura of light and shadow in the room. The noise of the market could no longer be heard from here and despite the sunny day, the room was semi-dark, cool and calm, and fairly ancient.

'Why didn't he choose to sit in the front room?' Millie whispered to Savitri.

'That could be the waiting room…I'll find out about that for you,' Savitri whispered back.

Maya stepped forward and got herself down to the man's sitting level. His eyes were still half-closed.

'Hari Om, Hari Om, Hari Om,' he chanted. 'The world is tainted…it is in dire need for regaining its pristine purity,' he paused and dipped back into mindfulness.

'He can speak English,' Millie said under her breath.

'And he speaks very well,' Savitri said.

Nimu sat down in front of him and uttered with great respect, 'Baba', then he pointed at the visitors. The sage opened his eyes fully. He briefly inspected them and fixed his gaze at Maya as if to say,

'Go ahead, speak your mind.'

Maya told him about indistinct images of strange people and places that showed up in her imagination during meditation. Her enunciation implied that she was just beginning to have some faith in the man, hoping that some guidance or satisfactory answers could emerge from him.

'Haar din, haar pal nayi batein hotey rahi,' Baba stated in a hushed voice.

Millie looked at Savitri inquisitively; she needed an interpretation of what Baba had said. Savitri whispered near enough to her ear, 'It means *every day, every moment new things are happening.*'

The man made circular movements with his right index finger on the space between his eyebrows and spoke in a pensive tone, 'When your third eye activates, you are in an altered vibrational frequency, you then function from within your mid-brain, and you experience things that you haven't experienced before.'

He then slowly chanted a verse in Hindi.

Janta ki awaaz mein kabhi kabaar ek shakti hai,
Unch ki sankhya mein kum ki bhavna hai
Vishnu ki duniya unhein ek din jaagta hua dekhegi
Aur rashtra ki utthan ke liye wohi behter hai.

Nimu dutifully repeated the verse a couple of times like an obedient student who had just memorised his lesson and was eager to retain it in his memory through repetition.

'The world will only experience what you have foreseen during meditation and what I have just said when certain conditions are met and when the left and right hemispheres harmonize. Human discernment is still miles away from that,' Baba apparently said this to Maya.

'Sir, could you please explain this a little more clearly?' Millie asked.

'There are signs for those who listen, there are signs for those who reason and there are signs for those who reflect. Hari Om, Hari Om, Hari Om.' Then he looked at all three women and said, 'Rise above your sorrow.'

'How can we do that, Baba?' Maya asked.

'Acknowledge your sorrow, feel it in your heart and move on,' Baba replied.

Then he directed his gaze towards Millie and Savitri and said,

'Stop by the woods, watch the birds fly, listen to the waterfall, smell flowers, taste a sweet corn, embrace a tree, embrace someone and praise the Lord.'

He closed his eyes to meditate. This was his way of saying goodbye to them. The holy paint stripes on his forehead were shining like neon lights; this was as if to mark the end of the conversation and the beginning of the next segment!

Maya then asked Nimu what Baba had meant by certain conditions and the harmonization of the left and right hemispheres, keeping her voice down. Nimu whispered back, saying that he was not sure but that she would come to know about these things in due course as people always did. Savitri also had a little conversation with Nimu in her native language.

It was getting late; it was time for them to return home. Maya left some Rupee notes in front of Baba without a word. Nimu picked up the notes and studied them from all angles in the dim light with wonder in his eyes. Maya thought he was checking their authenticity. Millie thought he was being rude. Nimu carefully put the money back and led them out of the hut.

'I feel like having an ice cream now,' Millie said.

'Same here. I'll make nice aromatic *sharbat* with ice cubes for us when we get home,' Savitri promised.

Nimu went back in and sat in the front room; he did not know how long he relished looking at the busy scene outside. Suddenly, he felt a tap on his shoulder.

'Hamey wapas jaana hai,' there was urgency in Baba's voice. He repeated, 'We need to return.'

✧

Sitting in the auto-rickshaw, Savitri helps Maya to remember the poem Baba and Nimu had recited. It was a short verse and was repeated by Nimu so it is not that difficult to recall it. Savitri endeavours to interpret it for Millie, 'The voice of people seldom has ah....,' she pauses for the right words.

'I think the verse has a deeper meaning. Give me some time to work on it,' Savitri says.

'But I found the sage pretty vague…Don't you think so, mum?' Millie asks.

'I'm not sure, but Mill, you're the one who's interested in these things, aren't you?'

'Yeah, but I need more information.'

Despite the elusiveness, what they experienced in the hut was intriguing. Savitri tells them that she managed to find out from Nimu about Baba being farther away from the entrance: the trip from the entrance to the main part of the hut through the alleyway symbolized the journey from the outer to the inner world of consciousness. It was meant to prepare them to go deep inside their inner selves although this may not have the desired effect on everyone. 'Because, as Nimu put it, *hum sab alag alag hain*, meaning *we're all different*,' Savitri concludes.

Millie says that the sage did not elaborate much on what he had said; the contents of his speech were rather sketchy. Savitri tells her that most sages are like that; they give the enquirer an idea or two to ponder upon yet they don't give away the whole truth which they themselves are seeking throughout their lives; one has to embark on one's own spiritual journey with an open heart and mind in order for things to come to light for them in due course. Maya smiles, Savitri's explanation rings a bell with what she has been experiencing recently.

'Remember, who he said the signs were for? Those who listen…' Maya jogs her memory.

'Yes, er… those who listen and reason. What was the other one?' Savitri asks.

'Those who reflect,' Millie replies.

Savitri plans to go back to Baba to get to know him and his work better although she keeps this to herself, not exactly knowing why; she wants to solve the apparent mystery without involving others. Above and beyond, she is more than a little influenced by Millie's scepticism so she wants to investigate the matter further.

The late afternoon creeps in like a homing pigeon. The sun rolls behind the buildings, leaving long and thin strokes of copper glow on the white bed of clouds, far beneath which the auto rickshaw proceeds through the noisy bedlam of Delhi traffic.

○ ○ ○

Chapter 10

'IRRASHAIMASE.'

The waiters and waitresses shout out the word at the top of their voices the moment Sayed and Leon enter Shunsai restaurant inside the conference hotel in central Tokyo. Welcoming customers with *irrashaimase* and taking care of them from the moment they enter the restaurant are of the greatest importance to the restaurant staff. They obligingly lead their new customers to the seating area. Real looking plastic food items on pretty plastic plates are on display inside a glass show case; this is a novel way of acquainting customers with the appealing assortment of food on the menu.

Leon and Sayed settle down on their seats and browse through the menu.

'Mmm, the miso soup looks good as a starter. What is it made from?' Sayed asks.

'It's usually made from soybean paste, dashi soup stock, tofu and chopped fresh green onions and there are other varieties,' Leon explains. They place an order for the soup.

While sipping the savoury soup, Sayed looks around and appreciates the restaurant's pleasant ambience. The street outside is full of commotion.

It is now lunch break.

✿

The green conference has started in the conference hall inside the hotel. There is a tall building opposite the hotel where models of green cars, in other words, environment-friendly cars, are on display in its spacious open-plan foyer. An extensive paved yard links the hotel and the building; participants will have the opportunity to go back and forth to enjoy the whole event. The convention is mainly centred on environmental issues, eco houses and future merchandising products such as green cars.

The statistics released in the morning session in the conference hall concerning the effect of carbon dioxide discharge on the environment were as alarming in Japan as in the UK. Measures taken in Japan in an attempt to reduce such discharge were addressed in the session. The session also incorporated screenings of clever uses of renewable energies, using minimal technology. The one about an eco-house in Kunitachy city was particularly interesting. The title of the show was displayed as:

Taiyou to kaze to mizu ni aisareru ie.

The house was shown from all angles beginning from its top. This was specially built to make full use of natural light, water and wind. No electric illumination was used during the day and the early part of the evening. The sunlight reached every part of the house through continuous panels of full-length frosted windows; the sunlight also entered the house through the skylight on the rooftop and permeated the floors beneath through partly frosted glass floors. During the day, the heat was accumulated in the rooms through closed shojis – they were traditional sliding screen doors; this arrangement provided warmth in the cool evening.

In the summer, a water sprinkler on the rooftop kept the house cool; the used water was then recycled and the process continued. The wind-power mechanism allowed small windows around the top of the house to open and close mechanically, ventilating the whole house. It was indeed…

…a house that is loved by the sun, the wind and the water –
taiyou to kaze to mizu ni aisareru ie!

During the morning break, Leon and Sayed ran into a Mr Yoda, one of the automobile executives in the show. He agreed to see them after the conference and arrange a date and time for a formal meeting to discuss pertinent issues. Leon insisted that he would prefer a meeting with him tomorrow afternoon, if possible, as he would be off to Siem Reap soon. This was his way of getting things done more quickly.

Mr Yoda, a short and stout Japanese man with rosy cheeks, had taken to the enthusiasm of the two Brits. He appeared optimistic despite the fact that automotive industries worldwide were going through financial and environmental crises.

The restaurant is now full of other conference members.

'So how are we going to request more information from Mr Yamashita?' Sayed asks Leon while eating sushi. Mr Yamashita is the chairperson of Japan Automobile Makers Association; a meeting with him was already arranged from London by way of emails and faxes.

'We'll see. They usually don't say *no* to requests. They will go as far as saying: *It's under consideration* or *it's inconvenient*,' Leon says. The time he spent in Japan enabled him to understand the culture and customs of the country to some extent.

'Hmm. So you mean they usually say *yes* even if they don't mean it.'

'Possibly. They don't normally offend people by saying *no*.'

'So if, for example, I ask: *Do you think it's a good idea*? Even if they think it's not, will they still say *yes*?' Sayed is curious.

'Well, they may hesitate to say *no*. You should then rephrase your question in their favour and ask: *Do you think it's a bad idea*? And their answer will be an inevitable *yes* if that's how they see it.'

'Then we should ask: *Could we please have your company's research report on green cars*?'

'Well, the answer could be, '*It's under...*''

'*Consideration*,' Sayed completes the sentence.

'Yeah, they're generally very courteous, they'll not openly insult you with negation.'

Leon is fascinated by Japan and its culture. After successfully majoring in Environmental Geography and East Asian Studies at Hertford University in Oxford, England, he was in favour of going to the country not merely to live there but also to get the feel of the country and its fascinating culture. His interpreting job in Tokyo was organised by the London branch of a Japanese agency. The Japanese language was part of his degree programme so his language skills and his passion for working in Japan assisted him in getting the job. The position was interesting and varied and so were the venues where he worked.

He lived in a bedsit with an adjoining bathroom. The rent was paid for by his company; affording a place near central Tokyo would have been beyond his means. The studio flat he lived in had four settings. Pressing of a few buttons on the wall would drop or lift wooden screens and partitions to reveal some furniture items, a small fridge and a cooker. They would cleverly appear as and when required and transform the place into a bedroom, a kitchen, a lounge or a dining room. He admired his resourceful landlord for the technological advances; he thought of introducing a similar system in London. This could prove advantageous to some congested parts of the city (this had never been actualised except for his own studio flat that he later bought in London and had some identical interior features installed in it).

Travelling from his flat to many places inside and outside Tokyo on account of the job was convenient. The train station was nearby and the trains were fast and frequent.

✪

Lunchtime will soon be over. Waiters and waitresses are at their customers' beck and call; they are keen to impress them with their quality service.

Leon is now finishing off the last bit of his succulent grilled chicken. After lunch, they will be off to the tall building opposite the conference hotel to view models of environment-friendly cars. Then they will be back to the conference hall in the hotel for the last show of the day.

The spacious lobby in the tall building has black and white square-tiled flooring and white walls with a high ceiling; the place channels an air of welcome to visitors that came from far and wide. In the middle of the grand space, four models of cars are displayed; they heighten the enthusiasm of the spectators who are currently congregating around them, pointing at their favourites that suit their tastes and expectations. Sayed and Leon join the crowd to inspect the models. Leon takes out his notebook and jots down some useful information from the descriptions exhibited. Sayed picks up some informative leaflets from a nearby metal stand. They are ready to go back to the conference hall.

✪

The conference hall is full again with delegates from Japan, America, Germany, France, Britain and Italy. Incidentally, not many people from Japan's neighbouring countries have joined the seminar. The host speaker mentioned in the morning that the event would probably be made more international next year in a much bigger venue. He said that this would depend on the success of today's event.

The screen in the hall goes brighter with the subtle running sound of the projector. It first shows the fascinating logo for going green. Then the internal mechanisms of the cars that were on display inside the foyer of the tall building are cast on the screen with detailed description narrated in Japanese. Members of the audience can use their audio headsets and choose their preferred languages: English, German, French or Italian. Next interesting segment contains zero-emission cars powered by alternative energy sources, like battery and electricity; some such cars will be available in Japan in the near future albeit in small numbers.

After the presentation, the management executives of Honda and Nissan briefly talk about turning fuel crises into opportunities and about their companies' strategies for introducing future cars. Finally, the panel's discussions and queries from the audience revolve around future industry trends, the availability of the cars for the general public in Japan and in other countries and the government's policies on the scheme.

✿

At the end of the conference, Mr Yoda says that it is *inconvenient* for him to see Sayed and Leon tomorrow afternoon. He apologises for this and gives them his business card. He asks them to ring his secretary to make an appointment with him at a convenient date and time, assuring them that this will be before Leon leaves the country. They have a consolation - they are going to see Mr Yamashita the next morning. Isaac had fixed this appointment for them before they set off for Tokyo. Meeting Mr Yoda, if that happens, will just be the icing on the cake.

✿ ✿ ✿

Chapter 11

GEMMA'S ACKNOWLEDGING SMILE SATISFIES THE woman, who is looking for a *yoga buddy*, that she has found the right person.

'Hi, my name's Jocelyn. I'm from New York City.'

Jocelyn has deep-set blue eyes and tanned skin. Her slender and toned body reveals that she does physical exercise of some kind. She appears cheerful and forthright.

'Hello, I'm Gemma from London, England,' Gemma extends her hand towards Jocelyn to shake hers.

'Nice meeting you Gemma. Isn't it a great show?'

'It is indeed. Did you come to the show last year?'

'No, this is actually my first time in Rome.'

'Really? I've visited Rome a few times, but this is my first time at the show. So what's this thing about *yoga buddy*?'

'Oh, I need a yoga buddy for a session over there,' Jocelyn points at the nearby encircled space labelled with the words *Partner Yoga*. They have kept the English words.

'It's a sorta sacred practice of yoga and it's done in pairs. I need someone the same size as me to do the practice. You seem to fit the bill. Would ya like to pair with me?'

'Sure. Let's go.'

☼

The yoga instructor Praneeta is an English speaking Indian woman. The session has just started and, fortunately, there is enough space with spare laid-out yoga mats. Jocelyn and Gemma take up their place. An assistant translates Praneeta's instructions into Italian for the Italian speaking participants. Praneeta says that the practice starts with *pranayama* that means breathing in certain ways and *asanas* - coordinated body movements and postures.

'You support and counterbalance each other in paired yoga asanas. These asanas promote a deeper understanding of the body, mind and spirit,' Praneeta explains. 'While this may seem complicated at first, with practice, it will become easy and enjoyable,' she assures the participants.

Two assistants step on a slightly raised platform to show the yoga postures. Their demonstration is well synchronized as if they are two halves of a whole. Friends and companions attempt to copy them. Praneeta goes round and verbally guides or praises her students. Balancing and co-ordinating postures, pulling and pushing with hands and feet trigger a lot of giggles and mistakes but Praneeta is right - it is fun!

'No, no, hold my left hand with your right hand,' Jocelyn corrects Gemma. Another time Gemma says, 'Hang on, I'll balance you with this scarf.' Someone Gemma hardly knows becomes her transient friend through the synchronised fun yoga. She is not planning to get to know new people at this point in her life; this does not stop her from having a good time in doing something new and interesting.

The practice goes on for half an hour and at the end of it, strangers, friends and partners feel their bonds of friendship and love strengthened.

'That was cool, wasn't it?' Jocelyn says.

'It certainly was,' Gemma agrees.

'Would ya care to try some delicious raw food?' I came here yesterday so I know quite a few stalls around here.'

The two women go back to the stall area to find the food stall selling raw chocolate brownies. They are rich and delicious protein chunks with bits of Peruvian raw chocolate, almonds and raisins. Smaller pieces of them are placed in a stainless steel bowl for tasting. Gemma picks up a piece of brownie from the bowl and slowly chews it to savour its taste.

'Mmm, it's chewy, nutty and chocolatey! Love it,' Gemma says. 'What are you doing next, Jocelyn?'

'I'm gonna go to the sacred space.'

'What's that?'

Jocelyn says that it is a sacred space for doing meditation in one's own time. People may also want to take a few moments to send out their good wishes and blessings to the world.

'Is it sign-posted?' Gemma asks.

'Oh, the place is girdled with arched bamboo sticks – you can't miss it. The inside of it is lined with a mat, cosy cushions, fragrant sticks, naturally formed stones, singing bowls and chiming bells,' Jocelyn informs.

'I've already had a taste of meditation so I'll let this one pass,' Gemma opens up the programme booklet. 'What else have we got here? ...There is Quantum Yoga, Qi Yoga, Yin Thai Yoga, Kundalini Yoga and Gong Bath. Won't be able to do all of them.'

'That's why I came here yesterday. There are long queues for most of them. You may not get a space in the practice area if you stand far behind in the queue. Do the ones with shorter queues,' Jocelyn advises. She steps forward. She halts and looks back:

'Oh, don't forget to try out Yogi Tea.'

'Where's that?'

'It's kinda near the entrance. There are samples of Breathe Deep, Green Energy, Ginger Lemon and more.'

Gemma plans to sample them on her way out. Having a taster cup of revitalising, calming tea will be a nice way to end the day. She will get some if she likes the taste. This is one of the attractions of the show – you get to taste, smell or try out things before you decide to buy or not to buy them.

'Thanks Jocelyn. Glad to have met you.'

'Same here,' Jocelyn grins and disappears into the crowd.

☼

Gemma's chattering mind has calmed down through relaxation exercises, but Mabel is frequently coming to her mind.

Mabel was a regular church-goer; she had unwavering faith in God most of the time; at other times, she was not so sure if He was really hearing her out. Gemma learned about Mabel's last visit to St. Paul's cathedral in London from Carina, their Portuguese neighbour.

Mabel invited Carina to accompany her to the cathedral. Carina was an admirer of the historic house of worship; she appreciated its architecture, greatness and beatitude; she was not confident enough though to go there on her own so she gladly accepted the invitation. Little did she know that Mabel had a reason for the visit. Mabel strongly believed that if she lit a candle at St. Paul's and said her prayers, they would be answered.

☼

Mabel and Carina came out of St. Paul's underground station and slowly made their way to the cathedral. Visitors thronged near and upon the wide steps of the building.

Having paid the entry fees, they entered the cathedral and walked towards the middle of the endless hall. Carina was awestruck by the magnificent arches, high ceiling and the décor with the delicate scent of candles and the aura of the place itself. The echoes of guides' voices and people's steps against the high ceiling created an air of mysticism. Mabel drew closer to a large volume of the Bible inside a glass box under the sharp gaze of a statue of an Eagle. She stood there for some time while Carina roamed about watching and admiring the place. Mabel finally found her way to the candles and lit a few of them in exchange for some coins. She then whispered a prayer:

Our Father in heaven, please bestow upon my family your divine guidance and blessings. Please bless my children with what I failed to bless them with. Please hear me out, Father, in the name of our Lord Jesus Christ. Amen.

She reached out for a tissue to wipe off her silent tears; she felt Carina's comforting stroke on her right shoulder. Carina's tearful eyes looked into hers and said, 'Your children are fine, more than fine, and you just know it.'

☼

Jocelyn was right. There are long queues in front of most of the sessions. Gemma scours the place and finally tracks down a shorter queue, it will start in twenty minutes. She waits in the queue. The writing on the nearby wooden stand says *Mantra di guarigione.* An Indian man, standing in front of her, initiates a conversation about the practice. He tells her that the practice involves chanting a healing *mantra* and that *mantra* is a word or groups of words chanted repeatedly by the followers of Hinduism or Buddhism to encourage concentration in meditation. These words are usually in Sanskrit - an ancient language of India in which legendary poems and Hindu Holy Scriptures are written.

When it is time, the participants move near the dais and sit on the mats with legs crossed. Gemma has become used to the sitting position by now. All these sessions come with soothing background music that fits in well with the mood, setting and the activities. A man of medium height with toned physique and bronze complexion called Matteo begins the session by breathing deeply and chanting the mantra, *Har, Haray, Hari, Wahe guru*, very slowly and tunefully. He then breaks down the meaning of each word in English, pausing every so often to speak in Italian:

Har: the primordial potential – the seed of all creation;
Haray: the creative force;
Hari: the manifestation of 'Har' through the infinite wisdom of Haray;
Wahe guru: the feeling of ecstasy for the process of all creation from 'Har' through to 'Hari'.

Wow, this is a-w-e-s-o-m-e!

The mantra allows you to perceive the process of creation that flows from the seed potential to its manifestation through the infinite wisdom of God.
The chanting and remembering all aspects of God - the creativity of God, the joyfulness of God, the beauty of God will generate feelings of love, peace and joy within yourself. This will allow the creative energy to flow into your life.
When you are feeling down or just want to uplift your spirit, chant this mantra and you will be in bliss; you can chant this anytime for inner peace and happiness.

Matteo then shows a sequence of arm and hand movements that involve tapping on knees and shoulders and then clapping. He performs the exercise with the mantra, first in slow motion and then at a faster speed. Gemma observes the routine; she is not so willing to join in but the participants' concerted effort inspires her to give it a try.

Everyone is now chanting the mantra with the synchronized exercise. For Gemma, everything else shuts out in the background –

the music, the noise from other nearby activities. The collective chanting and tapping seem to be coming from a far-off place.

The atmosphere is filled with elation;
…emotions intensify,
…and vibrations of the incantations develop into higher frequencies.

Everyone is now chanting:

Har, Haray, Hari, Wahe guru
Har, Haray, Hari, Wahe guru
Har, Haray, Hari, Wahe guru
Har, Haray, Hari, **Wa**he guru

This goes on for some time and like the gushing of a suppressed spring, Gemma weeps uncontrollably. Her arms now feel incapacitated, she can no longer continue with the ritual. With lumps in her throat she utters a single word:

'Mum.'

✿✿✿

Chapter 12

'AUNTYJI, I WENT BACK TO BABA'S DWELLING OUT OF curiosity, but there was no trace of him or Nimu,' Savitri announces.

'I had a nagging doubt that they were fake,' Millie says.

'But...they may have moved to another part of the city,' Maya reasons.

'I thought so, but nobody in the area has ever heard about them or seen them.'

'What about the hut?'

'Yeah, it is there but a nearby vendor told me that it had been empty for a long time. The owner of the hut went away on Kashi yatra, you know, it means a long pilgrimage to the holy city of Kashi. A big rusty lock was dangling in the middle of the front door. Isn't that strange?'

'I'm sure there is a logical explanation to all that,' Maya suggests.

'Maybe, I'll do more research on that,' Savitri says.

'You and your research,' Rani beams with a warm smile.

Savitri is giving Rani a head massage using the wholesome Amla hair oil under the late-morning sun out in the courtyard. This is encircled by red-brick walls with a metal gate at the front, a kitchen in the corner and a single-storey red-brick house at the back. Savitri is carefully parting Rani's grey-black hair from the crown of her head down to the back of her neckline; she is then rubbing the parted hair pathways with the herbal hair oil. Its odour is pleasantly overpowering.

Rani is sitting on a low stool near the sacred Tulsi tree that is on a pedestal in the centre of the patio. Savitri has settled herself in a chair behind Rani so that she can do her job properly. Maya and Millie are sitting on weaved cane stools opposite them, basking in the sun, enjoying the leisurely moment and wondering about the Baba episode. Enticing smell of food from the pot on the clay stove in the kitchen is travelling all the way towards them. Shruti, the producer of the flavour, is happily cooking and singing away in her native dialect.

✿

For Maya, visiting Delhi was a trip down memory lane. Her initial constrained feeling during meditation linked with what she had heard about Archana's (her mother) life and with her own life as a child. As she progressed through the guided meditation, the feeling wore off; she was released from the tightened grip, she was freed from her distant past.

Aunt Rani, now in her early seventies, has maintained fairly good health despite a little discomfort from arthritis. She is still as affectionate and true to her sense of responsibility as ever.

✿

During Rani's stay in London, she continued to provide financial support to her parents who lived back home in Delhi. Her husband Thomas did not quite comprehend such practice and regarded this as a means to cripple her parents' own abilities to live their own lives; he never made this a big issue though as both of them were careful enough not to intrude on matters concerning their respective families.

Her father, Randitya, had a house built in Arambagh Road in Delhi and moved into it with her mother, Pavitra, from the shanty town they earlier lived in. The expenses for building the house were met partly by Rani and partly by the money Randitya earned as a book-keeper in a small publishing company. Archana, Rani's younger sister got married and left home.

Rani was unable to ignore the fact that her father afforded her and her sister an opulent lifestyle in their birth city that altered virtually overnight into unforeseen circumstances. As children often do, Rani saw the turmoil as part of her own fault; it fostered guilt in her mind. Supporting them financially later in her adulthood made her feel better, and now she is reaping the benefit of this by living in her parents' house. She is now the happy owner of it.

✿

Rani was glad to have come back to her homeland after Thomas' death. Both her parents had passed away by that time. She could not bear to continue to live in their London flat that she shared with Thomas - her *dear Tom* - who stood by her through thick and thin; she decided to spend the rest of her life in her hometown. Having this in mind, she sold the flat in London, gave Maya a part of the proceeds and with the rest of the money, she bought a small farmland

74

near Delhi. Workers were employed to run the farmland based on fifty-fifty profit-sharing agreement. She had inherited Shruti, the long-serving housekeeper, who was the only resident in the house after her parents had passed away. Shruti was truly relieved to see Rani!

Savitri and her five-year-old son, Ranjit, later came to live with them. She did not have anywhere else to go when her world had turned upside down. She now takes care of the household and oversees the running of the farmland. In return, she receives love and guidance, and a shelter for her and her son. She also works part-time for a government agency that works towards reducing poverty and increasing employment in the city.

✧

The energetic little Ranjit appears on his three-wheeled bike and goes straight towards Maya, 'Auntyji, can I come with you to London?' Savitri uses the endearment to address Maya. He is simply copying it, stressing on the suffix –ji that is meant to show respect to elders.

'Don't be naughty Ranju, go and play with your submarine you made yesterday,' Savitri mildly reproaches him while rubbing the hair oil in Rani's parted hair.

'You're welcome to come and visit us in London, darling,' Maya says. Ranjit's small face lights up with innocent excitement.

'I'm not sure about that, Auntyji. Naaniji will be all alone,' Savitri sounds unsure.

'Aunt Rani will come too,' Maya says.

'No, no my dear. I have had my share of stay in London. I'm all happy and settled here.'

'Well, in that case, we shouldn't leave you.'

'Come on Savi, I'm sure Naaniji will be all right, won't you Naaniji?' Millie asks Rani hoping to receive an affirmative reply.

Rani is a mother figure to Maya and that makes her grandma (Naaniji) to Millie. Millie now knows that great aunts and uncles are regarded as grandparents in this culture. Visiting her ancestral home and spending time with her extended family have become quite meaningful for her; she has even picked up a bit of the native language!

Rani assures them, 'Of course I'll be all right. And don't forget my dear old Shruti will be with me…Savi, you should go; you need a break.' She adds, 'I will pay for the trip.'

Savitri's nimble fingers stop massaging Rani's head; she blankly stares into the distant horizon. Rahul hoped to send Ranjit to London for higher studies the moment he was born. Savitri found this ludicrous, but that was what he was like - planning far ahead of time.

Savitri's ebullient guise typifies the native proverb:

Ek rangina vyaktitya dukh ki chhaya chhupati hai – a jovial personality masks the shadow of sadness.

By being sunny and sportive, she hides her grief she has been silently nurturing since the day her husband, Rahul, simply disappeared off the face of the earth. There was a rumour that Rahul took the rap for his father's alleged misconduct in an ill-reputed group he belonged to.

Savitri once tearfully asked Rani, 'Why do people penalise the innocent for someone else's misdeeds?'

'People create these unfair rules, dear,' Rani tried to reason.

'Can't they undo it?' Savitri asked in desperation.

'It's easy to do but difficult to undo. Difficult, but do-able,' Rani comforted her.

✿

Ranjit gets off his bike and cajolingly pulls Maya with his little arms; he wants to show her the submarine Savitri was referring to. Maya gives in to the child's insistence and gets up to follow him indoors.

'Auntyji, whatever you say to him, he will come up with *what* and *why* questions,' Savitri warns her.

Maya smiles dotingly. She has become fond of the clever little boy.

'Okay, little pickle, show me your submarine.'

'What's *little pickle*?'

✿

Ranjit proudly exhibits the submarine he has made by stacking small and big empty plastic bottles and binding them together with sticky tape. He plays with it for a while and then shows Maya a picture he drew earlier with his coloured pencils. It is a picture of Santa Claus and his elves. It shows Santa in action. The cryptic artwork of a five-year-old needs some explanation.

'Tell me about your picture,' Maya says.

Ranjit points at the fat-bellied Santa and says that he is busy drawing sketches for the toys. The elves are gleefully producing them in a magic machine. Dancing and singing ladies wearing red and white check dresses and white aprons are wrapping them up and piling them into the sleigh, ready for dispatch. Unspoilt joy and pure innocence are central to the picture. Maya reminisces about her own childhood when trivial things made her happy.

'Has Santa ever visited you, Ranju?' Maya asks.

'No,' comes the subdued reply.

He thinks that Santa does not know his way to Delhi so he has never got him a present. Maya mentally plans to organise a trip for Ranjit and Savitri to London. That would probably make up for Santa not finding his way to Delhi!

There is one elf in the picture working away from the other elves.

'And who's that?'

'That's my papa.'

'So he has joined Santa's company, eh?'

Ranjit abruptly asks Maya, 'Some people took my papa away. Are they bad people?'

She carefully sits him down on her knees and explains, 'No one is born bad, darling. It is their preferences for actions that make them appear good or bad.'

'Why?'

Maya feels a lump in her throat, she tries to withhold tears of compassion for this boy. How can she possibly explain the conundrum of life in a way that a five-year-old would understand?

She tells him that everyone begins their life journey with a heart full of love and a mind that is forever curious; and as they grow up, they absorb some good things and some bad things from around them. They slowly grow into adults as expected by other adults. Some have opportunities to continue to nurture love, others may stray from it. Some may foster hatred towards themselves and others, incited by their own inhibitions and made-up rules! Perhaps they have forgotten that they began their journey with an enormous capacity for love and joy in their hearts.

'I'll never forget that,' Ranjit assures her.

☼

Out on the patio, Millie and Savitri are enjoying Rani's company. Shruti has joined in after her cooking and singing rituals. Rani is now telling them a story about heaven and hell in English for Millie's benefit. Shruti has heard the story many times in her native tongue. She is rather taking delight in listening to a foreign language she can hardly decode.

...And then Swamiji asked Lord Shiva, 'Lord, please show me what heaven and hell look like.' Lord Shiva smiled and with his raised index finger, he created an image of a door. 'This is hell', he said. The door flung open and it revealed a room. In the middle of the room, there was a long dining table with chairs around it. The skinny inhabitants of hell were sitting on chairs. On the centre of the table, there was a big pot of steaming hot and delicious soup of the day. The soup was served in their respective bowls. Despite the sufficient amount of soup for everyone, they looked starved. Each had a spoon with an unusually long handle awkwardly tied around the arm. They could scoop up some soup from the bowl with the spoons but couldn't get them to reach their mouths because the length of the spoon handles prevented this so they remained unfed, malnourished and miserable. They continually quarrelled over who had more or less soup and who had a bigger or smaller bowl; little did this help them to satisfy their hunger.

Swamiji then said, 'I have seen hell, now Lord Shiva, please show me heaven.' With another wave of his finger, the Lord showed him heaven which looked identical to hell with a roomful of residents, bowls of soup and long handled spoons tied around their arms. 'I don't understand Lord,' said a confused Swamiji, 'How come heaven and hell look exactly the same? What's the point in calling them heaven and hell if they are the same?'

Lord Shiva smiled again and said, 'Look closely into both, my child, and see the difference for yourself.' And the Lord made both heaven and hell come forth in front of Swamiji. Swamiji peeped into both over and over again but failed to mark the difference. Lord Shiva said, 'Can you not see that…'

Savitri chirps, 'Oh, I know, I can use this metaphor to explain Baba's rhyme...*Unch ki sankhya may kum ki bhavna hai, Vishnu ki dunya unhe ek din jagta hua dekhegi.*'

'Shhh, let her finish,' Millie is rather chafed at the interruption.

Ranjit hops into the courtyard with Maya behind him. Shruti and Savitri head towards the kitchen to organise the delicious meal for everyone.

Millie stays behind to listen to the end of the story.

Chapter 13

'IN ACTUAL FACT, GENTLEMEN, THIS WILL JEOPARDIZE the future of the fuel industry,' Mr Yamashita, the chairperson of Japan Automobile Makers Association, speaks politely in his native accent. He briefly sheds light on the implausibility of the green-car idea and how this will put the fuel industry at risk. He is in his late forties. His grey-black hair is neatly brushed back. He appears busy and his mind is racing along to the next task of the day.

'No matter how concerned we all are across the globe and however much we research on cutting-edge mechanisms of low-emission vehicles, the fuel industry will go on for a long time to come,' Mr Yamashita says.

Sayed throws a cautious sideways glance to catch Leon's attention. He finally has a chance to talk,

'We are not debating all that Mr Yamashita. Despite what you're saying, Japan has taken measures to produce green cars in a bid to reduce harmful emissions and this was mentioned at the recent green conference.'

'Yes, you're right there and we're currently working on the idea, but I maintain that there's no immediate solution to the problem. You see, our hands are tied,' Mr Yamashita explains. He further suggests, 'One feasible solution could be the launching of much finer quality lead-free petrol and diesel. What do you think? '

'Sounds fair enough,' Leon says.

'Perhaps this will help.' Mr Yamashita then directs his remote control towards the erected screen next to him and turns it on. The presentation that appears on the screen is about the research on advanced, environment-friendly fuels that provide more power and efficiency to the vehicle engine. The fuels also prevent the forming of deposits that can impede fuel injection into the engine. The interaction of the fuels with intricate mechanisms of cars becomes animated on the screen. At the end of the show, the chairman provides the men with a summary of the presentation.

'Thanks. That was quite informative. Do you have any research report on green cars? Sayed asks.

'Yes, we do. We issue a quarterly Green Strategy report that contains everything about the development of fuels and cars,' Mr Yamashita informs.

'Could we please have a copy of that, if that's okay with you?' Leon asks.

Mr Yamashita picks up the phone and calls his personal assistant. A petite, young Japanese woman walks into the room. She stops near Mr Yamashita's desk. She is wearing a black midi skirt, a red blouse and a smart black jacket. Her red lips match the colour of her blouse and her varnished nails. She smiles at Sayed and Leon with a quick bow. She is holding a personal organizer and a pen and is patiently awaiting her boss' instructions.

'Gentlemen, this is Miss Tanaka, also known as Jenny,' Mr Yamashita then speaks to her in Japanese.

'Kono danseitachi wo jimusho ni tsureteitte *Green Strategy* no houkokusho wo ichibu watashite agete... Mochiron eigo no ne.'

Leon repeats Mr Yamashita's words in his head in English:

'*Take these gentlemen to your office and give them a copy of the Green Strategy report...in English of course.*'

From Sayed's initial bewilderment followed by his sigh of relief on hearing the words *Green Strategy*, Leon assumes that he understood the gist of what the man has just said.

'Jenny will take you to her office and give you a copy of the Green Strategy report,' Mr Yamashita says.

'*I know,*' Leon mutters under his breath. He feels that it is not necessary for Mr Yamashita to know about his knowledge of Japanese as the man is perfectly bilingual.

The secretary walks up to the door where she halts for Sayed and Leon to follow her.

'Please don't hesitate to contact me if you have further queries. By the way, Jenny speaks English to some extent; however, she understands more than she speaks,' Mr Yamashita smiles. Then he says, 'It was nice meeting you, gentlemen. Have a safe journey back home.' He cordially shakes hands with the men followed by a brief bowing.

Jenny leads the men to one of the cubicles in a large open space outside Mr Yamashita's small office. Other cubicles are staffed with workers, the majority of whom are male. They are working mechanically, making and receiving calls and working on computers. There is a certain degree of noise from the commotion. In the well-lit interior of the building, it is hard to guess the time of day.

'Miss Tanaka....,' Leon begins.

'Me, Jenny,' She corrects him.

'OK, Jenny. We hope that the report has also got some information about the latest findings,' Leon speaks slowly and clearly.

Jenny looks puzzled but exhibits a cursory smile. She asks them to sit in the narrow seating corner in her office and vanishes into the space beyond it. She returns a few minutes later and announces what with gestures and limited knowledge of English that she has got a copy of the old report; she could not find the current one. Leon insists on obtaining the recent report and, much to Jenny's surprise, he now speaks in Japanese. Jenny gasps in disbelief and agrees to contact them immediately if and when she finds the report. Leon gives her his business card. Sayed follows suit. Jenny collects them with great care and inserts them neatly into her personal organizer. She hands out the old report to Leon who has now become less persistent. He receives this with thanks.

✿

Leaving their worries behind, Sayed and Leon travel towards 'Hachiko' – the statue of an Akita dog outside the busy Shibuya train station in Tokyo. The story of the loyal dog called Hachiko was commemorated in this statue. Leon tells Sayed the story. Hachiko used to wait for his master at the station every day. He continued to wait for his return for a decade at the same place and time; he was unaware of his master's sudden death. The dog kept waiting until the day he also died.

The statue, that honours the devotion of a dog, encourages human connections by becoming a landmark for a rendezvous. Many friendships and dates start from here; this has become a common meeting place for thousands during the course of the day; *meet-me-at-Hachiko* has become a catchphrase. Sayed and Leon decide to roam around from here. They playfully follow Hachiko's fake paw imprints that lead from below the statue to the station.

☼

Later in the afternoon, they unwind in the hotel lounge after having a quick dip in the swimming pool.

Isaac has been kept abreast of their day-to-day progress in Tokyo. He asked Sayed to pack up and come back, leaving Leon to deal with Mr Yoda, the man they met at the conference.

'What's up?'

'Nothing much. Just thinking about Gemma.'

'Thinking or worrying?'

Leon and Sayed have a close enough friendship to occasionally share their personal concerns. Leon is the one who usually lends an ear to Sayed though Sayed is aware of a silent discord between the siblings: Leon and Gemma. Sayed does not know the reason behind this nor does he want to know. He has his own issue of growing up in two diverse cultures. At times he feels neither here nor there. Leon helped him to recognise the advantage of perceiving sentiments inherited from both cultures.

☼

Sayed was born and raised in the East End of London. He is the youngest child and the only son of his parents. They travelled from the district of Sylhet in the then East Pakistan to London with their three young daughters. They took refuge in London in the early seventies from atrocities against the civilians in East Pakistan. After the bloodshed of many, a new country – Bangladesh – was born.

Sayed's father, Rahim Miah, worked in a restaurant in East London. After having saved enough money, he opened his own restaurant. His mother, Maryam Bibi, was a good cook so they did not have to hire one. This helped them with keeping the expenses down. They were hard working and God-fearing people, and following the prescribed ways of their religion in a foreign land was their prime concern. Although they had little institutional education themselves, they valued education a great deal and encouraged all their children to go for higher studies. Education started at home when their eldest daughter Fatima taught the younger ones how to read and write in Bangla, their first language.

83

Sayed loved all the attention during summer holidays in their homeland. When the dust settled, the family did visit the country from time to time. It was fascinating for him to know that some of their relatives viewed London as a city that existed in a fairyland – a city made of gold and silver – and its people as living beings out of this world. They would often ask questions in their regional dialect:

Are they like us?
What types of clothes do they wear?
What do they eat?
Do they have lots of money?
Do they care about their loved ones?

General expectations of the answers were more disposed towards differences than similarities. With regard to the last question, Sayed believes that everyone cares about their loved ones irrespective of their background, faith or culture; the ways of caring may differ. Here is his best friend and colleague, Leon, sitting in front of him, worrying about his sister. Leon was right, being brought up in two cultures helped him to grasp sentiments of both!

✿

'No, not worrying, just a little concerned about an estranged sister,' Leon says in answer to his friend's question. The fleeting sign of tension on Leon's face disappears. For no apparent reason, his fond childhood memories take him back to the days when he played with his little sister Gemma with their cuddly toys, despite their three-year age difference. They never got bored and used their imaginations to their full potential while playing with their toys.

Mabel would always be there for them in the background, loving every moment of their silly role plays. She would comply with their every whim and buy things for them within and sometimes outside her means. She was, however, anxious and, to an extent, fearful of how her husband David would react for splashing out money on them. He would often say, '*If you have some spare cash, pay the bills.*' He justifiably did not see the relevance in spoiling the kids when holding on to every coin was pertinent for a family that struggled to make their ends meet. Mabel had reasons for dealing with the children the way she did – she compensated for the impact of their fateful marriage on the children by being laid-back with them in most things.

On Leon's 10th birthday she bought him a Play Station game. She thought twice before taking the plunge; she asked for Gemma's opinion. Young Gemma behaved like an older sister, 'Are you kidding? He has been dreaming about it since he was six.'

Young Leon could not believe his eyes when he saw the much-adored gift. Little droplets of happy tears rolled down his cheeks. 'Is this really for me?' he asked.

One chain of thought takes him to another - to that great time, effort and care Mabel put in to bring them up, to each and every one of his viola concerts and parents' evenings she attended. Without her he could not be where he is today.

✡

'Anyway, we're going back to London,' Sayed changes the topic.

'You are. Not me.'

'Just kidding. Have you called Millie?'

'Not yet.'

Leon will stay a bit longer to see to the project in hand. He does not have anything else to do other than meeting with Mr Yoda. He called Mr Yoda's secretary and got a date for the meeting. This will happen in three days' time so Leon plans to climb his much revered Mount Fuji the following day.

'The Mount is locally known as Fujisan. The word Fuji is a native word that means *eternal life*,' Leon explains.

Leon was 19 years old when he first ascended the mountain; he was then on a four-month student exchange programme organised by Hertford College, the University of Oxford in England, and Kwansei Gakuin University in Osaka in Japan. With three of his friends, he decided to celebrate the end of his stay in Japan by climbing its highest mountain. He climbed it again three years later and, on both occasions, he told Mabel only after he had completed climbing otherwise she would have been worried sick.

The second time around, Leon stayed in Japan for two years.

Leon has convinced Sayed to go hiking with him with the assurance that he would be in good hands. Besides, summer is the right time for the hike when all amenities and services along the routes up to the top of the mountain are available.

'What's so special about Mount Fuji?'

'The Mount is my inspiration.'

'Inspiration for what?'

'For reaching the top.'

✿

During his second stay in Japan, Leon had heard Japanese folklores from Aika, his girlfriend, and there was one about *inspiration*.

Many years ago, there was a king that ruled the island of Honshu in Japan and one day he announced that whoever, among the eligible maids in the island, could successfully complete a task set by his minsters would win the prince's hand in marriage. The task was to make a fine silk thread go through a narrow passage inside a stone ball. The surface of the ball was very rough and uneven; the inner passage from one end to the other was more serrated. None of the eligible maids succeeded in doing the task that looked simple enough at the beginning; the king was on the verge of giving up hope.

One day a milkmaid came round with a pot of honey, a silk thread and a honeybee. Everyone was curious to see how she would meet the challenge. She slowly poured some honey into one end of the hole of the stone ball and let it trickle through to the other end. She then tied the thread around one of the delicate legs of the honeybee and gently pushed it into the hole. The bee kept licking the honey until it came out of the other end taking the thread along with it.

The milkmaid completed the task successfully and, by the royal command, she married the prince and became known as the Milkmaid Princess. Aika ended the story by saying that the trickle of honey was the bee's inspiration and winning the prince's hand in marriage was the milkmaid's inspiration. Leon found the story rather childish but interesting and Aika was such a good storyteller, he could listen to her for hours. However, she had another reason for telling him the story.

✿

'OK mate, don't forget you have two missions to accomplish,' Sayed recaps.

'Two?'

86

'Yep, two: re-conquering Fujisan and meeting Mr Yoda. Which one is more difficult? Hard to say.'

Leon finds the comment amusing.

'But I don't get it...if you've already climbed the Mount twice, why do you want to climb it again?' Sayed asks.

'You know, there is a saying - *you are wise to climb Fujisan once and a fool to climb it twice.*'

'In that case, I am wiser as this is going to be my first climb.'

Leon pats Sayed's back in jest, 'Maybe the person who came up with the quote never climbed it himself... or herself?'

✿

Leon goes over essential things for the tour and mentally compares one route with the others in order to choose the best and shortest route to the summit as this is going to be Sayed's first climb. Leon is confident about his past climbing experiences which were at times close to danger.

'Cambodia is my next port of call, why don't you come along? Leon suggests.

'Slow down, mate. You know I don't have a visa to Cambodia and I'm not as resourceful as you are.'

'Relax, chum. OK, maybe you're a bit resourceful.'

'Just enough to hike along with you.'

'You'll be a bit more of that when you dig out the current report from Jenny,' Leon winks.

'Maybe, but I'm not sure who will get that call first, you or me,' Sayed winks back.

✿✿✿

Chapter 14

RANI'S STORY IN LONDON BEGAN WHEN SHE CAME TO the city for higher studies. She met Thomas at the Queen Mary University of London. They were very good friends among other mutual friends; their friendship turned into something deeper without them realizing it. This only came to light when another friend casually commented on their feelings for each other. Rani wanted to return to Delhi after completing her studies. Destiny had other plans - Thomas proposed to her in the cool shade of the university campus. Rani accepted. They got married soon afterwards and settled in a flat that Thomas owned. The flat was on the ground floor of a block of high-rise flats on the corner of Streatham Common North and Streatham High Road in the south-west part of London.

Rani and Thomas, two people from diverse cultures, bound by love, had respect and appreciation for each other. Thomas, ever-smiling and content, was a happy man. More often than not, he would go along with what Rani said or preferred. He would rather concentrate on his work and left it to Rani to oversee most things in life.

☼

'Maya, would you like to come and live with us in London?' Rani asked.

'To the dream city?'

'What makes you think that?'

'Mum-mi told me. I also see nice pictures in my head, I really do,' young Maya's eyes lit with excitement. Rani felt that Maya was quite thoughtful and imaginative.

Maya's fondness for the city was passed on to her by her mother, Archana. Reading Rani's detailed letters made Archana grow a penchant for the city. She nurtured the hope that one day she would emigrate to London with her family.

After Archana's untimely death, Rani travelled to Delhi to escort Maya to London. As Maya was left with no proper guardian, Rani and Thomas decided to adopt her. This would, in a way, fulfil part of Archana's dream and part of Rani's own longing – she wanted a child of her own but she could not have one because of a physical disorder. If adoption was to be considered, she might as well adopt her own sister's daughter who was left orphaned at the age of twelve. More importantly, there was a pressing need for Maya to leave her homeland as soon as possible; had she not left Delhi at that point in time, she could have faced consequences similar to what her mother faced.

✿

Maya had a wonderful time in London. Because of the time well spent with her aunt in the kitchen and uncle in the garden plot, she developed a passion both for cooking and growing herbs and plants. This eventually inspired her towards securing a position as a chef in a café.

Thomas took great care of his share of the plot surrounded by a wire fence behind the block of flats. Maya would often sit on the garden bench, daydreaming and feasting her eyes on intense florets of hydrangea in blue and lilac, pressed closely against each other, and on the delicately scented jasmine on the trellis. Within wide-ranging fragrances of flowering plants and herbs, she could make a clear distinction between the sharp smell of rosemary and the spicy flavour of coriander or between the sweet-scented lavender and mildly elegant parsley with her eyes closed. The distinct scent of these herbs, the fragrant honeysuckle and easy-to-grow Viper's Bugloss attracted honeybees and bumblebees that carried the powdery pollen in the grooves of their tiny, spiky legs and accelerated pollination in their garden.

Apart from consciously using her sense of sight, sound, smell and touch, Maya was blessed with savouring moments of taste. There was nothing like relishing plump and juicy, red strawberries with fresh cream or a bowl of thick soup made from striped, water-logged vegetables of squash variety – the fresh produce of the garden.

✿

At a Christmas party in her friend Sarah's house, Maya met Jonathan Morgan. He was of medium height. He had wavy, roseate hair and a kind face. Coincidentally, it was the same man she had met briefly a couple of weeks earlier. The transitory encounter with him on the underground train left a lasting impression on her mind.

As the sweet memory of an otherwise ordinary event was almost fading away, fate had brought him back to her life.

'Have we met before?' Jonathan asked.

'I suppose so. And this time, the seat is yours. I won't take *no* for an answer,' Maya replied. Both laughed.

The atmosphere at the party was intoxicating; the festivity trailed on into the small hours of Boxing Day. She did not plan to stay that long; she was aware of her aunt's concern about her staying out late, but she lost track of time and because of the typical inaccessibility of transport that night, she accepted Jonathan's offer for a lift home in his car. They sailed through the traffic-less roads. Foggy beams of street lamps nebulously lit up the streets. The sky was cloudy and dark. The living room light was on when Maya reached home. Rani was awake.

'Thanks a lot,' she whispered and before Jonathan could say a word, she swiftly got out of the car and slipped through the front door like anxious Cinderella. This was rude, she later thought, but she wanted to be present indoors as quickly as possible to assure Rani of her safe return.

✿

They first met on the underground train at Russell Square on the Piccadilly line when Maya was returning from an open air show of song and dance. Jonathan was holding the hand-strap to balance his weight on the train in motion. Maya had just grabbed the only seat available without much consideration for the needs of other passengers. She opened a book to read. A sudden jolt of the train made her look up and they noticed each other. Realising that Jonathan deserved the seat as he had got on the train first, she hesitantly offered it to him. Jonathan politely refused as he was getting off at the next stop. They then engaged in a brief conversation. Jonathan appeared gentle and debonair in those few moments. The train stopped. He got off.

An elderly lady, sitting next to Maya near the window, was attentively protecting her blue coat from getting crushed. She got off at the next stop. *If only she had gotten off earlier*! Maya thought.

She jotted down a poem in her diary later in the day. She drafted and re-drafted it until she was satisfied with the final draft. One day, Aunt Rani found her reeling the poem off.

'May I hear it?'

'It's just one of my poems,' Maya blushed.

'That'd be nice,' Rani assured her. Maya read the poem with a hesitant start:

You got on the train just before me.
I hopped on it and grabbed the only seat,
Not having a care in the world for others.
There you were, standing tall,
Gentle and calm.
Mortified by my manner,
I offered you the seat.
You smiled and politely declined.
We exchanged greetings
And a few patchy words.
The train halted at the next stop,
Nice to meet you, you said.
Nice to meet you too, said I.
Then you mingled with the platform crowd.
The fleeting encounter for ninety seconds
Felt long and sweet.

'That's nice, Maya. Who's the lucky fella, if I may ask?'

✿

'May I have the privilege of exchanging phone numbers?' Jonathan asked at the Christmas party. Maya would normally not give her phone number to someone she had met for the first time. It was indeed the first time; the brief encounter on the train was just a first sight. Every day so many people are bumping into each other, who cares to remember? With Jonathan, she felt she had known him for a long time!

In time, they navigated their relationship to the next stage. Her good feelings towards him at first sight (and subsequent sights) turned into love, but her sense of responsibility towards her aunt and uncle barred her from committing fully with Jonathan.

'Don't worry about us,' Thomas would reassure her. 'That Jonny boy surely loves you.'

'But I don't want to leave you,' Maya would raise as objection. She was happy to remain with her God-sent parents for as long as she could. Thomas looked affectionately at her and his kind gesture assured her that everything was going to be fine.

Thomas' reassurance led her to contemplate marriage when Jonathan dropped the bombshell. He was trapped in a loveless marriage to Maureen. Like parting clouds they drifted apart to a point where living separately was the only amicable solution. He made it clear to Maya that it was her who he loved and who he wished to spend the rest of his life with. Maya, on the other hand, detested continuing to stay in the relationship; she felt betrayed by his secrecy.

A year later, she found newly divorced Jonathan emaciated and depleted from the divorce settlement.

✿

Maya is trying to meditate, but the lulling words in the guided meditation is making her fall asleep. She sits up straight and turns the player off lest she falls in the grip of sleep again. She decides to be her own guide and imagines hearing a distant voice in her mind. She tries to get into the meditative state again; her eyes are still in a drowsy mode. The guiding words run through her mind.

Close your eyes.....
Take a deep breath...
Put aside your present string of thoughts and just relax...
You will soon take an awesome journey to a place of your imagination...
You can go to amazing places in your imagination...

The mental citation seems to be coming all the way from behind the mountains, hills, meadows, cities and it finally enters into her room by which time it dies down.

Do you see any changes?
What did the people of the city do to bring about the changes?

The recollection of those questions helps her to get into a trancelike state. She conjures up images of people living close to beautiful valleys, natural fountains, reservoirs and interesting routes through the woods. A sudden flow of the static energy in the switched off television alerts her. She is not far from dozing off again.

'Mum, you should keep your eyes half-open while meditating to avoid falling asleep,' Millie once suggested.

Maya heard or read somewhere:

Praying is talking to God and doing meditation is God talking back.

Since she is not being able to carry out the latter without falling asleep, she might as well talk to God so she decides to pray instead. She sits down on the prayer corner in front of Lord Krishna's miniature image.

She prays:

Lord Krishna, thank you for these uplifting experiences. I intend to continue to receive more of them, grow into them and be in a calmer state of mind in my day to day life. During my waking hours, I am still downhearted with past memories and uncertain future. I know you are there – within and without - but I don't always feel this. There is a difference between knowing and feeling. I want to feel your presence. Please Lord, fill me with your presence.

Maya remains still to receive any form of answer. Nothing happens - no whisper, no small voice. Was she just speaking to the brick wall?

Aunt Rani once said:

When we pray, we expect immediate results but God works in a mysterious way. We need to place our trust in God and be patient.

Maya stands up from her prayer position, half-believing that one day the Lord will respond to her prayer in His own divine way.

○○○

Chapter 15

IT IS REALLY NOT A COMPLETE CLIMB. MOST CLIMBERS start from the 5th station of Mount Fuji. Highway buses take hikers up to this station. Four trails around the mountain branch out towards the 10th station – the pinnacle of the mountain. Each trail has its own 5th station.

Leon and Sayed are wearing layers of comfortable clothes (bulky clothes, according to Leon, may impede the journey) and hiking shoes; they are carrying hiking sticks. Leon prefers to travel light, taking only the bare essentials such as a map, a flashlight, water, money and some onigiris - they are tasty and convenient to carry. Sayed wants to get oxygen canisters in case they need them near the top of the mountain. Leon thinks that given the hot clear day in mid-July, they will be able to do without them; there are plenty of shops at the stations where they can get the canisters, if required.

'Got the camera,' Sayed checks his own list of bare essentials.

'Good, and I want to capture my thoughts too,' Leon shows his pocket diary and pen, and slips them back inside one of many pockets around his jeans.

They arrive at the bus station on time and find some empty front seats in their bus. The bus makes its way towards their destination. When it reaches the foot of the mountain, it begins its long ascent on the route that leads to the wide parking lot on the 5th station of the trail called Kawaguchiko trail. Shops on the station have colourful arrays of expensive gifts, souvenirs and indispensable things for the journey.

As the packed bus crawls on the winding pathway around the mountain, Leon says that many prospective trekkers come to one of the 5th stations, buy some souvenirs and go back down. That's as far as they go up to.

'I could be one of them, you know. At least, I can claim that I've climbed Fujisan,' Sayed says.

'You're not planning to desert me. Are you?' Leon asks.

Sayed grins playfully. He is happy to sit near the aisle with passing scenes through wide windows on both sides of the bus. It is deliciously warm today. Sayed looks forward to completing the first round of the journey.

✿

The bus wheels make a heavy gravel-crushing sound signalling the imminent halt on the 5th station of the Kawaguchiko trail. It is 6 p.m. and most of the shops are open. They hop off the bus and land on the parking lot. Other highway buses have already arrived.

Sayed says in ecstasy, 'Wow! I'm on Mount Fuji! I made it! I made it! He stretches his arms up in the air to take in a lungful of pure, fresh air.

'C'mon, it's only half the battle or a quarter to be precise!'

Each time Leon climbed the mountain, he felt as overjoyed as Sayed and each time it felt all new to him so he can understand Sayed's enthusiasm.

Excited hikers from all over the world are trickling through the buses onto the parking lot. Some disperse in all directions; others go to nearby shops. Leon and Sayed follow the latter and enter a shop. It is filled with interesting souvenirs, flags, T-shirts, carvings and beautifully wrapped up food for gifts; all are tagged with sky-high prices. The vendors have arranged them in ways that everywhere shoppers look, they will catch something to feast their eyes on, something interesting to buy. Consumerism in Japan is designed to be impressive, innovative and effective.

A tuneful laughter hovers in the air and soothes Leon's ears. He spots a young Japanese couple in the carving section. The woman is marvelling at one of the statuettes on display.

Strangely enough she sounded like Aika.

✿

He went out with Aika for six months and on the day that was destined to be their last time together, he could clearly see in her eyes that she wanted to break up with him. He just sensed something strange in the air. She was so sweet and caring; she thought he was the perfect guy for her, but she had marriage in mind like the Milkmaid Princess in the story she once told him. Her expectations did not match with those of Leon's at that time. She was after settling down in life; Leon, on the other hand, aspired to move up the

95

career path. For her, it was either make or break. Leon did not see this coming.

☼

'We shouldn't stop here for long Sid. Let's get going if we are to reach the top on time to catch the sunrise,' Leon says.

Sayed is unmindful of Leon's urgency. He is fascinated by something he has just spotted. 'Look at this T-shirt, Lee. What does it say?' Sayed asks.

He points at a white T-shirt that's hanging down from a rail. Leon lifts the corner of it to have a full view of a beautiful Japanese calligraphy in flaming red against white.

'Let me see....erm, it says:

Anata wa mainichi jibun wo hitasu...Nanikani jibun wo hitasou...Anata ha aisuru...'

Leon reads part of the message out loud and part of it inaudibly.

'Sorry, I didn't quite catch your mumbling,' Sayed humours.

'Okay, let me say it clearly for your understanding...hehe...but this seems a strange message for a T-shirt,' Leon jots the full text down in his diary. 'Just give me a minute, I'll work it out,' he says.

Sayed quickly takes a picture of it and a couple more of other exhibits. He believes that the text on the T-shirt could well be of some significance. He recalls a strange message in Bangla on a little decorative clay pot in a gift shop in Cox's Bazaar - the long sea beach along the Bay of Bengal. The message said:

Nodir eparer dheu bohey oparetey,
Bhalo holey bhalo, mondo holey mondo, tah jodi janitey.

Sayed runs the message in his head in English:

Waves on this side of the riverbank surge towards the other,
Good begets good, bad begets bad – if you would only care.

He bought the pot for amma, his mother during one of his trips to the place and carefully carried it in his hand luggage for a smooth relocation. Amma loved it so much that she hung it in a criss-cross rope-holder over the kitchen entrance. The proverb was stored in Sayed's memory, as every time he went past the pot its rounded bottom slightly caressed his crown. He now wonders if there is a link between the messages from two countries in the same continent!

✿

'We must start climbing now,' Leon declares.

They go outside the store and join the hikers on the rocky trail. Trampled rocks generate mass rhythmic beats under people's feet.

'Got the map?' Leon asks.

'Sorry, left it on the bus,' Sayed says apologetically.

'Don't worry. I've got one. Just stay together. We may even follow a group that has a guide.'

The climb is not as easy as it sounds and getting to the top from the 5th station takes an average person about 9 hours. The first half of the ascent is uncomplicated. The route is wide and less steep, and the hikers march together towards a common goal.

✿

The two men start hiking. They go past the 6th station. They occasionally stop here and there for a drink of water or to take photos, carefully avoiding the routes that have signs for possible gusts of wind and falling rocks.

'Awesome,' Sayed looks down and points at a conical reflection of the peak of the mountain on the passing mass of silvery clouds. The overhead clouds that were visible from the ground level are now hanging below them. Sayed has never climbed a hill before let alone a mountain. His heart is filled with ecstasy for the pure, intoxicating view. He keeps clicking his camera like an excited child!

They wind their way around the 7th station. It is getting dark and a beam of light shines from the level area of the station. A log cabin becomes visible; the light is coming from it. Sayed feels a bit queasy.

'We'd better take a break now,' Leon says.

A young Japanese man comes out of the cabin; he seems to be a member of staff. He is friendly and welcoming.

Leon waves his hand and asks, 'Mada aite masu ka?'

The man replies, 'Hai, aiteimasu yo.'

'Asked if they are still open and yes they are, as you can see,' Leon interprets.

97

The man ushers them inside and takes them to wooden stools installed in the corner of the cabin. The cabin is lit with lanterns that are hanging down from horizontal wooden beams, creating a semi-dark aura inside it; it also has a Tatami room at the back that can be booked for getting some rest or sleep. There is a carefully mounted fireplace in the cabin with a crackling fire. The place is quite crowded. The dry wooden smell of the cabin with its warm fire invites them to a welcome break!

Now is the time to eat some onigiris – Leon thinks. Onigiris - rice balls - are wrapped in nori (edible seaweed) and filled with delicious salmon flakes. The tantalizing ricey smell of onigiris transports Sayed to his own childhood when amma used to feed him and his older sister Rasheda together. Amma would get a plateful of rice and top it up with some lentil soup and carefully chosen chicken pieces from the chicken curry. She would then lovingly mix them together, craft small balls and deposit them into their little mouths by turn. The siblings competed with each other as to who could eat the highest numbers of rice balls.

At this moment in time, Sayed does not want to eat anything. He feels sick and weary.

'Hey, you okay?' Leon asks. Sayed nods.

'Here's the translation of the lines on the T-shirt,' Leon passes his diary to Sayed thinking that this may divert his mind from feeling poorly. Sayed inaudibly mouths the words:

You are soaking yourselves every day
Into things you love to hate.
Let yourselves soak into things
You would hate to love.

'It's a strange message. I wonder what it really means,' Sayed says.

✪

In order to view the sunrise, some of the other climbers set off at around 7 p.m. from the 5th station but Leon did not want to risk missing it so he had started climbing earlier with Sayed.

Darkness is now setting in and the winding rows of climbers, carrying headlamps and torches, form a procession of lights. From a distance, they bear a resemblance to flashing fireflies swirling around the dark mass of the obscure mountain.

They reach the 8th station at around 1:30 a.m. The steep slope in front of them becomes crowded as Kawaguchiko trail meets Subashiri trail. The last one-third of the journey is the most gruelling. The twilight begins to get fainter, masses of clouds make the visibility poorer and they only have the glimmer of a small torch light to guide them, a torch light whose battery will soon run out.

The temperature drops,

darkness deepens,

they shiver with cold despite many layers of clothing.

As they press on towards the summit, hope begins to fade, but they keep going. Sayed feels weary. His face becomes pale. Leon suggests going back to the Tatami room to rest and, if necessary, going back down afterwards. After climbing this far, Sayed does not want to quit, he is determined to reach the top. He prays in his mind:

'Oh Allah, all praises are due to you. Please grant me the strength to complete the journey and bring into my experience one of your countless spectacular displays of nature. Thank you Allah, for all your blessings.'

His prayer fortifies his faith and hope. He keeps moving with his fellow climbers. His sheer determination and the firm support of his companion keep him going. Trails from all directions end at a set of uneven steps with guarding stone lions on each side. The steps creep up towards the Tori Gate, the final destination. At about 4.15 a.m. they reach the top, just in time for the sunrise.

'Hey, you made it Sid!' Leon says with pride. The crowd roar with overwhelming joy and laughter. They catch a glimpse of the first thin red light of the sun on the horizon. Like an artist's random brush strokes on a canvas, the light blends in with the backdrop of the early morning grey-blue sky. It gets thicker and then within a nanosecond, the sun peeks its nose above the massive sea of rolling clouds; it keeps growing. Everyone gapes at the spectacular show without blinking so that not a part of it is missed!

The rising red sun is free from all obstructions; its splendour and radiance are deluging all with soul-expanding experience. Sayed absorbs its healing energy. It now dawns on him what Leon had meant about inspiration, about reaching the top of the mountain. Physically reaching the summit heightens his mystical persona. He is now full of admiration and gratitude towards the Manifester of the great show. The mountain slope and the distant hills blend in with the misty surroundings, creating a surreal world where only beauty, eternity and unanimity can exist. The meaning of Fuji – eternal life – now becomes clear to Sayed.

Reaching the apex is more rewarding than the terrifying experience of the long climb itself. Roars of excitement from people and the clicking of cameras say it all. Sayed sits on a rock, still weak from exhaustion and sickness. He is glad he has made it, he is glad he did not give up. Leon takes charge of Sayed's camera; he wants to capture the unforgettable moment for his friend.

Leon is back to his adventurous past with the challenging present and future.

✧ ✧ ✧

Chapter 16

MR YODA'S OFFICE IS IN SENDAGAYA WITHIN SHIBUYA ward. It is not too far from Leon's hotel. He hails a taxi well before the appointed time for the meeting as the roads can get crowded around this time of day. It is now late afternoon. The taxi driver nods with a friendly grin and halts his car near him. Leon gets in and tells him where to go. Taxi drivers here are polite and formal, and they seldom talk to their passengers unless it is necessary.

Sayed is on his way to Delhi. He will stay there for a day or two and will fly back to London with Millie. Leon thinks that all in all, the mission has been quite successful what with the stimulating and informative seminar and the meeting with Mr Yamashita. Jenny did call Leon after all! She found the latest Green Strategy report and agreed to fax it to their London Bridge office with a hard copy to follow; and now this forthcoming meeting with Mr Yoda will be top-notch – the big boss could not be happier!

The superb models of the cars he saw at the seminar captured his imagination. These cars combine two or more distinct mechanisms aimed towards less fuel usage, less emission and rapid acceleration. In addition to the conference, one-to-one discussions with Japanese executives have additional benefits – one can get more information about pertinent matters and find ways to act upon shared interests and beliefs.

He gazes at the passing scenes from inside the car and mentally rehearses his conversation with Mr Yoda in line with his own expectations of the outcome of the meeting. He believes that the contents in the old strategy report Jenny provided will come in handy. The report highlights the plan for introducing new refined fuels for cars, but it does not give a time frame for this; this could well have been included in the new report. There is an interesting piece of information in the old issue relating to recycling of old cars. The process involves having hazardous car parts removed and reusable parts recycled. Some of these reusable parts are being stored in a compressed form in the hope that they will be put to good use in the future!

Leon's mind is racing along the lines of thoughts on the impending meeting; this time, he will adopt a different approach and will not ask Mr Yoda straightaway for any facts and figures. A sudden jolt of the car shifts his thought patterns. He has been away from home for a while. He wonders how Millie's trip to India went. He has not thought about her consciously all this time. He knows that she is anxious about anything and everything, especially about him!

It was a different story when they first met. At that time, she was rather annoyed and irritated by his friend's foolish behaviour.

✿

There was a rare dolphin show in London Zoo. The smart marine mammals were showing off, jumping, twisting, twirling and diving into the water tank like mermaids, and the apparent mischievous one among the dolphins was splashing water in the *splash zone* like a naughty child. They were praised and rewarded with fish by their female trainer. Some spectators, sitting in the zone at the front row, wore waterproof coats, others either did not mind getting soaked or they did not have a choice as drier seats at the back were taken up. Sayed and Leon were among the spectators in the front row.

A mother, sitting in the splash zone, cloaked her son protectively with a plastic cover while he eagerly waited for more dolphin acts. The naughty dolphin was flipping backwards when it decided to splash water on Leon and Sayed. They quickly got up to track down drier seats. They found seats on either side of Millie who was sitting a few rows behind their former seats. Millie half-smiled at them. She did not bother to move up; her focus was on the show.

A lonely looking seagull was trying to catch a fish or two while they were tossed in the air for the consumption of the water performers. The bird failed to catch the one it was after; the fish landed near the edge of the pool where the trainer was standing. The bird stepped cautiously towards the fish, hoping that the trainer would ignore its motive. The trainer's attention was solely on the show, she shouted out instructions to the dolphins; the bird flew away.

Sayed was blabbering away about how intelligent dolphins were, how they used ultrasound to locate members of the pod; they could even read other dolphins' minds and they were actively aware if one of them was hungry, physically hurt or in danger. While conveying this message to Leon, Sayed's eyes fell on Millie and he completed his sentence,

'...unlike some human beings with icy exteriors.'

Millie was by then offended and annoyed with the uninvited meddlers. Her ready reply with a hint of sarcasm articulated that these dolphins were not intelligent enough to escape captivity imposed on them by some inconsiderate humans. She then abruptly got up and walked away from her seat.

Leon met Millie again in the library inside the Victoria building; he apologised for his friend's behaviour. He came to know that Millie worked in one of the offices in the building. He told her that she could join Isaac's team if she wanted to. She said she would think about it. She eventually joined the team.

¢

Leon becomes aware that his taxi ride to Mr Yoda's office is taking longer than usual. He asks the driver what is going on, 'Dou shitan desu ka?'

The driver sounds anxious, 'Anohitotachi tsuite kite masu yo.' He alerts Leon that the occupants in the car behind are following them. Leon sees no relevance in the suggestion; the driver may have misconstrued this, someone is probably taking the same route as theirs. Leon swings round and looks through the rear window. He expects to see a flow of normal traffic of the day but to his sheer surprise, he does not see any cars at all or any other vehicles for that matter. The road behind them is empty!

Leon wonders if this is a tactic of the taxi driver to prolong the journey so that he can charge an inflated fare, but the man's nervous response tells him that there is something wrong. He keeps calm and asks the driver to take one of the side streets, 'Wakimichi no hitotsu wo iku.' Their change of direction will ensure if an interested party is indeed following them. The driver does as he is told.

After what seemed like ages, they finally reach their destination. Leon gives him the fare and asks him to keep the change. The driver is glad that the chase is over and thanks him for the tip; he quickly disappears through a narrow lane apparently to avoid the chasers.

Leon enters the ground floor of the office building and walks towards the reception. The male receptionist warmly receives him and gives him directions to Mr Yoda's office. Leon takes the lift and reaches the office.

Mr Yoda is not there. He left a note for him!

✿ ✿ ✿

Chapter 17

BACK IN HER FLAT, MAYA IS SOMEWHAT ANXIOUS; HER motherly concern over Millie is the apparent reason for her anxiety. It was Millie's decision to stay behind for a few more days and return to London with Sayed. Maya's thoughts then deviate around her childhood days. These thoughts almost always transport her back to the stories about her grandparents, about their grand life in Muzaffarabad, about their hardship when they had to leave their homeland with two young daughters – the youngest was her own mother.

✿

Pavitra Suri, Maya's grandmother, packed the essentials and sold other valuable items and jewellery at ridiculously low prices so that she would have some money available for the family to keep them going during their dreaded journey from Muzaffarabad to Delhi. It was not easy for her daughters - Rani, then seventeen and Archana, fifteen - to leave an affluent life and relocate somewhere unknown and unfamiliar. Pavitra consoled them by saying that it was a matter of escaping from an unsafe to a safe place.

All their servants gathered together to bid farewell to their dear masters being unsure about their own fate and safety. The head of the servants, Mano, insisted on coming with them to help them with the relocation. Maya's grandfather, Randitya Suri, declined his offer, but Mano's persistent pleading compelled him to take him under his wing.

A muezzin was calling for the night-time prayer from the minaret of a nearby mosque when they set off. It was safer for them to leave at that time. It cost them a fortune to cross the border and head towards Delhi via Srinagar in the Indian region, using multiple modes of transport: overloaded buses, trains, trams and bullock carts. On their way, they hid in deserted houses that once belonged to people who were also probably on the run like them. They struggled through solitary tracks in deep green forests and went without food and drink for days before they reached the old part of Delhi.

Although Maya did not experience any of this herself, the tale of her family's predicament was engrained in her mind which often surfaced while she meditated. She heard horror stories about Jammu Valley in Kashmir where the lives of refugees crossing their paths from both the countries in search of safe shelters were in jeopardy. In the process, the innocent lost their lives in the hands of merciless opponents; parents were separated from their children and families went missing in the wilderness. Maya felt sad for these people; at the same time, she was profoundly grateful to God for her family's arrival in Delhi, exhausted, wounded and hungry but safe.

Randitya had a distant relative, Mohandas, in Delhi who was kind enough to put them up for a while. Mohandas was poor himself with limited resources and space; he had his own large family to care for. Soon afterwards, Randitya and his family moved out and settled in a small bedsit in a shanty town. In the end, their faithful servant and friend, Mano, left them - he did not want to be a burden to them. He remained in contact with them and some years later, left his orphaned daughter Shruti in their care. He knew his child would be in good hands. Shruti became their housekeeper and she remained a spinster for the rest of her life.

Negativity set into their impoverished life. Judging and emotionally hurting each other became the norm in their household. Pavitra blamed God and His *hopeless* servant Randitya for the uprooting. She maintained that they should never have left Muzaffarabad - it was the biggest mistake they had ever made. Randitya, on the other hand, faulted her for not being supportive enough. These scenarios were inconceivable in Muzaffarabad, in their welcome abode of peace, love and harmony.

Archana decided to get married to a clothes merchant's son and lived two blocks away from her parents' home in the shanty town. She was the one who had an eye for fashion and style; she dreamt of marrying a rich man. She married Prince, but it was only by name. Soon afterwards, Prince detached himself from the family and lived like a fugitive, dodging from members of opposing political parties. His involvement in politics was based on the *do-or-die* philosophy that brought forth a great deal of peril to himself and his family so he stayed away from them, occasionally dropping by when he felt it was safe.

Prince knew that, Maya, his dearest daughter, loved reading so during one of his rare visits, he got her a book she yearned for.

'Maya guriya. Idhar ah,' he called her dotingly.

'Bapu,' Maya ran towards him.

'Yeh terey liye hai,' he sat her down beside him and gave her the book. Maya was overjoyed.

She read the book over and over again; a character in the book reminded her so much of bapu. She treasured it in her wide-ranging collection of things.

Prince hoped that one day things would get better so that he could live a normal life. It never happened.

☼

Archana took care of her disabled father-in-law and, in her spare time, she would lend a hand to the workmen in the shop, sewing, cutting materials and taking orders. She was far too exhausted to mind Maya who would often go to bed without food or a proper shower. Maya developed the habit of having one or two meals a day. When years later Rani and Thomas tried to convince her to eat more, she would often refer to Archana's words of wisdom:

People do not die of hunger, they die of gluttony.

Rani, on the other hand, did not consider marriage as an only option to escape from their altered situation. She continued to study hard in the face of adversity. The grant she was awarded by her local college contributed towards her successful completion of education at the institution. Her passion and aptitude for higher studies led to her getting further scholarship and a place in a London university. Rani did not return home after graduating at the university although that was her initial plan. She married Thomas; simultaneously she secured a training contract in a law firm in London. Her dear sister Archana was always in her mind.

Archana kept dreaming and hoping for an affluent life like the one she had in Muzaffarabad!

☼

Rani was horrified to see the condition orphaned Maya was in. The twelve-year-old girl was left with the responsibility of looking after her sick grandfather and the shop, with little help from her fugitive father who ultimately stopped visiting them. There was a rumour that he was prosecuted by the secret army.

Rani appointed Shruti on a part-time basis to nurse Maya's grandfather and escorted Maya to London. Randitya and Pavitra were relieved as they were able to do little for their granddaughter - Maya.

✿

The phone rings in the early evening. Maya picks it up, it is Millie calling from Delhi.

'Hello, mummy,' Millie sounds worried. She calls her *mummy* as she did in her childhood when she was in distress otherwise, it is just *mum*.

'Hello Mill. What's wrong?'

'Listen, Sayed can't get hold of Leon who's supposed to be in Cambodia by now. He is not picking up my calls either.'

'Take it easy, Mill. Maybe he is busy or his mobile phone is out of order,' Maya comforts her.

'No, no. You don't understand mummy, it is totally unlike him. If he is busy, he'll say so,' Millie pauses, then she says, 'Can you meditate? See, if something comes up in your mind.'

When Maya described an office building that appeared vaguely in her mind's eye during meditation, Millie was amazed. The details matched the exterior and interior of the building in Victoria where Maya had never set foot. These images showed up in Maya's mind when she was asked to imagine an old city in the guided meditation.

Maya has not done this before: meditating and having visions at will. Millie is putting her trust in Maya, hoping to get some information through a way considered fly-by-night in the domain of logic and reason. Perhaps Millie is worrying unnecessarily. *Wait a minute. Is she in love with Leon?* Maya thinks. She will not be surprised if she is. The endless time Millie had spent with him during and outside office hours may have brought her emotionally closer to him without her actually realizing it until now.

Maya wonders if Leon feels the same way about Millie. Maya is happy and relieved in the midst of the turn of events; Millie has found her soul mate!

'I'll do my best, darling', Maya assures Millie. 'But can't guarantee a satisfactory outcome,' she adds.

✿

Maya plays the meditation disc. She is unable to concentrate with scores of questions running in her mind. She visions absolutely nothing. One thing she has learned from this activity is that one cannot force this to happen. She needs to relax, which is currently impossible. The unexpectedness of the situation and her inability to relax finally lull her into a slumber. She dreams fragmented and unrelated segments of scenes where there is a car chase; the car that is being chased is the mirror image of the one that is chasing it and then the picture loses its shape and turns into a blanket of obscurity where time and space merge into a single existence. Fragmented flashes of some strange and happy people appear in another part of her dream.

Maya wakes up into an alpha state, the state one is in just before falling asleep and on waking up. She does not remember seeing anyone she knew in either car; Leon was certainly not in there. She is uncertain about what to make of the dream, it was like a wild horse, haphazard and random. She goes back to sleep and slowly drifts into the Theta mode, the light sleep mode. In this mode, she is in a place where she has never been before. A cool wave takes her to a wintry snow city. Even in her dream, she shivers with cold; her slumbering body huddles into the duvet for warmth. She faintly hears a sweet Chinese melody!

✿

The chirping of morning birds wakes Maya up. Her recent dream was vivid but the memory of it is progressively fading away. A sudden thought enters her mind. This thought is not the usual one that leaps aimlessly in all directions and anchors with other thoughts. This one is isolated, this is a calm, small voice in disguise that may nearly have escaped her attention; this is perhaps the answer she was seeking when she prayed – *Please Lord, fill me with your presence.*

The small voice whispers:
Just trust your knowingness and stay connected.

Maya momentarily feels the divine presence in her heart that whispers again:

109

In your knowingness, there exists the one who will listen, the one who will reason and the one who will reflect!

Maya feels the urge to see Rosie, her supervisor, work colleague and friend, and tell her all about her recent experiences - *is Rosie the one who will listen, reason and reflect?* Maya thinks. She decides to wait until Millie returns. There is so much to tell Rosie. She is the kind of person who glows with compassion. The way she drags each word at the end of a sentence is quite melodic and it shows her loving concern. Rosie is always there for her.

Maya often wonders as to why Rosie is so different from others but then again, *everyone is different* – Maya reasons. But why is her name *Radiant Rosie?* Maya wonders again!

✿

Radiant Rosie was the only child of her parents; she travelled from Sierra Leone with her father, Tranquil Trevor, when she was five. Her mother, Norma, died a few months after giving birth to her. Tranquil Trevor played the role of both a father and a mother to Rosie. When he fell ill in his old age, Rosie nursed him until his last days. She never married; the only family she has is her adopted daughter Tania who lives in another part of London with her husband and her son. Rosie's friends and work colleagues have become her family.

Rosie is always engaged in doing something in her spare time. She has done endless courses on photography, flower arrangements, painting - one after the other. In addition, she does gardening, window shopping and explores new avenues in town or in her imagination. If anyone wants to pursue anything from do-it-yourself tasks to having the best cookies that would perfectly complement a cup of tea, friends and colleagues would say,

'Ask Radiant Rosie'.

✿ ✿ ✿

Chapter 18

WHAT WITH ON-GOING ROADSIDE WORK AND THE diverted traffic lanes, Maya's short car trip to Coombe Wood in Croydon becomes a long one. She is not accustomed to the long winding routes in this part of Croydon; the signposts for traffic diversions are not properly visible at the intersections. Once she gets out of the maze, she will be happy to reach the site she chose for the rendezvous.

The beautiful gardens in Coombe Wood belong to Coombe Wood House surrounded by a vast stretch of land in the county of Surrey. The gardens are arranged in terraces with seasonal flowers, shrubs, perennial and ornamental plants and trees, a rockery and a pond with a waterfall along the garden front. The topmost terrace of the gardens leads towards a woodland.

✿

Maya picked the site for the get-together at Rosie's recommendation. She met Rosie after Millie had returned. Maya told Rosie everything about recent events in their lives. Although Maya was not aware of Leon's soul-searching experiences at that point in time, she assumed from his long absence that he too had a story to tell. Rosie compared their experiences with isolated pieces of a jigsaw puzzle in need of being pieced together to form a bigger picture.

Rosie said:

Put the art and artistry together and see what happens.

Interestingly, Rosie equated them and their recent experiences with *the art* and the well-laid out gardens in Coombe Wood with *artistry*. She said in her tuneful voice:

The art and artistry are but one…
So are the dance and the dancer…
The song and the singer…

What a fascinating way of looking at things! Rosie was probably doing an excessive study of art, craft and music! So Maya thought!

✿

It is unusually warm and sunny this Saturday when Maya would otherwise have been at work. She has taken time off work for a couple of weeks to be with her specially invited guests from Delhi. She did not waste time and soon after coming back home, she organised the sponsorship letter to speed up Savitri and Ranjit's visit to London.

Ranjit was excited all the way from the plane ride to Maya's doorstep! Finally, the duo are in their fantasy land where streets are believed to be made of gold and houses are made of silver, where Santa Claus drops in through chimneys and makes every child's wish for gifts come true. Savitri thought these were true as a little girl and so does Ranjit who is still in the innocent crook of childhood.

Maya set off in her car under the autumn sun with plenty of time on her hands; soon afterwards, she got stuck in traffic. Gemma and Millie must be in the garden café by now catching up with news. That is where they are supposed to meet first. Sayed is with Savitri and little Ranjit; they are visiting some of the city's attractions. They will soon join the group.

Leon will also be there. He has returned from Cambodia.

✿

After what felt like going round in circles for ages, Maya drives past the Lloyds Park tram stop; the tram journey would have been much quicker. She will shortly be at the entrance of Coombe Wood gardens on the junction of Coombe Lane and Conduit Lane. This part of the suburb is not too far out from the busy town centre, yet it gives a misleading but pleasant feeling of being in the countryside.

The entrance to the gardens is through the free car park. The pond is on the left-hand side immediately after the gateway; it is the habitat of insects, large goldfish, water lilies and other fish of varying sizes and colours. The water is moss-dark and a riveting miscellany of water creatures are peacefully co-existing and thriving in it. The sound of the waterfall at the back of the pond creates an intoxicating lull in the environment. A toddler spots a tiny frog on one of the lily pads on the pond surface and runs jovially towards the wire-net barrier. His father quickens up his paces behind him, picks him up and sits him down on his shoulders. The bedlam scares the frog away and, like its instantaneous appearance, it disappears into the pond with a splash! The path beside the pond leads to a tree-encircled single-storey building; the café is attached to the building.

The first terrace of the gardens is opposite the pond. This is lined with arrays of pink, white and purple lisianthus and colourful hydrangea and freesia. The subtly scented blossoms are planted amidst skilfully trimmed round clusters of green shrubs. Uneven stone steps by the shrubs and an adjacent slope for the ones who prefer a smooth ascension, lead upwards to other terraces and finally to the top of the gardens containing a small shelter. Various paths branch out from here to the woodland. Maya's plan is to get everyone gathered around here and sit on the benches arrayed in front of the shelter if it shines or huddle up inside the shelter if it rains. Fortunately, that honeycomb fiery ball - the sun - is up and shining!

Behind the shelter, there is an ornamental tree with evergreen leaves. It is very old. Its trunk is short, thick and streaky. A blast of thick, dark brown branches growing spindly at the tips protrudes aimlessly towards the sky. One can easily climb the tree and perch on one of the branches. Millie did this many times and hung down from the branches like a monkey!

✿

Maya finally reaches the car park. It is fairly full. She finds a space between two cars and skilfully gets her car into it. She rushes out of it and glides past the pond towards the café where she hopes to see Gemma and Millie - the first group of the troop.

She opens the glass door to the cafe. The room is small with a serving counter and some tables and chairs. Afternoon hospitality has already started in the café with a few dispersed customers in the room. Some are sitting at the tables, waiting for food, others are standing at the counter ordering food and drink. Maya checks the time, she is about forty minutes late. She looks around; there is no sign of the girls. Perhaps they got tired of waiting and ventured out into the gardens. Where can they be? She has not told them about the meeting place at the top of the gardens. In her haste, she left her mobile phone at home. She decides to wait here for a while in case they return. They are surely somewhere up the slope; a quick flash in her mind bears an image of one of the girls sobbing profusely. Who is that and why is she crying? She shakes off the image from her mind and plonks down the food basket she has brought on the table; this is filled with snacks for the group. She sits down on the chair and out of a sense of habit takes hold of the menu in front of her.

'Ma'am, 'tis for yer.'

A young waitress appears with a tray; there is the traditional English cream tea on it: a pot of tea and an upturned white teacup on a white saucer, a delicious hot scone on a plate and small pots of strawberry jam and clotted cream on the side. She places each item neatly on the table.

Maya is surprised. She looks appreciatively at her favourite food. She is not hungry right now but for the cream tea, she always is.

'There must be some misunderstanding, I haven't asked for this.'

''Tis from yer daughter.'

'How do you know I'm the right person?'

'Why, you look exactly like yer daughter, only a wee bit older.'

Maya finds the compliment flattering.

The girl continues, 'She wants yer to 'ave tea and then join 'em at the top of the gardens.'

The girls may have gone there as it is a common meeting site or it could be a pure coincidence although Jonathan used to say:

There are no coincidences, Venus darling, everything happens because it is meant to happen; you and I were destined to meet, and that was not a mere coincidence.

She suddenly feels the pangs of separation; she pines for Jonathan, for softly resting her head on his wide chest, for hearing his sensual voice and for his happy co-existence. She recalls Baba's advice, '*Rise above your sorrow.*' She softly whispers to herself:

I'll keep the sweet memories.

A distant bird tweets, a light breeze through upper sashes of the windows strokes her hair and she almost hears a whisper in the wind:

Me too.

✿

Sublime crumbs of the scone with the jam and soft clotted cream dissolve in her mouth with each sip of refreshing English breakfast tea – they perfectly fit in with one another and are in perfect harmony with the pleasant setting of the room. Maya finishes her tea quickly as she is already late. The rest of the group will be here any moment.

The adjoining narrow side slope is a quicker route to the top of the gardens, but she decides to go there through the beautiful garden terraces. She avoids the route with uneven stone steps by the flowers and shrubs lest she stumbles over in her haste, and strolls on the parallel, smoother gradient. Then she goes past the expansive lawn, on her right, lined with papery anemone, colourful chrysanthemum and lavish herbaceous plants. She slides past sweet-scented sweet peas and enters into the rose garden through the garden arch. Sparse roses are beginning to wilt away at this time of year. Come the rose season, the abundant blossoms will spurt out of their dewy buds!

Maya finds Gemma and Leon standing in front of the shelter. Where is Millie? She cannot locate her within the range of her vision. The brother and sister, oblivious of Maya's presence, are having an emotional reunion. Gemma is sobbing and repeating, 'I never hated mum, I never hated mum.'

'Shh, I know, Gem,' Leon comforts her.

'We tend to dwell on our misunderstandings and differences throughout our lives. We stick to these petty, stupid ways and now I'm thinking that when life is taken away, we're left with nothing, nothing at all,' Gemma says between sobs.

'You know what? Mum would have been very proud of you.'

Gemma looks at Leon with enquiring, tearful eyes.

'Because you're blossoming like a flower.' Leon continues, 'From now on, let's focus on our similarities rather than differences.'

'We can try,' Gemma sighs.

115

'And remember, we can paint that picture in black, white and grey with blobs of red, blue, green and yellow,' Leon reminds Gemma about what their mother had once playfully suggested.

Maya goes behind the shelter to look for Millie. Millie is leaning against the trunk of the ornamental tree, staring blankly into space. Maya saunters back to where Leon and Gemma are standing. She puts the picnic basket on one of the benches.

'Mrs. Morgan,' Leon notices Maya. Gemma, still sniffling, walks towards her to greet her.

'Glad both of you could make it,' Maya says. 'Leon, there is someone else to see you,' she channels her gaze to where the tree is. Leon walks towards the tree. Millie emerges from its side. They pause and look at each other.

'Hey,' Leon greets her.

'Hey,' Millie mumbles. After a long pause, she murmurs, 'You didn't call me for two whole months!'

Leon quickens his pace towards her and tentatively rests his hands on her shoulders. He then tenderly draws her close to him and says, 'I'm sorry Mill and for God's sake, one woman at a time.'

Gemma and Maya burst into soft giggles.

Millie coyly buries her face into the embrace she was so longing for. Leon savours the moment for a while and then gently cups her face into his hands, and plants a tender kiss on her lips in the honeysuckle scented wind.

'I love you,' Leon says.

'I love you too,' says Millie.

Leon and Millie, with their hands clasped, sit down on a nearby bench. Leon signals Gemma and Maya to join them. He then addresses the group.

✿✿✿

Chapter 19

THANK YOU MRS. MORGAN FOR ORGANISING THE GET-*together. I am glad you did. I know I did not keep in touch with you* (Leon looks at Millie and Gemma) *for a while but you were always in my mind.*

When I was done in Tokyo, I flew to Siem Reap in Cambodia and then, on the spur of the moment, I decided to extend my stay there. There may have been reasons behind this or maybe there were no reasons at all; and much to my surprise, Isaac, our boss, granted me further leave of absence. Perhaps he recognised my need for space and time.

I'll tell you about the days I was away from my familiar world. However, today I'd like to go further back into my past. Where shall I begin from? My childhood? I don't think I have ever shared these thoughts with anyone before. My fond childhood memories go back to the time when I played with Gemma with our cuddly toys. Despite the three-year age gap between us, with me, being the eldest, we never got bored and used our imaginations to keep ourselves busy. We made our toys come alive, as all kids do, by making up stories, inventing names for the characters, squabbling over what the ending of the story should be and settling down for a rushed finale.

Dad was busy with work and could not always be there for us, but we knew he was there behind the scenes to care for us, to provide us with what we needed. Mum was always at the forefront. I remember the great time, effort and care she put in to bring me up into what I am today. Her sheer belief in me helped me to achieve my goals. Without her, I could not be where I am today. I have her to thank for all she did for me, but I can't do that now even if I wanted to so I would say if you want to appreciate someone, just do it; don't wait for tomorrow or next week or next month. If you can't say it, show it through your actions – you can hug them or give them flowers or take them out for lunch, not only on Mother's Day, Father's Day or 'something' day! Extend your appreciation over other days. Every day can be 'something day', can't it?

Anyway, I feel Gemma is right in saying that we typically focus on our differences rather than our similarities, but I'll put it slightly differently: we tend to look for what is going wrong in our lives rather than what is going right.

When I was growing up, I lived in fear of disappointing my parents, especially my dad, in terms of choosing the right path in education and profession. Mum helped me to set my mind at rest. Despite her own personal unhappiness, she made me realise that being in a state of happiness is one of life's true joys. If you are doing something that you enjoy, it does not matter how difficult or easy it is, you will always feel refreshed and content.

However, mum slowly began to drift away from us; if not physically, at least mentally. I became resentful; little did I see things from her perspective; she had always put us before her happiness – it was time she had hers. Gemma was in the same boat as me. I resolved the matter by keeping to myself; she rebelled. In the end, I held Gemma responsible for adding to mum's misery. I was hardly aware of Gemma's own angst at seeing mum wither away from inside, bit by bit.

As individuals, we are more in discord within ourselves because, I think, we're able to perceive only a fraction of the whole picture. This is the problem in our human culture. Nevertheless, I must say that I learned to accept good things and challenges in life through the insights of my loved ones who led me to regain my poise after stumbling over.

As for our business trip to Japan, it was overall a successful one. I have always maintained a degree of fascination towards this country whose people work towards achieving common goals; they also have their own hopes and dreams. Mother Teresa once said:

What we are doing is just a drop in the ocean but the ocean would be less because of that missing drop.

The saying reminds me of the Japanese people - together they make the ocean, yet they are individuals in their own rights. In today's climate, when the inclination is about focusing on where the world is heading towards, I prefer to think where I am heading as an individual. This is the reason why I have an affinity with these people.

One afternoon while I was still in Tokyo, I went to Mr Yoda's office to meet him as previously arranged but he was not there. This was generally unlike Japanese people. When they give you their word, they keep it under all circumstances. Strangely enough, he left a message on a piece of paper for me that said:

Dark forces are against us, better interpretation awaits you in the temple of Angkor Wat!

The temple of Ankor Wat is in Siem Reap in Cambodia. I will tell you about it in a minute. Mr Yoda knew I was going to Siem Reap as I had told him about the trip during our prior brief encounter. I wondered what he meant by dark forces and what Angkor Wat had got to do with all this! Nothing else was in the note; there was no date for another meeting or no hint about why he cancelled the meeting. His secretary did not have a clue as to where he was at that moment!

Staying in Tokyo for an indefinite period of time hoping to meet with him was not a good idea so I went to Siem Reap as previously planned. I felt so peaceful once I was there. I just needed a break from the world I had known and Siem Reap was just the right place: a lush green quiet spot on the planet. It helped me to put my perspective of life back on track.

The following day, I had an elephant ride which was great! Elephants are very loving and gentle creatures. You can't help but feel this when you are near one. It was also funny because the elephant I was riding on was hungry so it took a detour to find some coconuts to eat and it stopped when it found them! Talk about only humans being capable of taking detours! Afterwards, the elephant-driver caressed its trunk and they exchanged the common language for 'let's go'.

During my stay in Siem Reap, I visited many magnificent temples. Scores of temples were built there and also in other parts of Cambodia. They date from the 9th to 14th century. They are in dense tropical jungles surrounded by moats and reservoirs. These temples are works of art and are incredibly big. I wonder how men had built them with their own hands all those years ago in deep forests without the help of any modern technology. The awe-inspiring temples exude charm and beauty of a lost civilization. Contrary to Greek or Egyptian ruins, these shrines are still holy places for worship for thousands of Buddhists and Hindus. Tourists from far and wide also visit them.

Angkor Wat, the biggest religious monument in the world, built in the early 12th century, specifically captured my attention. This was the temple Mr Yoda mentioned in his note so I was determined to go there. One has to be physically fit to take the endless journey to the central shrine and climb steep stairs to reach the top of it. Imagine doing this a number of times every day! The worshippers do this tirelessly to care for the needs of their gods. They mark their devotion with incense burners whose divine fragrances bring in a mystical environment in the shrine.

On the endless walls inside the shrine, there were stone carvings of both Hindu and Buddhist myths. If Gemma was there, we could have pieced together some of the stories just as we did with our toys in our childhood! I was trying to unravel a specific scene on the wall containing statuettes of celestial bodies and a long line of warriors. They were involved in a tug of war. Some warriors were on large elephants and horses. The carvings were lifelike and overwhelmingly beautiful and ancient!

A guide appeared from nowhere and introduced himself as Nhean. He was wearing a deep orange attire and seemed to be in his late twenties. His head was clean-shaven and his English was good enough for me to understand. He was frequently checking a strange looking device. He was perhaps measuring distance he covered on foot although he was not covering any distance at that moment!

He told me that the story on the wall was about the churning of the sea of milk by the gods to produce the potion of life. One of the by-products of the churning was the creation of beautiful deities called 'apsaras'. Like angels they floated majestically between the water and the sky, living on the celestial elixir. They were able to change their shapes at will and they often visited earthly mortals.

There were also untiring demons trying to cause turbulence in the process of creation. The gods felt threatened and they competed with the demons in the galactic tug of war using a massive serpent as a rope. According to the mythology, this continued for a thousand years. Then the gods defeated the demons, goodness prevailed and divine peace was finally restored.

It was an insightful story but if the gods were meant to be greatly mightier than the demons, how could they have got involved in a war for as long as a thousand years? I posed the question to Nhean. He pointed at the bottom of the frieze where there was an image of water that showed the reflection of the whole scene, but this was ruined in places. He said that the gods did not take any notice of the reflection in the water and that was one of the reasons for the long-drawn-out war. I did not fully understand what he meant by that. Nhean read my mind and said that from the physical reflection of your actions, you can see if things are going right or wrong. The demons and the gods were too busy fighting, they didn't have the time to notice what was going wrong because of their actions. He said that there was another reason for the prolonged war. The story was getting rather complicated so I didn't press him for the other reason, but he did bring it up later on.

I suddenly remembered Mr Yoda's note. I was trying to see the connection between the story and the note as it contained the words 'dark forces'. If it was meant for me to decode the myth about the gods and demons, then this was nothing new; this was, in fact, a well-known old myth! Besides, it felt absurd for an executive to avoid seeing me, mention dark forces and direct me to a fable that existed in an old temple!

Nhean appeared somewhat mysterious inside the semi-dark walls of the temple. He was telling me the story and, at the same time, keeping part of it in suspense; he would probably pass for a mystery story-teller or for a mystery role in a thriller film. Perhaps it was his way of keeping his clients engaged. However, his further interpretation of the story was quite interesting. He said that the world itself had been going through turbulence for a thousand years in terms of self-induced and natural calamities, but humanity was now at the gateway of a peaceful era; the peace process had already begun. This would continue for the next thousand years and beyond! I told him that I wouldn't be so sure about that. The current state of the world did not give the slightest inkling of reaching a peaceful *era. I didn't want to offend him so I said that stories and parables were inspirational, but they were far removed from reality. Nhean asked me, 'Don't we all create our own reality?' I said that we probably did, but it was not that simple. Besides, if the process of the desired change had already started, then it was painfully slow and it may not be evident in our lifetime. Nhean reminded me of the quote: things may get worse before they get better. According to him, the peace process could be fast-tracked by learning from our past errors, applying what worked and shedding what didn't. 'We're doing this all the time,' he said. By 'we' did he mean the worshippers at the temple?*

A tad dramatic approach aside, Nhean seemed to be a clever guy. He thought that this was the time to reflect on all that had been negatively affecting us and our Mother Nature - one way or another - greed, misuse of resources, clash, unrest, fear, wars, and so on - and to actively find ways to overcome barriers caused by these situations. We would then be able to move towards accelerating the peace processes. If we continued to gravitate towards unrest, then like the tug of war in the story, we would remain in misery forever.

'And that will not bode well for us or anyone else for that matter,' Nhean concluded.

Millie interrupts Leon at this point, 'What was the other reason for the prolonged war?'

Leon replies, 'Oh, Nhean said that the increasing disparity between the gods and the demons arose from the sense of being separated from one another. By connecting with each other and sharing all that they had, the problems would have become non-existent; but I did not see how the gods and the demons could possibly connect and share, given their positions as divine and evil, although, for me, it was just a story.'

'They could've, at least, co-existed peacefully,' Gemma comments. Maya nods in agreement.

'I guess so,' Leon says. '…Nhean also mentioned that there was a third reason that correlated with the first and the second.'

'He does sound mysterious,' Millie says. Leon continues:

Anyway, in the end, I found Nhean's interpretation of the story of the gods and demons quite insightful! Surprisingly, he mentioned a theory propounded by a British scientist that inspired me to find out more about his work while I was in Siem Reap. I'll elaborate more on this in a minute.

My encounter with Nhean got me thinking for the whole time I was there – if an average guy could think this way in a remote part of the world, perhaps we could also think seriously about the issues that are affecting our world one way or another and actively do something about them. It could start with something very small!

When you view things from different perspectives, they frequently show up in your life. It's like when you hope to see a car in a particular shade, it becomes visible everywhere! They were there before, but you only notice them more because of the change in your perception. Likewise, I came across many regional people in Cambodia who spoke about a new era and a new world.

Nevertheless, I have been deeply absorbed in my own story, please tell me about your own thoughts and ideas, about what you think we can do together, maybe in small steps, so that we can be those drops in the ocean without which it would be less. That's what we should be doing here, right Mrs Morgan? (Maya nods.)

By the way, something strange happened to me in Cambodia. I didn't give it much thought at that time! When I was at the airport waiting to fly back home, I probably dozed off in the passengers' lounge. Out of the blue, everything around me turned brighter and more colourful as if a film crew had directed a spotlight towards me for a scene to be shot.

A tall and slender man wearing colourful clothes walked towards me, a subtle glow was emitting from him or was it from me? I wasn't sure. He seemed quite friendly, cheerful and carefree; he was smiling broadly and he rather looked like the character of Bert in the film Mary Poppins. This refreshed my memory of the integrated cartoon scenes in the film that portrayed an imaginary fun-filled land. I noticed his big eyes and the space between his eyebrows as it was unusually wide. He said that flash dancers would arrive soon and that they were so good! He also told me that he had left his lunch at home; he could 'zoom back' and get it, but he would be spoilt for choice anyway in flash parties. He wasn't speaking much, but somehow I understood what he was trying to convey. I specifically remember the strange terminologies he was using like 'flash dancers' and 'flash parties'. I didn't have a clue as to what on earth he was talking about. I looked for the things he mentioned not knowing exactly who or what I was looking for. When I looked back, the man was gone and the brightness was gone too! Was I daydreaming? I had never had this sort of experience before: it was so vivid. Maybe it was a hallucination! But why on earth would I have that either? All I can say is that it was stranger than fiction!

Chapter 20

'YOU COULD WELL HAVE BEEN REMOTE VIEWING,'
Savitri catches the last bit of Leon's story and expresses her opinion.
She shows up with Ranjit and Sayed. Ranjit races towards Maya
clutching his fluffy teddy bear; he prattles excitedly,

'Auntyji, I saw Santa's reindeer.'

Chiming of everyone's laughter echoes in the air. Sayed picks him
up, proceeds towards the ornamental tree and sits him down on a low
branch. Ranjit looks cute in his bobbled woolly hat and padded coat; he
is well equipped for the cold weather in London. Everyone mills around
the tree. Maya introduces Savitri and Ranjit to Gemma and Leon. After
exchanging greetings, Leon says to Savitri, 'You were saying something
about remote viewing.'

'Well, from what I heard, you could have been pretty much in a half-
asleep mode in which you either saw a segment of the past or the future.
I tell you, I'm saying this from my own experience,' Savitri looks
meaningfully at Maya and Millie.

'So you've done your research, eh? Millie humours. She says, 'As
far as I can remember, we weren't in drowsy modes in the Delhi market
for the remote viewing to have happened to all three of us.'

'It was awfully hot that day, remember? And one does feel drowsy
in unbearable heat,' Savitri explains.

'Sounds like time travel to me,' Sayed comments. He is not quite
clear about what the women are talking about.

'Well, it was kind of that…the realm of the mind is not only
confined within the brain, you know, it stretches beyond it, plugging us
into the past and future,' Savitri says.

Every day, every moment new things are happening - Maya recalls
what Baba had said in Delhi. She offers her own interpretation centred
on this adage and her own recent experiences:

'Yes, strange things may happen when we are at the junction of
different levels of consciousness.' She continues, 'Anyway, the reason I
asked you all to come here is for you to have, if you like, a reunion and
to discuss and reflect on your recent enriching experiences. I'm sure

something good will surface from this and you can, as Leon put it, be drops in the ocean of goodness. Let me know what you have come up with as I'd like to be part of this too.'

Maya then helps Ranjit to get down from the tree branch. She tells him that she will take him to the central library inside Croydon Clocktower. 'I will take you to the children's section, and we'll read story books together, and then we'll have yummy food at the Clocktower café. Okay, little poppet?'

'Yay,' Ranjit's small face lit up with excitement.

'Tomorrow, we'll go to Hamleys,' Maya announces.

'What's Hamleez?'

'It's a v-e-r-y big toyshop in London. You'll see loads and loads of toys there.'

'Can I have one?'

'Of course darling. You can have more than one.'

Ranjit chuckles with joy.

'No more than one toy, Ranju,' Savitri warns.

'We'll see,' Maya says. She hands over the picnic basket to Millie. Maya takes another look around her. This section of the garden overlooks carefully laden oval-shaped rose beds.

'And if you care for a hot drink and a piece of cake, there's a café down there. Will catch you later.' Then the two glide down the side slope towards the garden gate, leaving *the art and artistry* behind them.

Savitri calls out from behind, 'Don't be naughty Ranju. Listen to Auntyji.'

Savitri now fully notices the ornamental tree, its short, stocky trunk, and protruding branches. She asks Millie mischievously, 'Are you thinking what I'm thinking?'

Millie throws a perplexed look.

'Remember, what Baba had said? *Embrace a tree, embrace someone?*'

Millie grins. They both race towards the tree and give it a hug, then rush back and give cursory hugs to their bewildered audience.

☼

Gemma's attention falls on the shelter in front of her. It is a small wooden shed with just enough space for a bench. A three-year-old girl is inside it, peeping through the window. The wooden beam above the window has started to rot; the white paint on it is peeling off. Her mother is standing outside the shed. In a quilted blue coat, blue tights and black buckled shoes, the little girl is the child version of a young lady.

'Let's play hide and seek. Shall we? Shall I count from 1 to 5 or 1 to 10?' the mother asks.

'1 to 10,' the girl replies boldly.

'Here we go, 1..2..3...,' the mother starts to walk away from the shed. The next moment, the girl bolts out of the shed.

'Mummy, it's cold in there.'

One moment earlier she was willing to play but now she equates her mother's moving away from the shed with her being left alone in the cold.

'You want to come with me? Alright, darling.' The girl hops into the safe shadow of her mother and the two disappear into the pine forest.

The small shed reminds Gemma of the saying she came across in Rome. 'Let's see if I've improved my Italian.'

'La casa è dove si trova il cuore, e dentro al cuore esiste l'uomo saggio.'

Gemma interprets the line:

'The home is where the heart is and inside the heart there is the wise man.'

She tells them that, in the saying, the home is compared with the body that contains the heart. A wise being (*l'uomo saggio*) exists in the heart. This wise being in the heart, in other words, in the inner layer of consciousness, is the true self, the higher self, the soul or whatever individuals prefer to call it.

'I picked up the phrase in Rome. I thought it was quite interesting. To avoid repetition, let's just refer to *l'uomo saggio* as *it*. *It* always makes sage choices, but we're not consciously aware of *its* existence,' Gemma says.

'What inspires *it* to make sage choices?' Sayed asks.

'Devine wisdom,' Gemma replies.

'And knowledge?' Savitri asks.

'Knowledge is experiential whereas wisdom is the application of knowledge based on good judgements and decisions,' Gemma says.

'In other words…,' Leon attempts to comment.

'In other words, knowledge tells us that a tomato is a fruit and wisdom lets us decide whether to put it in fruit salad or not,' Millie speaks for Leon.

'Yeah!' Leon agrees.

In the course of their discussion, it comes to light that the true self in the deeper layer of consciousness is infinitely wise. False garment of fear and natural inclination towards despondency tend to propel one away from paying attention to *the wise being*.

'We are conditioned to live in fear. Just like a fly, yes a fly that lives in its tiny world of endless fright!'

'That's quite intriguing. Oh, the mention of food is making me hungry. What have we got in here?' Sayed peeps into the food basket. It contains cling film wrapped homemade sandwiches with a selection of fillings: tuna with sweetcorn and mayonnaise, chicken with sautéed red peppers and balsamic-glazed onions, and cream cheese with cucumber and tomato slices. There are also packets of unsalted crisps and small bottles of water. Everyone digs in.

✿

The autumn sky is now pale blue with sprinkled rain-clouds. It will soon be drizzling. The stillness of time takes them into the rose and ornamental grass garden. What is left of withered roses blends in with the subtle autumn scent. Bunches of ornamental pampas grass nearby stand tall and sway in the air in a bid to invite the endless sky to come down and join them in the joyous festivity. The shimmering grey-blue sky receives the offer with a smile!

'Wow! Heaven on Earth,' Savitri exclaims. Her amazement propels her to link the scenic beauty with the story about heaven and hell. She repeats it for everyone's benefit and then solves the mystery of the long spoons tied up along the arms of the residents of both:

…*heaven and hell*!

✿✿✿

Chapter 21

PEOPLE IN HELL COULD NOT GET THE LONG SPOONS TO reach their mouths so they remained hungry and miserable whereas those in heaven, in a similar situation, stretched their arms and learned to feed each other so they were happy, well-nourished and content. That was the subtle yet profound, life-changing difference between heaven and hell.

Savitrti sees a link between the story and the Hindi verse recited by the mysterious Baba in Delhi. She ran through the English translation of it many times in her mind. She recounts this now:

The voice of people seldom has power,
The ones high in number are low in spirit.
Lord Vishnu's world will one day see them awakened.
And that is better for the rise of nations.

Savitri explains that people in a country are high in number, but they seldom express their views about what goes on around them (perhaps a few of them do) which accounts for why they are low in spirit. They are the silent majority - their hands are tied with inhibitions and situations deceptively beyond their control like those in hell. Although they may not necessarily be in a hell-like situation, they are at times isolated and disconnected; their arbitrary ways of dealing with problems sometimes make them miserable and unfulfilled. Their awakening will happen through collaboration with each other like the ones in heaven - a little adjustment in heaven reversed the situation that also existed in hell. The world is now in dire need of such adjustment. The story and the poem share this common message!

Savitri adds that according to Baba, certain conditions need to be met in order for *the rise of nations* to happen. 'But he didn't specify the conditions,' Savitri says.

'Let's ask Mrs. Morgan. She may have better ideas,' Leon suggests.

The group now wander into the winter garden. Colourful heathers are in full bloom. Sprightly stalks of Chianti, the late yellow-brown blooms of the sunflower variety, swing merrily in the wind. A lady is sitting on a bench nearby; her brown umbrella, brought in anticipation of the usual drizzles, is hung loosely on the bench arm. She is busy writing in her notebook. Dry autumn leaves on the ground take off in the wind and swiftly drift past the rim of her printed, ankle-length cotton skirt.

Beyond the gardens, many pathways fork out towards the woodland full of towering pine trees with deep, cool shade dancing beneath them; the sunbeam, trickling through the closed canopy of pine leaves, pitches in with the merriment. The light and shade offer a restful break to strollers and joggers. They can also sit down and have a momentary rest on the fallen tree trunks that border the sides of the pathways.

✿

From the pinewoods, they journey towards the rock garden. The rock garden was accidentally discovered by the workmen who were clearing the dense forest while laying the gardens. Alpine plants with tiny little blue and yellow flowers sprout through varied sized rocks in the garden. The rocks are ancient; they have been soaking in the rain and shine, gathering moss. The group stay there for a while, musing on and absorbing nature's felicity.

'Ah, this rock garden puts me in mind of the Japanese proverb, remember, Sid?' Leon recites the English version of the short poem:

You are soaking yourselves every day
Into things you love to hate.
Let yourselves soak into things
You would hate to love.

What Leon reads in the poem is that people are generally exposed to things that they absorb on a daily basis. These could be pieces of news, news about economic depression, crime, war and so on. They don't particularly like to read or hear about them every day, but they do it anyway – this is the norm they feel at home with, this is the *love-to-hate* part.

By the same token, they have had enough of what they have been soaking in for so long but for some reason or other, they don't want to admit this and continue to do what they *love to hate*.

'But good things are also happening every day,' Savitri says.

'Yeah, but how much of that comes to the forefront?' Leon asks.

Sayed says mockingly, 'Perhaps it will be weird if news breaks out about thousands of aeroplanes taking off and landing safely or about the majority of the seven billion people not killing each other.'

'Well, joking apart, we're informed about good things too,' Savitri says.

'Yes, but a little sweetener is served in a large ball of misfortune!' Millie replies.

Sayed asks, 'Don't we hear about what's actually happening around us?'

'Yes, we do…this is because fear breeds more fear. The same goes with hatred!' Gemma says.

Sayed remembers the Bangla proverb on the clay pot he bought for amma. This spurs him on to talk about it as it goes with what Gemma has suggested; something within urges him to wait for the right moment.

Leon continues with his explanation, 'Deep down in our hearts, we want to hear about something good, but this may go against our common expectation of hearing the norm which is predominantly negative in nature, hence the phrase goes: *you would hate to love.*'

✿

The group decide to end their excursion in the café. There is a narrow slope to the left-hand side of the rock garden that leads to the café; there is not enough space on the slope for two people to walk side by side. Leon, Millie, Savitri and Sayed form a single line to climb down the slope with Gemma at the front. The slope is lined with big and small flowerpots, constricting the path even more. Colourful primroses in the pots are dancing merrily in the wind. Gemma stops for a while to admire the pot garden. The rest halt behind her.

'*Now is the time*,' Sayed hears a small voice. He recites the English translation of the proverb on the clay pot,

'Here is one that you may like,

'Waves on this side of the riverbank surge towards the other,
Good begets good, bad begets bad – if you would only care.'

Sayed says that the metaphor in the saying implies that what happens in one part of the world somehow affects the other. The nature of the effect will depend on the nature of the cause, as in the poem – *good begets good, bad begets bad.*

'I was sceptical about the saying. Now, it kind of makes sense,' Sayed says.

'My papa used to say something similar,' Savitri says. She recalls,

'Sahi raha par chalne ka natija sahi aur galat raha par chalne ka natija galat-hi hota hai.'

'What does that mean?'
'Difficult to translate. It goes something like this:

The consequence of treading on the right path is positive and the consequence of treading on the wrong path is negative indeed.'

'As Dr Emoto claims…our positive or negative thoughts or words have corresponding effects on our surroundings,' Leon says. Millie agrees. She can vividly recall beautiful pictures of frozen water droplets that were exposed to words of love and gratitude prior to being frozen, and disfigured pictures of water beads that were impacted by words of hatred. Millie talks about Dr Emoto's theory to the rest pausing every so often for Leon to fill in.

Leon also acquaints his friends with the British biologist, researcher and author Dr Rupert Sheldrake's theory of morphic resonance. It was Nhean, the guide at the temple, mentioned the scientist's findings. Leon explains that the morphic resonance is a process through which characteristics and habits in living organisms and in matter are acquired across time and space through self-organising collective memories that exist within the morphic field so what crops up in one part of the field has a bearing on the other; this, in turn, links with Sayed's proverb.

'Keep in mind that as with any findings, there are critics who look for inconsistencies in them. Give them a hundred years, people will be singing their praises.'

'What about the one with glycerine?' Millie asks.

'What about it?' Sayed enquires.

Millie tells them the story about crystallization of glycerine. During the first forty years after glycerine was discovered, it was widely accepted that it did not form any crystals. Then something very strange happened one day that changed its characteristics everywhere in the world!

It is now drizzling. Savitri flips her umbrella open. The rest are happy with tiny pearl droplets of the light shower. The soft drizzle slowly turns into rain.

Inside the café with steaming cups of coffee, slices of moist carrot cakes and banoffee pies, they explore a rainbow of possibilities and ideas in light of their wide-ranging adages and sayings.

Sayed remembers the lines from a song in which the Indian Nobel laureate Tagore visualized a perfect world. He recites a couple of lines to his baffled audience,

'Amra shobai raja amader ei rajar rajot-tey
Noiley mo-der rajar shoney milbo ki shortey.'

'That's poetry for my ear but not for my understanding,' Gemma comments.

'Oh, they're a couple of lines from one of Tagore's many songs. He probably wrote it during the British colonial rule when the reigning king in Britain was the Emperor of India,' Sayed says. He translates the lines:

'We are all sovereigns of this land,
Why else should we tune in with our king?'

'If you read between the lines, it implies that we are all equal,' Sayed explains.

'Nice. Sounds like a perfect world to me,' Savitri utters with a sigh.

'Too perfect. Who would've thought such a place would exist during the colonial reign?' Sayed remarks.

'All great people have dreamt the same dream. Martin Luther King also had a similar dream,' Leon says.

'An ideal world exists only in a dream,' Savitri thinks out loud.

'That's it – *dream* – this will be one of my themes,' Gemma says excitedly.

Leon is perplexed, 'What do you mean?'

He is about to indulge in his habitual thinking: *that's very Gemma-like, always acting on impulse.* He averts his own impulse to be judgemental and attempts to think positively about her and about everything!

Gemma continues,

'My expectation of a perfect world stems from the cartoon films I used to watch as a child. Unlike my friends, I always felt sorry for Tom, the cat, in the Tom and Jerry cartoon. If the cartoon began with Tom sleeping peacefully and Jerry, the mouse, coming up with mischievous ideas, it would result in them harassing each other. I would often wonder why Tom couldn't carry on sleeping peacefully for the rest of the 5-minute cartoon. As a child that was more desirable for me than grasping the selling point of it.

The cartoon wouldn't have been popular if Tom slept undisturbed throughout the running time of it. But what if Tom travelled to a wonderland along with Jerry? What if this land revealed amazing aspects that we have never seen before? I used to have these thoughts as I was growing up.

In reply to your question Leon, I'll probably be organising an event in which 'dream' will be one of the themes. That's all for now.'

✿

All the while they are mirroring each other, relating each part of the garden to their hopes, songs and poems as if they are being inspired by some unseen forces. More discussions lead to Jacob Newman's connections with media groups; these groups are hungry for new ideas. Leon and others could provide the media with new ideas – they go on at length about their new ideas. Savitri thinks of doing something similar when she gets back to Delhi.

'Our ideas are not completely new. They will just add a few drops to the ocean,' Gemma says.

'Yes, but the ocean will be less because of those missing drops,' Leon remarks.

'So to sum up, I'll quote something I picked up in Rome,' Gemma says.

'What's that?' Millie asks.

'Energy flows where your attention goes.'

The chorus of evening birds echoes over the woods and hills as darkness falls.

✿✿✿

Chapter 22

MAYA READS A NEWSPAPER ARTICLE THAT SAVITRI has recently sent her from Delhi.

Four slum areas, three on the edge and one in the centre of Delhi, are added to the welfare provision scheme undertaken by government agencies. These urban slums are renovated with the help of these agencies. Representatives of the agencies train youngsters, aged 11 to 18 in these slums to clean up their spaces and to help with recycling glass and plastic bottles. Building construction workers, appointed by the agencies, then convert glass bottles into sand-like particles that are used as part of building materials. Plastic bottles are turned into durable corrugated sheets for the roofs. A portion of the materials is then donated back to the slum residents who, with the support of the workers, rebuild their flimsy houses.

Youngsters have also been encouraged to form self-help groups in their own respective regions to make their dwellings better places...

The article further informs that high school students educate local youngsters in their spare time in exchange for some pocket money from the organization's charity fund. The programme also includes distribution of seeds and plants to the residents in slum areas so as to encourage them to grow their own fruit and vegetables and sell any surplus to the nearby street markets.

Savitri is now involved in the project mentioned in the article. She was able to convince her bosses that her pleasure trip to London had some business elements in it that could be useful for the project. Her lively personality and her long-term service in one of the government agencies afforded her the opportunity to become an integral part of the programme.

Savitri later phones Maya.

'Has Millie read the article?' Savitri enquires.

'Yes, she has. She'll call you anyway. Just so you know - her friend Anne is doing a documentary film on women's rights.'

'Nice going! Let me know how it went as we may not have the privilege of accessing it. By the way, Sayed may stop by for a few days on his way to Sylhet. He says he has some news for me.'

'Hope you don't think I am prying, is something going on between you two?'

'It's nothing like that, Auntyji,' Savitri blushes. 'Besides, I'll never forget Rahul.'

'Savi dear, moving on in life is not about forgetting Rahul.'

'I know, let's face it, Sayed and I belong to different cultures and faiths.'

'Love conquers all, my dear ... love conquers all,' Maya says.

'Anyway, tell me more about events in London,' Savitri makes an effort to stray from the topic.

'Well, Daily Herald is getting an influx of good news, I believe,' Maya updates her.

'I'll also tell you about something a-m-a-z-i-n-g at my end, but you go first,' Savitri says.

Maya fills her in with similar news to the one Savitri has sent her; as if by the power of morphic resonance, the positive flow of events are causing outreaching effects across the world. She tells her about young volunteers who are working for the Blue Badge Club. These volunteers endeavour to keep their respective neighbourhoods in the south-east and south west parts of London nice and clean. The Blue Badgers are also working in partnership with Age Concern. They visit elderly people and do the gardening and other odd jobs for them. Shop vouchers and free train tickets to Europe are given out to them as rewards and prizes!

Voluntary groups have always been working tirelessly throughout the country but, in most cases, they have remained unnoticed and unsung. Their work is now beginning to get noticed.

Maya reads out an extract from another story, included in Daily Herald, to Savitri:

Children at St. Mary's Orphanage in Hounslow demonstrated their generosity by skipping lunch for a month and saving money for the families of the lost fishermen in Plymouth. The members of staff also participated in the scheme. They donated 20% of their salary for that month. A group of staff and children went to the Prime Minister's residence to hand in a cheque for £2,500. The PM welcomed the generosity! He commented that this was a shining example and an unforgettable moment for all. His culinary staff entertained the special guests with freshly baked scones, strawberry jam and tea.

'That's so sweet,' Savitri says.

'And what's your amazing news?' Maya asks.

'It's about a remote village in Kerala. It is simply out of this world and unheard of, in this day and age.'

'Really? What is it about?'

'Well, I'll send you a copy of *The Delhi Post*,' Savitri maintains a degree of suspense. 'By the way, can you remember more of your recent dream that you were talking about the other day?'

'I only remember some scattered scenes and some words. I wish I'd written it down while it was still fresh in my mind. It was really sad and scary!'

In her dream, Maya was running fast in an open space, gradually picking up speed like a fast-moving aeroplane on the runway, ready to take off. Then she found herself floating in the air and zooming past a boundless ocean. Rolling and roaring, dark tidal waves beneath her seemed treacherous. It was overwhelming and frightening. She was scared stiff in her dream as she was gradually losing speed and was on the verge of falling into the ocean. At that very moment, her feet touched the ground.

✿

Charlotte Creek, the sub-editor of Daily Herald, needed a credible explanation from Jacob Newman for the inclusion of news about enriching events and opportunities at home and abroad. Jacob had skills and expertise from diverse arenas of his working life based on his past involvement in the media and his current role in Isaac's *dream team* (as coined by Isaac himself). He told Charlotte that more good news would be a welcome break for the majority who are inundated by a plague of sad and gloomy news; they would love to read about positive things that are also happening in the world.

Charlotte pointed out that there was already a section in their weekend issue that incorporated news about art and theatre, finance and other community news and events. Jacob debated that although such news did exist, it was infrequent and did not actually represent the wider picture. Most happenings - beneficial, stimulating and inspiring - remained backstage. These could often open doors of opportunities to many. Leon and Millie also met Charlotte and discussed the benefits of the inclusion of wide-ranging news about positive events and opportunities in the tabloid. Charlotte finally agreed to go ahead with the project on a trial basis.

The advert for the inclusion of such news in Daily Herald stated:

You create ripples of good news - we take them in. Tell us about the success, progress and opportunities in your community.

Surprisingly, educational institutions and low-profile organizations were great sources of such news; they continued to send in news items with photographic evidence: some were interesting, some were regular and some required sorting.

Sayed gathered and sent in some amazing international news articles for the overseas news section! There was one about gardens that floated!

Another project of the Bluebell group in a village of Barishal, Bangladesh proved successful. Visiting members of the group showed the natives how to build floating gardens that survived in floodwater and provided food for the villagers. Lots of easily available home-grown materials like bamboo, tree branches and twigs, cow manure, water hyacinth etc. were used to build such gardens.

Mohsina Bibi, one of the village enthusiasts, involved in building a floating garden, said that surplus fruit and vegetables were sold in a nearby open bazaar. The spokesman of the Bluebell group said that this system would be copied in other countries that are prone to flood and rising sea level.

The project had turned apparent misery into a healthy survival!

The article included a glowing photo of Mohsina in one of the gardens, holding a freshly picked vegetable of the zucchini variety! Behind her, there were composites of more floating gardens separated by floodwater!

☼

'What's Gemma up to?' Savitri asks.

'Oh, Gemma...she liked Leon's story about flash parties. She's planning something exciting – watch this space!'

'Cool. And Leon?'

'Well, he is in the process of designing a web...web...weblog that will invite people to comment on environmental issues and possible solutions.'

'Will his work colleagues support this venture?'

'I'm sure they will.'

'Auntyji, Millie told me that she was going to promote healthy eating through her departmental website. Isn't that cool?'

'Yes, that's very much like her.'

'How is your meditation going?'

'Going well, but there is a minor hiccup in another area I've set my heart on.'

'Hiccup?'

☼ ☼ ☼

Chapter 23

IN THIS GUIDED MEDITATION, YOU ARE GOING TO ENJOY focused relaxation by breathing deeply and doing simple calming exercises.

Find a comfortable sitting position. Your spine should be straight without straining. Clasp your hands and place them on your lap, palm sides up.

When you are ready, close your eyes.

Imagine breathing in a healing blue light. Inhale deeply into this light, hold it to the count of 3-2-1; exhale fully.

Meditation music in soft notes gets drowned in the noisy mise en scène in the Ashcroft Room in Fairfield Halls in central Croydon. Maya is offering guided meditation to the participants coming in singly or in pairs. The room is deluged with a mixture of sounds from adjacent stalls. She continues:

In a moment, I am going to count down. As I count down, focus only on my voice, and as the numbers decrease, you will reach a calmer state of mind.

Here we go:

7 – Breathe normally. Focus on your breathing.

6 – Just taking a break from the outer world.

5- You are going with the flow.

4- Taking just a moment sinking inwards.

3- going deeper and deeper.

2 – Any aches or pains you may have are disappearing.

1- You have come to a place of peace and harmony deep inside you.

Your thoughts are calmer. Your breaths are slow and steady.

Imagine that stretching in front of you is a vast golden beach. Feel the warmth of the sand under your feet. You feel a tingling sensation in your feet.

Maya had briefly outlined her philosophies in a leaflet she designed herself. It showed images of desk workers confined in office cubicles alongside a contrasting picture of a group of people deeply absorbed in yoga and meditation. She coined the idea of offering the calming exercises to people who remained within four walls of offices for a large part of the day. The text in her leaflet said:

Are you sitting all day at work?
No time to breathe deeply?
We will bring the relaxation exercises to you!
Breathe, relax and energize!

She did not mention *meditation* in the leaflet. The word is unfamiliar to many; for some, it is a process that makes you lose control of your mind. In reality, it is the other way round – people gain control of their minds by doing it!

Maya wrote to Eleanor Hatfield in relation to her ideas she expressed in the leaflet. Eleanor worked for a business organization; she was responsible for staff's health and well-being. She replied to Maya suggesting a date and time for a meeting with her to discuss the possibility of having her staff do the calming exercises during lunchtime. Eleanor's office was on the 6th floor of the ten-storey building in central Croydon that held at least sixty desk workers inside designated cubicles. The building resembled an upright matchbox from a distance. It housed a thousand members of staff altogether, working for various government, semi-government and business organizations.

✿

Maya gained access through the front desk and took a lift to the 6th floor. Office cubicles on this floor were just as Maya had imagined. Mazes of cubicles, devoid of fresh air and natural daylight, created a night-like effect with glaring ceiling lights. She gasped for breath; she had never stepped into a confined place like this before. The office ambience somehow fitted in with the rhetorical question in her leaflet: *No time to breathe deeply?*

Maya halted for a few moments in front of the cubicles. She imagined a different scene from the one before her. In her imagination, the workers suddenly got up from their seats, stretched their arms and legs, danced in time to music and smiled at each other; then, after ten minutes of the enthusiastic ritual, they went back to their respective desks, refreshed and revitalised!

Eleanor Hatfield was apparently impressed by Maya's leaflet and enthusiasm. Eleanor, a bubbly woman of small build, welcomed the idea of having her willing staff do the exercises to de-stress and relax, with a few of them to get started.

She commented on Maya's leaflet, 'This looks all so good.' Then she asked, 'May I see your certificate for teaching meditation?'

'I don't have a certificate, but I have been practising meditation on my own and with a small group at my workplace,' Maya said.

'Our hands are tied, you know. We run everything by the book. Why don't you take up a meditation course and become a teacher? It'll be easy for you since you've already been doing this.'

Maya took her word for it. She began a meditation course with an additional component - yoga. When she was halfway through the course, Eleanor asked her to run a meditation stall in Ashcroft Room on the Staff Well-being Day. Eleanor hired the room for the event.

✿

Ashcroft Room is a spacious room in Fairfield Halls. The building of Fairfield Halls is a stone's throw from the matchbox building where Eleanor and her staff are based. Other named rooms and spaces in Fairfield Halls are available for hire and for various purposes: theatrical shows, weddings, on-going art exhibitions and parties. The vast space in the foyer holds a gift shop and the reception desk; beyond the foyer, on the upper level, there is a bar and a café with adjoining toilets. Passages and stairs on this level lead to the rooms and spaces for hiring.

Inside the Ashcroft Room, there is a food corner with a wide selection of sandwiches, fruit and drinks for the staff; they will have their lunch break there. There are other stalls in the room - stalls with information about various courses on offer in and around Croydon: golf, Pilates, yoga and other well-being courses.

It is becoming increasingly noisy in the Ashcroft Room. People are coming and going, murmuring, feet-shuffling – the commotion is not exactly conducive to meditation. Maya was aware of this in the morning before setting up her stall and asked Eleanor for a quieter corner. Eleanor was busy organising the whole event; she did not have time to pay attention to Maya's request.

Maya was not very happy when she saw the layout of the stalls on the map that was posted to her a few days earlier. The space allocated for playing golf was practically inches away from her stall. She did not have a clue as to how she was going to get her clients engaged in doing meditation when a prospective golfer might shout with excitement for shoving the ball into the hole for the first time.

✪

To Maya's sheer surprise, some first-timers reported after meditation that the noise in the room did not bother them at all; for them, it felt as if it was coming from a far-away land. A young woman said that she actually felt a tingling sensation in her feet when Maya had said:

You feel a tingling sensation in your feet.

Millie visited her briefly in the morning to help her set up the stall. She spread out a white piece of cloth on the oblong table and decorated it with some multi-coloured gemstones, unlit scented candles (lit candles were not allowed in the room as they could be a fire hazard) and a small potted plant. An image of a woman on the laptop screen, sitting cross-legged on a beach with her eyes closed complemented the decor. She discreetly took a picture of Maya from behind while she was doing a session with a participant who seemed blissfully lost in stillness!

✪

Maya continues with the current meditator:

Listen to the sound of the waves. Listen to the birds. Here, you are safe, peaceful and happy. There is a deck chair in the middle of the beach. Walk towards it. Sit on the chair.
Devote this time just to yourself, you really deserve it.
The bedlam of your daily life is now far behind you.
I will leave you for a few moments so that you can enjoy your time here.

If your mind wanders, come back to your breath.

The meditation music is coming from the laptop CD drive. The subtle flow of musical notes is permeating into the heart and soul of the participant. After some time, Maya slowly counts her back up to the waking world.

✿

Maya has allocated 15 to 20 minutes for each meditation session, long enough for the first-timers. For some, it is an extraordinary experience, for the others, it is different and nice. Maya is optimistic about the new door of opportunity that is about to open to her. Eleanor walks past Maya's stall several times and notices the positive response of her staff to meditation despite the uproar from the golf spot nearby.

'When can we have this blissful experience again?' an eager participant asks after the session.

'Eleanor will do something about it, I'm sure,' Maya replies.

Eleanor remains indifferent in contrast with her initial interest in the matter. For reasons unknown to Maya, Eleanor never contacts her afterwards.

The world at large is not ready yet for meditation, for a quiet mind!

✿ ✿ ✿

Chapter 24

A PLETHORA OF GOOD NEWS ABOUT POSITIVE EVENTS
and endeavours slowly and surely spread across the morphic field.

✿

'Paul, come quick...this may interest our Chris!' Grace turns the
volume up of the afternoon Community TV news:

*Stallworth Manor College is in search of future motor racing
drivers – the likes of Damon Hill, the Formula 1 motor racing
champion. To this end, the College will be introducing a new course
on motor racing. Enthusiastic course organisers are expecting to
train the next Damon Hill through the Young Driver Coaching
Programme.*

*When the course starts next September, it will become unique in
the whole country. Here is what Donna Crowe, the college's Skills
and Enterprise course coordinator said earlier on* (a video clip of
Donna Crowe appears):

*'We trust that the course will be very popular. We will indeed go
out to the race track and work with young people. Most of the
students who will be on the course will not be in the college
buildings so we will take education to the site, both theoretical and
practical.'*

So watch out Damon Hill!

The newscaster concludes the show with the final phrase and a
smile!

'You're right there. Chris might like it; not sure though if Lillie
would approve of it,' Paul sounds unsure.

'We'll see. She may consider it for her dear son once she finds
out more about the course,' Grace is hopeful.

✿

'Mum, there will be a new school down the road, I can go there all by myself,' Jamie calls out. Sitting in his wheelchair, he leans forward to turn the volume up on his mini-radio placed on a low table. The news goes on:

...The plan was announced by Councillor Monty Seville. He states that investing in education has been the council's priority. The New Star Academy will be built on the disused land where Redbridge railway station once stood. It will be a secondary community school that will take in pupils of all abilities and backgrounds. All pupils will be motivated to be confident and independent in order for them to attain their own holistic and academic goals at their own pace. Learning will be incorporated in the curricula in ways that are achievable and rewarding. School policies, curricula and teaching methods will reflect the motto: Every... child... matters.

Here is what Mr Seville said, (an excerpt of Mr Seville's speech is broadcast) *'These children are our future leaders, workers and carers so it is crucial that they are motivated and encouraged to reach their full potential in all areas of learning. I fully believe that they will benefit from school ethos individually and as part of the rising new generation.'*

The school premises and equipment will be user-friendly for students with physical and learning difficulties, and special classes and sports for them will form part of the curricula.'

'You don't have to come out of your morning shift at the grocery to drop me off at school,' Jamie pauses for a moment and says in a melancholy tone, 'But the school will open next year.'

'That's great Jamie. You'll go there next year.'

'If I'm still around.'

'Course, you will,' Mum says, holding back her tears.

'Mum.'

'Yes, sweetheart.'

'I don't like my school.'

'Why is that?'

'I hate Physics, Chemistry and Biology. They're hard.'

'Darling. Your physiotherapist studied these subjects to get qualified; she is now helping you to get better.'

'What damn use do they have for me? I'm not going to be a therapist. And I don't like History either. What's the point in learning about the date of the Battle of Hastings?

'I'll speak to your teachers.'

'No use. Bet they can't do anything.'

☼

Radiant Rosie takes some non-perishable food items to Reeves Food Bank - the food bank where donations of food are collected and distributed among people who live on the street. Doreen, her neighbour, informed her about the food bank. The organization is run single-handedly by Sabena with the assistance of Jack. They work together with other charitable organisations of semi-government and private nature. When food stocks reach rock bottom, these organizations refer the homeless to Sabena.

The tall red-bricked building stands on Reeves Corner in Croydon. It is adjacent to a twin building of the same height and features, separated by a common yard. Rosie enters the yard; signposts for other community support are visible from here. There is no one else around; the yard feels abandoned and deserted. She walks up to the end of it; the wooden door to the food bank is on the right. It is flaky and blue; there is a notice on it. The ink mark on the notice is faded. It is difficult to guess how long it has been sitting there. From its dull colour, it is evident that it might well have been there for some time.

There is a food container at the bottom of the door.

'Tinned food, some of which may have passed its sell-by date, is deposited in the container outside collection hours; it simply vanishes by the following morning,' Doreen had told her.

A young girl of about eighteen, wearing a grubby jacket and tattered jeans, is peeping into the container in the hope of finding some food. There is none left. Rosie pulls out whatever she could from the food bag she was carrying and promptly hands them out to the girl. The girl grabs hold of them and bolts out of the place in a flash!

Rosie reads the message on the door. She is terribly shocked by its content. There are so many shops, restaurants, supermarkets and cafes around this place, how could this have happened? She hesitates, then she knocks on the door. Jack opens it.

Chapter 25

IN ORDER TO RECOLLECT HER RECENT DREAM, MAYA sits down on the floor in the lotus pose, keeping a pen and a notebook handy to scribble whatever she could call to mind. Retrieving memory from the conscious level of mind is not easy especially after a substantial lapse of time so she gets herself into the meditative state. The subconscious mind holds a reservoir of memories and the way to reach it, is through meditation.

The dream reveals itself to Maya one more time during her mindfulness practice.

✧

In her dream, when her floating-self touched the ground, she found herself in a bizarre place. It looked war-torn, destroyed and deserted. Prince, her father, emerged from one of the shattered buildings, and then her mother, Archana, followed by other despondent inhabitants of the land. Even in her dream, Maya felt sorry for her parents and their companions.

Prince communicated with Maya by means of a defaced round clock. He kept the clock rolling towards her, conveying a silent message through it that urged her to go to a temple nearby and find a sacred script. In this script, there were instructions on how to liberate them from their misery. Time was running out for them. They were quickly approaching the point of no return where they would be doomed forever. It was crucial for them to come out of their perilous situation as soon as possible.

In the following segment of her dream, she was in front of an ancient temple with a pointed tower. She opened the creaky entrance door and stepped inside; she heard her own scary footsteps: ...*tap*...*tap*...*tap*. Time stood still. Everything was rolling in a slow motion. There was no one else around; it was dark, damp and cold inside.

In the corner of the spacious ground floor hall, there were some pitchers lined up in a semi-circle around the base of an image of a deity. She could not clearly see the face of the deity. Somehow she knew that her parents worshiped her and that the holy script was inside one of the pitchers. Maya, however, had an odd foreboding that the deity would punish her for taking something out of the pitcher that did not belong to her, but she was desperate to do anything to free her parents and their cohorts from their precarious situation so she frantically searched for the script inside all the pitchers. The clock was ticking loudly and menacingly - *tick-tock, tick-tock, tick-tock* - in the background. The time was running out! Finally, she could fish out a crumpled page from inside a pitcher at the far end of the line of pitchers that said *Save Mother Earth*, she tried to read the rest of it; it was elusive and illegible.

Maya heard a rustling noise...was it a bird or a wild animal, or another intruder like her? She dared not turn round to see what or who it was. Instead, she swiftly put the page back into the pitcher and scurried upstairs. There was another big, empty hall on this level. The floor was made of ruined stone slabs and in the middle of it, there was a fountain mounted on a waist-high stone pillar with a stone bowl. No water was coming out of the fountain, but the bowl held a small amount of stagnant water; the fountain itself was dirty and was covered with moss. It had stopped flowing ages ago. She leaned forward to look inside the bowl and saw her own distorted reflection in the water. There were some engravings at the bottom of the bowl that said *Connect and Share*. Slow ripples in the water barred her from reading the rest of the text. Muffled sounds were coming from multiple invisible sources that sounded like *me, me, me*.

Maya finally made her way to the inside of the tower. Leafless branches of an oak-like tree entered into the tower through broken windows and cracked tiles. They kept growing and growing, filling in the empty space. Nature appeared to have got out of hand. Lines of ants were crawling over and around the branches. Flashes of animals and trees, small and large, were appearing and disappearing in quick succession along with prolonged groans that sounded like '*save us, p-l-e-a-s-e save us*' – the groans echoed on the walls. Maya shivered with fear and tried to escape from the scene. She felt debilitated.

Then somehow (as happens in dreams) she was downstairs again! A giant honeybee was hovering above her; like her, it was trapped inside the temple. Maya groped for the exit but failed to find one.

She looked up. On the ancient stone ceiling there was a short message:

Look for the gateway to love and gratitude.

The words began to pulsate, revealing a glimpse of a group of people in an open space who were happy together, who thrived and prospered in their land. The sky was deep blue; clear water in the stream was flowing beneath. A jovial man was sitting on a rock surrounded by his admirers. He held a book in his hand. He was reading from it to his avid listeners. Surprisingly, these listeners were all children. Maya did not quite grasp the content of his speech, but it channelled a sense of harmony and tranquillity. She caught a word or two; there was a specific word that echoed in her dream: *repetition, repetition, repetition.*

She kept praying for her parents. Her painful past that remained dormant in her memories for so long was alive again in her dream!

✪

Maya becomes alert again, her eyes are half-open. She picks up the pen and the notebook to jot down something very fast without thinking. She then opens her eyes fully and reads out what she has just written:

Save Mother Earth.

Connect with your inner self. Connect with others.

Crying out: me, me, me.

Share resources. Share joy.

Learn from and take care of nature including animals.

Gateway to love, compassion and gratitude.

Repetition.

Maya takes a deep breath; she gets up from her cross-legged sitting position and sits at her desk. She now expands her notes. Her keywords and phrases inspire a flow of writing:

We have long been mistreating and misusing Mother Earth and its resources, littering the land and sea, generating harmful substances, producing a massive amount of products for consumption that are disproportionately distributed across the world.

151

We have become isolated from our inner selves and from our fellow beings. At conscious level, we do not know how to connect, how to share, how to rise together. We are like time-worn stone fountains alone in the middle of nowhere, crying out 'me, me, me' like an old broken record. We look for happiness outside ourselves. The light of felicity comes from within us; it then spreads out and connects all.

We need to identify our similarities, acknowledge our differences, and connect with each other, for distancing from one another gives rise to nothing but misery, conflict and confusion. Peace and unanimity will be restored when greed and fear are outshone by love and gratitude; and when we achieve this, sharing and caring will become normal phenomena in our world.

We can learn from innate messages in nature: the plant kingdom and the bees, the ants, the way they work together - they collect their food to share. If you place an obstacle in front of a worker ant, it will ride over it or work its way around it but it will never run away from it. They may have less intelligence than humans, but they are more disciplined.

Nature in its pristine purity is harmonious – there is no competition, compulsion, greed or disharmony in nature. We are continually spoiling its normal state of being. We have now almost reached a pinnacle whereby nature will destroy us if we do not take care of it or follow its principles. If we return to nature, nature will return to us, otherwise, like endangered animals, trees and plants, we will helplessly be calling out - save us, please save us - when nothing or no one will be there to save us.

If all else fails and if we are stuck in the complexity of inescapable circumstances, we can look for the gateway to love and gratitude that will lead us to a life we so desire – a life of love and compassion for all and gratitude for all. This is the world we want to live in. This is the world we can collectively craft because we are fashioned to do so.

(Maya recalls her father rolling a clock towards her in her dream. She adds another line to the text.)

We do not have much time really! We need to act fast!

Maya is pleased with her dream analysis. She wonders about the presence of very young disciples in her dream. Why were there no adults apart from the teacher? Why were the children so unusually attentive and still? And what did the old man mean by *repetition*? But, of course, such portents are not always clear to the dreamers! Maya intends to share this experience with Savitri and Millie.

She hopes that her script reflects *certain conditions* Baba Sattyaram had quoted. Nimu did say that things would come to light someday although she is still not clear about *the merging of the left and right hemispheres* that Baba had also mentioned.

Baba, real or not, gave her food for thought.

✪

Rosie is determined to write to a number of food shops including supermarkets in Croydon after her visit to the food bank. She sits in front of her computer in the comfort of her own home. She keys in the words that appear on the computer screen:

> *I am writing to inform you that I recently visited Reeves Food Bank in Croydon for the homeless with the intention of donating some non-perishable food items. This organization receives food from the donors and distributes it to the homeless. However, it broke my heart when I found a notice on the door that said,*
>
> *'We are currently closed due to the lack of donation'.*
>
> *Fortunately, a volunteer was in and he gladly accepted my trivial donation. When I enquired about the notice, he said that perhaps my food would contribute towards taking the notice off. Was it a sad joke or a harsh reality?*
>
> *I am sure, at the end of each day, you have surplus food. You can donate non-perishable food that is on their wish list and also include their link on your website for those who are willing to help. Please visit the food bank's website and check it out for yourself.*
>
> *Lack of donation will force the volunteers to shut down the place. The hungry homeless may not have elsewhere to go to.*
>
> *May God bless you and return your favour a thousand fold.*

✪✪✪

Chapter 26

MAYA DIPS INTO THE NEWSPAPER ARTICLE IN THE DELHI Post that Savitri has sent her. Maya often dreams about the existence of such a place on Earth as mentioned in the article.

In the cutting, there is a photo of banana-tree lines and a cluster of half-brick built houses - some with corrugated roofs, some with thatched roofs - behind them. Young children are playing on the narrow pathway between the tree lines. The picture reflects the ingenuity of the story.

The title of the article is:

A VILLAGE IN BHARATHANJALI THRIVES WITHOUT MONEY - by Mr Shehzad Khan

Maya reads on:

A village in Barathanjali thrives without money - a concept incomprehensible in this day and age! The remote village in the north of Kerela along the coastline has embarked upon a new deal. This is similar to that of the barter system that once existed or still exists in some places in the world. The system is about exchanging goods for other goods and services; the difference between the barter system and the system followed by the villagers is that one does not exchange goods in a single transaction; they give or receive products or services as and when required.

People in this small community offer their services or resources and get what they need in return without money changing hands. The roofer repairs his neighbour's roof for free and when he needs a can of fresh cow's milk or a bowl of fresh fruit or vegetables he visits his neighbour who has them. The neighbour may not be the same one whose roof he has fixed. A potter gives away his pots and gets fish for his dinner from his fisherman friend. They welcome their neighbours with a common greeting:

Namaste! How may I help you today?

The head of the panchayat, in other words, the leader of the village council, Mr Lakshman, says that mutual help and understanding form the basis of this new way of life. Further questions to him begin with 'how', 'what' and 'what if'. Mr Lakshman diligently answers each of them.

- How does the system work without money?

What is money? It's just a means of exchange. Money itself has no value, we just attach the value to it based on the commodities we consume and how frequently we consume them. Something that is priced at ten Rupee today will have a different price tomorrow. Furthermore, as long as money exists, there will be division, greed, scarcity and discord. Money is just a concept that we have created! It does have some practical benefit in the modern world, but we choose to do without it!

- What if some are tempted to only receive without giving anything?

We have thought about that too. Only those who provide services to the community are entitled to receive what they need – no service, no gain. The gain is not in the form of money, but it's in the form of things or services that you need at a given time. Besides, we take what we need not what we lust for. Once you know that your needs will be met only in exchange for goods and services, you are encouraged to serve others.

- And how does exchanging a bowl of fruit with having the roof repaired work? Isn't there a disparity between the two?

For us, the disparity does not matter; all that matters is what we need at any point in time.

- What about the old and the disabled who may not be capable of supporting the workforce?

We don't have very many of them. The ones that we have, are being taken care of by their younger family members.

- But how do you keep a track of the transaction with no specific system of record-keeping?

We know everybody here. It is a small community and the driving forces keep us going.

- What are the driving forces?

Trusting and willing to help each other are our driving forces. Moreover, we have always been self-reliant and self-sufficient but we didn't get good prices for our own crops from the local markets so we decided to help one another and consume our own goods that we produced; some manipulators out in the markets actively opposed the idea but we won in the end.

- What if the fisherman neighbour doesn't have any fish to spare?

Then we will go to another fisherman who has it. Do you always go to the same shop? Besides, we usually have enough to share as a result of a farming procedure that we follow.

- What's the procedure?

We will enlighten you in a minute.

- What about education and entertainment in the village?

Educated members of the community provide education to children in a primary school without any salary! The grateful and happy parents offer the teachers the essentials and much more! Open-air sports and competitions often take place for all to see and enjoy. We are considering the idea of employing teachers from outside the village for secondary school education!

The villagers do not always have surplus. They predominantly depend on the mass production of crops and in some years they produce smaller amounts, but they still have enough to share as a villager puts it, 'Everyone has the right to share the fruits of the world.'

They sell some produce to the outsiders as they need money for other services or raw materials that they do not or cannot produce. This practice will one day cease when they expand more and manufacture almost everything they need. The villagers are hopeful about this.

As promised, Mr Lakshman presents Mr Jayawant Trivedi who supervises the farming procedure as mentioned previously. The procedure relies on food waste management with cows, chickens, frogs, ducks and worms forming the integral part of the workforce. Jayawant and his team fulfil their duties by harnessing nature's blessings!

They begin their day by collecting discarded bits of vegetables from carefully designated waste bins. They use these as the fodder for cows. These cows are the ones that no longer produce milk and are considered useless by many so they spend their happy retired lives by just feeding on the discarded vegetables, resting and producing manure in eight hours. Through a chain of procedures with worms being the last in line, the manure is converted into wormy cast, also known as black gold. This is thought to be the best in the world of farming!

The rest of the fodder that cannot be given to cows is mixed in the compost pit where maggots are formed. Chickens love maggots! They happily peck at them and, in the following morning, they hatch good quality eggs! Their counterparts, ducks, eat throw-away parts of fish and vegetables and produce 24 eggs each, per month, instead of the usual ten. No machines have ever been invented that can eat maggots or fish and discharge quality eggs in large numbers!

Cows, chickens and ducks are day workers – they need to rest at night so nature has provided the villagers with night-shift workers and they are frogs and worms! Worms are involved in the process of making the black gold. Frogs consume the trespassers – uninvited flies and insects that are harmful to crops and plants.

This is simply amazing! People in neighbouring villages are considering following in their footsteps. This is a small part of Bhrathanjali that exists without money. The exemplary way of life in this small village is justifiably impractical to the rest of the world where everyone and everything revolve around money.

People here are not rich, but they are happy!

☼

Despite Eleanor's silence, Maya continues with the yoga and meditation course. The trainer is an Englishman called Lenny Brown; he is in his early fifties. Lenny talks passionately about manifold benefits of yoga and meditation. He tells his students that yoga promotes strength, flexibility and balance in the body; physical balance translates into balance in all aspects of life; meditation changes the brainwave patterns into an Alpha state that assists in healing and calming the body and mind - the combined practices lead to a state whereby every cell in the body is filled with more prana or energy. What originated thousands of years ago in the East is now being reinvented both in the East and West.

Lenny thinks highly of his students, thereby calling them *yogis* and *yoginis* (males and females who are proficient in yoga). At the beginning of each lesson, Lenny addresses the class:

Dear yogis and yoginis, this is not a competition so don't stress or strain your bodies, do what feels comfortable. Breathe, enjoy and smile. Use your letting-go muscles. You won't find information about these muscles in any books or websites.

Then he places his two index fingers on the raised corners of his smiling mouth and says, *'These are the letting-go muscles.'* After that, in his unhurried cheerful voice, he instructs and demonstrates standing and sitting yoga postures with deep oceanic breathing called

Ujjayi breathing. Every now and again, Lenny reminds his students to smile. Maya wonders why he values smiling so much when no one else bothers to do so apart from Antonios (so she thinks)!

Lenny explains that smiling connects people. *'Try smiling at a grumpy teller behind the counter, see what response you get,'* he jokes. He then recites a short poem:

Smile awhile
And while you smile, another smiles,
And soon there are miles and miles of smiles,
And life's worthwhile because you smile.

Another day he gives a scientific account of the benefit of smiling:

Smiling or laughing, ladies and gentlemen, releases the happy hormone in the body that generates an instant good feeling. The body's immune system improves if smiling is practised longer. People tend to smile spontaneously when they are little, but they gradually lose the skill as they grow older and finally, they forget to smile or smile only when the situation calls for it.

The session ends with a blissful experience of meditation that enables learners to further release emotional and physical tension. Maya later realises that yoga postures work well in preparation for an extended meditation session that she favours so she devises her own relaxation exercises in the hope of using them with the existing meditation group at her workplace. Antonios, a keen yogi, thinks this is a great idea and helps her to modify some of the exercises so as to make them more interesting and achievable. He has his mind set on becoming a yoga instructor himself in his own country, Cyprus. Antonios, a lean and tall man in his mid-fifties, who does not look a day older than forty, tells Lenny, 'It's never too late for doing something new in life.'

On the last day of the course, Maya gives Lenny a thank-you card and a scarf she has knitted for him. The card reads:

Thank you for teaching us yoga and meditation, thank you also for showing us how to hold a smile longer.

Lenny reads the card and smiles!

Maya has learned to smile again. Jonathan could not have been happier.

✿

'Going back to Cyprus next week,' Antonios says, sipping coffee in the Coombe Wood café.

'Good for you. Thanks for all your help,' Maya replies.

'Is that it?' Antonios asks.

Maya gazes at distant plants through the café window.

'Maya, you know, moving on in life does not mean forgetting your past - it means accepting it and embracing the joy that presents itself.'

Maya gave a similar piece of advice to Savitri! She is now at the receiving end of it!

I am embracing the joy, Antonios … in my own way - Maya says in her mind.

✿✿✿

Chapter 27

'THERE'S A VACANCY FOR A FUNDRAISER IN OUR department, you know. The pay isn't much but it is rewarding. Will you be interested?' Phillip asks.

'Sounds good to me. Will I qualify for it?' Gemma enquires.

'Well, you've been doing voluntary work and there is no harm in trying; think about it. Meanwhile, here you are,' Phillip unrolls a sheet with a collection of messages he has gathered for the special event and gives it to Gemma for her perusal. Her face lights up as she skims through them. Gemma is amazed by their inherent beauty and inspiration; they perfectly match her expectations. In one of their earlier meetings, she gave him some ideas about what she was looking for in them.

'They're exactly what I wanted, thanks Phillip, but how are you going to present them?' Gemma asks.

'Leave it to me,' Philip says.

✧

It was trying to rain early in the morning of the last Saturday of May - the juncture between spring and summer - in 2001. The weather has been vacillating between the prospect of rain and a wayward shine. Gemma is hoping for fairer weather.

She has never organised such a big event before - an open air charity event in the wide expanse of the pedestrian precinct in North End located at the rear of the Whitgift shopping centre, the hub of the shops in Croydon. This was the space where her mother, Mabel, drew her last breath. Grim reminder as it is, it will be perfect for a peaceful closure of Gemma's pent-up grief; at the same time, it will bring communities together.

The place is almost always busy with other regular events, shoppers and youngsters so it is the right location for the event. It starts from here and extends down to the Queen's Gardens nearby. The banner at the garden entrance says:

A day like no other.

The pleasant, persistent heat of the morning sun falls on Gemma as she checks the progress in the Queen's Gardens. The brass orchestra is playing behind the flowery circular patch in the centre of the upper garden. The patch is surrounded by a low brick wall. There are pathways branching out in all directions from here. Along the pathways, there are inscriptions cleverly written in heaps of white powdery stuff. These are the messages that Phillip collected and showed to Gemma.

Gemma walks around the writings on the ground, angling her body and neck to read them properly:

It took me so long to grasp this is what they call 'imagination', I thought I was strange!

Thunder clouds feeding on trees with forks of lightning, that's what I expect from life's challenges.

A swan's trail on water is what I want to experience when I look back.

For your dreams to come true, you need to dream first!

If I have a son, I will name him Dad after my dad and I will present Dad to my grieving mum and say, 'Mum, this is Dad'.

I knew I liked her because my lips trembled between being unable to speak and suddenly blurting out loving words.

Love and compassion will someday flow across the world.

'Phillip, these writings on the ground came out beautifully and although they are on the sides of the pathways, they may get trampled under people's feet,' Gemma expresses her concern.

'That's okay Gemma,' Phillip says. 'I'll be more than happy if only one person gets inspired by one of the messages.'

'Well, that person is standing right in front of you and there'll be many more, I guess!'

Gemma had to go through a number of recalcitrant council officials to convince them about the positive outcome of the charity event. It took her six months to receive their approval to use the open space in the town centre for the event; the officials made it clear that they were not going to fund the project. A female member of staff, however, kindly gave her contact details of Phillip and Katy who, she thought, would be willing to lend a hand in the project. This was a great help as Phillip and Katy not only assisted Gemma in organizing the event, they also made approaches to local businesses on her behalf to fund the event, some of whom came to their aid; they even let them use their transportable stalls for the occasion.

Katy and Phillip work for a local charity that provides temporary accommodation for the homeless. Gemma will donate a portion of the proceeds from the event to this charity; the rest will go to other local charities.

Katy has organised the bandstand show, a one-man comedy act, a dance show inside the Queen's Gardens and a short video screening near the entrance to the gardens.

What was meant to be a small project turned out to be a grand venture!

✿

Down in the lower terrace of the Queen's Gardens, an Indian comedian and actor is doing a one-man show with minimal props. He is currently making up the act by poking fun at his own accent. There will be a colourful Indian Bhangra dance afterwards - a folk dance from the Punjab region in India.

Katy's collection of short videos will shortly be displayed on the large screen. The screen is currently fluttering gently in the breeze; the whiteness of it is shimmering in the sunlight. Gemma had a sneak peek at the clips that were videoed randomly in the streets of London. There was this homeless elderly woman curled up in her blanket, sharing her cup of coffee with another homeless man on a cold wintry day. There was one with a young Somali girl who noticed a disabled man dragging himself along the road in heavy rain. The girl kept pace with him and covered him with her own umbrella, getting herself soaked in the process.

✿

The screen now lights up. The theme of the presentation is displayed:

A little act of kindness goes a long way.

The show starts with a popular song with the display of its lyrics. Gemma hums along with the song:

I'd like to build the world a home and furnish it with love,
Grow apple trees and honeybees and snow-white turtle doves.
... ...
I'd like to see the world for once all standing hand in hand,
And hear them echo through the hills for peace throughout the land.

When the song ends, deeply moving videos are shown on the screen, one by one.

Back in the pedestrian precinct in North End, there are stalls of international food, lemonade, toys and bric-a-brac. Local residents from all cultures and backgrounds have donated their unique offerings for the stalls. Some of them have also volunteered to sort out the donated stuff and run the stalls. Aleena has joined the group and has become a part of Gemma's own little Rome in Croydon; this time, she is Gemma's helper!

The merry-go-round corner for children is there, as always. A sweets stall is a new addition. Maya has introduced something new for this stall – sweets made from cookie dough, chocolate chips and marzipan. These are labelled as *Hansel and Gretel sweets*! Children and their parents are gathering happily around the place. The raindrop song is being played along with the revolving merry-go-round:

If all the raindrops were lemon drops and gumdrops,
Oh, what a rain that would be.
If all the snowflakes were candy bars and milkshakes,
Oh, what a snow that would be.

Millie has given a novel spin to the event by getting willing adults pose as Disney film characters. Sayed is impersonating Bert in the film *Mary Poppins* and Leon is Prince Charming. Persuading him to do the act was the hardest part Millie had to endure but she achieved this in the end by giving in to his counterproposal. Leon said he would only do this if Millie posed as Cinderella.

Sayed abruptly appears at the food stall with a broad grin and a fake expectation of receiving free food. Aleena and Rosie, working at the stall, participate in this fantasy game. Their refusal to give him free food prompts him to magic 50 pence for the food item and 20 pence for a can of lemonade from behind his ears. He does this several times and collects as many food items as he can. He then chucks them into his rucksack, dances merrily with the novice Prince Charming and Cinderella and strides towards those flocking around other stalls who are not able to buy food even at subsidised prices. They are homeless people. Sabena and Katy have invited them. Sayed distributes the food among them and then joins other Disney characters for more fun acts! There is Snow White, there is Winnie the Pooh, there is Tiger, there is Tinkerbell – children are crowding around them. The show continues.

People from far and near and from all backgrounds are chatting and having a great time, forgetting their differences or adverse life situations. It is also an opportunity for children to enjoy themselves, '...like I did when I was your age. What do you think?' Katy chats with a young girl.

'It's really nice out here, it feels as if everybody knows everybody,' the youngster replies cheerfully; her message speaks volumes, it is a rare experience in her life thus far.

Katy nods in agreement.

✿

Three men, dressed up as inflated honeybees, pedal around on child-sized bikes from North End to the Queen's Gardens in exhilarating speed and spirit. They stop at different places in the area, circle around people who are sitting or standing, collect money for charities and utter words in an amusing, high pitched squealing sound which is supposed to mean:

Thank you, that's so kind of you.

The non-stop music, coming somewhere from the middle of their bee-bellies, blends in well with their bee-language and the entertaining atmosphere! The honeybee men are incredibly comical! At the end of their cycling rounds, they drop three large sacks of coins in front of Gemma and disappear into the crowd. Gemma thinks Phillip has scheduled this act, Phillip thinks it is Gemma's idea!

Amidst enchantments and laughter, the evening crawls in. In the twilight, everyone packs up from North End and gathers in the Queen's Gardens. The brass band, still playing, sounds as if it is coming from the distant horizon – they blend in with the mood of the evening. The honeybee men return on their bikes from nowhere and circle around the Disney characters and the remaining laughing crowd.

At the foot of the gardens, Maya and Rosie hand out goodie bags to an orderly queue of homeless people for their future consumption. Maya's eyes moisten as these people silently appear one by one in growing darkness in the hope of receiving a windfall. They will go back to their makeshift homes, to lonely park benches or to their families with whatever they will have amassed today!

The final attraction of the event - the colourful fireworks - begin in the garden! The blazing fireworks sparkle in red, blue, green and yellow high up in the night sky and burst into each other in a thousand spikes, and then plunge into space and fade away before fresh ones arise.

The beating of drums, the dancing of colours and the humming of the crowd create an electrifying ambience. Everyone mingles with each other and the joy, the shadow, the sorrow, the merriment fuse together into...one...whole...existence.

It was indeed *a day like no other*!

✿ ✿ ✿

Chapter 28

IT IS LEICESTER SQUARE IN CENTRAL LONDON. NATURE has decided to bless this place with a sprightly, hot day. Haagen Dasz café stands on the corner of the square. After having lunch in Bella Italia, an Italian restaurant, Anne, Sue and Millie have come to the café to fill the pudding corners of their stomachs with delicious Haagen dasz ice cream.

Haagen Dasz café has taken advantage of the hot day to entice customers to indulge in the luscious, creamy ice cream along with hot and cold beverages. The decor and the surreal brown shade of the interior walls of the open-plan two-storey restaurant with angled ceiling lights are delightfully inviting. There is also a takeaway section on the ground floor.

The women settle on a sofa in the sitting area upstairs. The restaurant is quite busy with clients of all ages. Fragments of their small talk and laughter blend in with the rest of the sound.

'So how's the filming going?' Millie asks Anne while crunching on the crispy waffle dipped in the caramel sauce of the banana split.

Anne sips her Belgian mocha and replies, 'Going slowly. Some people are scared to voice their opinions.'

'They worry about their own and their families' safety,' Sue adds.

'Anyway, look out for it, it'll soon be aired,' Anne says.

'I don't watch TV a lot. Turn it on, and all sorts of miseries rave in front of you,' Millie says.

Sue has been relishing her coffee and cappuccino truffle ice cream with waffle pieces and nuts. She says, 'Don't they reflect on what's happening in the world?'

'As I see it, we're dwelling too much on negativity and by doing so, we're actually empowering it. It will lose its power once the majority of us learn to put our attention to things positive in nature. The world is a mirror of what we think, say and do, you know. Change that for the better, the world will change,' Millie says.

'Well, then millions of us need to act together in harmony. That sounds a bit too utopian, doesn't it?' Sue comments.

Anne voices her own opinion, 'What hasn't been working for the whole time the world has existed needs re-thinking, re-adjusting and renewing.'

'Who's going to do that? Where will it begin from?' Sue asks.

'It'll begin from us. Anyway, on a lighter note, do you know that Community TV is going to feature the World Culture Season?' Anne says.

'Who has taken such initiative?' Sue enquires.

'Well, as far as I know, Lambeth Council has decided to honour and explore the richness of the world's major cultures. Having that in mind, the council is going to organise massive events across the region. The first event will concentrate on African culture: its land, history, art, commerce and so much more and then the focus will be on Indian culture and so on. Other councils will also follow the practice.'

'Wow, sounds like Gemma's big venture in Croydon has made ripple effects,' Millie exclaims.

✿

On the bank of the lake, thick curtains of weeping willow sway in the wind, gently caressing the lake beneath in St. James's park in London; the dark green shadow of the trailing leaves quiver in rolling waves of the lake. Water-birds snuggle around the bank. The skyline view of Buckingham Palace through the trees transmits a sense of tranquillity and calmness.

Millie rests her head softly on Leon's shoulder. They are standing against the railing of the Blue Bridge across the lake. It is a pleasant public holiday Monday in August 2001.

'Mill, how did Emoto's book exactly help you to patch things up with your mum?'

'Well, mum and I used to argue a lot. It was our way of coping with the grief at losing dad, you know. Remember, Emoto's claim? The outcome of the use of positive words is always positive, likewise, negative words have the power to destroy. I finally realized what was happening between us after I read the book.'

Millie wanted to salvage what was left in their relationship so she began to explore more through inspirational and self-help books, cassettes and compact discs, covertly encouraging Maya to take an interest in them. Millie left them lying around in the sitting room.

Maya must have put them back to where they belonged countless times but what actually motivated her to use the meditation disc in the end, Millie did not know.

'Maybe she was finally curious to look at the stuff that interested you.'

'Maybe.'

Millie says that she finds Dr Emoto's theory of things happening in one part of the world affecting the other part the most intriguing. Leon correlates this with Dr Sheldrake's theory of *morphic resonance* – when the same thing keeps occurring over a period of time, a network of invisible resonance, in other words, a habit is formed and it increases the possibility of having the event occur again elsewhere, with ease.

'The phrase *the hundredth monkey effect* originates from here,' Leon says.

'Yes, the story of glycerine is an example of such phenomenon,' Millie mulls over the story about glycerine. Glycerine was discovered in 1779; it did not crystallize then and it maintained such behaviour for many years. Then at the onset of the nineteenth century while being transported from Vienna to London, all of a sudden, it began to crystallize and subsequently glycerine in other parts of the world started to crystallize as if its characteristics were responding to the wave of resonance instituted by the first batch of glycerine in Vienna. It is now generally accepted that glycerine forms crystals below a certain temperature.

The distant cries of seagulls and water-birds break the serene silence. Millie and Leon are revelling in nature's symphony.

'Lee...What actually happened to Mr Yoda? Why didn't he meet you as planned?'

'I was wondering about that too so I did a little investigation of my own.'

Leon made several phone calls from London to Mr Yoda's office in Tokyo. With what little information he managed to dredge up, he came to the conclusion that the man agreed to see him personally without consulting his superiors who considered this to be a breach of trust. These high-ranking people may have thought that Mr Yoda would release part or all of their confidential report to a couple of foreigners. Mr Yoda must have felt guilty afterwards and feared losing his job.

Leon believed that besides Mr Yoda's superiors, a third party in the upper echelons may also have been involved in the matter; the mention of *dark forces* in Mr Yoda's note gave this away. Mr Yoda possibly referred him to the temple story in Ankor Wat as he assumed that was where Leon would go while touring in Cambodia; it was the place that appealed most tourists. He expected Leon to be clever enough to apprehend his predicament by making a connection between the story and the note he left for him.

'He could have explained the matter to you directly. I still don't understand why he did this in a roundabout way.'

'Maybe he thought he owed me an apology or maybe he didn't want to go against his superiors by speaking to me again.'

'And what about the car chase?'

'To be honest, I didn't see any cars behind us. Perhaps the taxi-driver was tired so he imagined things or maybe someone wanted to scare us off, who knows?'

'Hmm...interesting! Spoke to Ranju over the phone. Guess what he asked me.'

'What?'

'If wars solved all the problems then, after years of fighting, why don't the problems go away?'

'Uh-huh...Our own little Socrates! What did you say?'

'Well, I said something like...um...the mass human consciousness needs to evolve in order to include better solutions in its experience.'

'Good thinking.'

'Although I toned it down a bit for him to understand I wasn't sure he got it, but he said he could get quarrelling people to become friends in a second.'

'And how could he possibly or impossibly do that?'

'He said he would put them in a room, tie them up on a sofa and get them to shake hands.'

'Ha, ha, ha...wishful thinking.'

'If only we could keep our childhood innocence alive. Erm...talking about wars, what was the third reason Nhean gave you for the dragging tug of war between the gods and the demons in the temple story?'

'Just as you said about mass consciousness, even the gods were often engaged in squabbles within themselves. That's why it took so long for them to defeat the demons. And you know what? Although it was a myth, I guess that in the end, the gods realised there were far more important issues to give attention to than wars, like natural disasters, diseases, poverty...'

'True. And when they finally won, the new tranquil era began. You know, mum often sees blurred images of a new peaceful world.'

Nuzzled in the beautiful aura of the park, Millie talks about Maya's new world. The lake beneath the bridge is tranquil and calm. A segment of the blue sky and the under-view of the bridge are reflected in trembling water ripples.

Not too far away, the Rastafarian sings:

Oh yeah, you are one God, one love, one hope.
You are my father, my shepherd.
You live through me, walk through me and talk through me.
Oh yeah, you are one God, one love, one hope.
Praise di Lord.

He has returned, as promised, at the mention of the new world.

☼

Maya, Gemma, Millie, Leon, Sayed and Savitri, each within and outside their routine of careers, are committed to creating a positive environment in and around their localities, year after year. Each time, their work exceeds the excellence of what they have done before. They still bask in the hope that their efforts will spawn an outreaching morphic field of inspiration.

'I don't see anything significant coming out of this, mum,' there is a tinge of desperation in Millie's voice.

'Don't despair, Mill. The world will wake up one day.'

'May not happen in our lifetime.'

'Look, we can continue to do our bit in our little world. Just one good thought, one good word and one good deed from one person – that's all we need, and if more people do the same, an awakening will slowly but surely take place.'

☼ ☼ ☼

Chapter 29

IT HAPPENS IN THE FIRST WEEK OF AUGUST 2011.
The sound of the mob dies down for a while and then their footsteps can be heard again. Stephen knows that the hooligans are upon them and they may barge into the house at any moment. He has to make a quick decision: either he should leave the house with his family through the overgrown wild thorn bushes in the alleyway at the back of the house or face the mob.

When Rosie visited her adopted daughter Tania, her husband Stephen and their son Samuel in Tottenham in North London, the riots broke out. In conjunction with mass intermittent rioting in many crowded places in and outside London, abrupt intrusions in households have become common features of the frightful event. Random arson attacks and the police's failed attempts to control the situation are recurrent incidents in these places.

Tania and Stephen's house in Tottenham is the young mob's current target.

Smoke is billowing from nearby shops. First, there is shouting, and then there is hurling of stones at the windows initiated by five or six youngsters who are still increasing in number. Stephen has never raised his voice before. He is a rather quiet man but today he gathers all his strength and screams at the top of his voice to drive the crazy mob away. Rosie and Tania are petrified; little Samuel freezes in fright and hides under his desk next to his bed. The mob, now bigger, is not backing off.

✿

Mobile riots – so they call it - since youths are using mobile phone devices and social media in an attempt to organize the ghastly event. Gangs of all ages and backgrounds also join in, on an impulsive spree, to loot shops and premises, helping themselves with what they cannot otherwise afford or what they can seize for the moment just for fun, causing further chaos. It lasts for a few days.

✿

'Riots in a civilized country?' Savitri is perplexed and shocked. Maya tells her that the underlying reason behind the shameful act was rather complicated. It was the young people's pitiful way of saying *hear me out.*

'Are you all okay?'

'Yes, apart from being a little scared but Rosie and her family got caught up in it.'

'Are they okay?'

'Well, they managed to escape with cuts and bruises but Tania and Stephen's house was in a total wreck.'

✿

In another part of the world, in Cairo, Egypt, a jubilant discotheque is in progress in the middle of a simulated oasis with palm trees and a flowing stream – a combined enterprise of man and nature. Tourists and natives alike have come together in the jollification.

There is a sudden blast of fire - the merrymakers, innocent passers-by, the magnificence, the beauty - all turn into a scene of burning horror.

Ramola, a peace activist, happens to be in the scene of horror. She is in the city on a mission; she left her children in the care of her mother. In order to escape blindly from the blast, she bumps into a terrified little girl whom she promptly grabs hold of and leads to safety only to realize later that her parents are missing!

✿ ✿ ✿

Chapter 30

IT WAS PREDICTED THAT WHEN THE MAYAN CALENDAR ended on 21 December 2012, the world would also end. How? No one knew. Perhaps a consistent shower of meteors would strike the earth or aliens would arrive from space and destroy the world.

There had been all sorts of predictions and speculations. Some thought the idea was lunatic and absurd while others did not give it a hoot and just got on with their lives. Some believed that if the world did survive beyond the stated period, a golden age would begin.

Amidst all speculations, the sun rose and set and the earth span on its imaginary axis as normal.

✿

Now that the Mayan calendar has ended, the earth is still rotating on its axis; the sun is still rising, and there are no signs of meteor showers or aliens. A new era has begun with more chaos, more confusion, more dispute, more destruction, more hatred and more natural calamities; they subside in one part of the planet only to spark off in another part of it.

People in anarchic societies are immersed in more miseries and mayhem; justice and injustice have no clear demarcation in some social groups. The world seemingly steps into more alarming and uncertain times. It is outwardly collapsing, one part at a time, and a great number of its dwellers are just the silent observers of the show.

Droplets of happy events are like insignificant, floating weeds on the vast, tumultuous ocean. The events take place in the form of the New Year celebration, diverse religious and cultural festivals and global sports competitions. The mass jubilation during this period spreads like wildfire; the momentary togetherness and brotherhood filter through shared awareness – the mass sensation sweeps the shore of life in joyous vigour like rolling waves pounding on the beach. The celebrations are little spurs in the dark like fireflies, a few of which emerge, grow in number and then they die out in seconds.

Little waves of peace and positivity occur sporadically and incoherently across the globe. Nothing much has changed; there is no golden age, no heaven on Earth. The world is still...the...good...old...world!

☼

Maya comes across a leaflet for the Ideas Fair that will take place in the Broad Green region in North Croydon. The leaflet reads:

Come along and:
• join the crowd who share the same interest;
• explore the funding opportunities for innovative enterprises;
• gain support and resources to materialise your passion;
• showcase your own unique talent.

The Ideas Fair will encourage local people to do something new and innovative for their community; these people are probably unemployed or they may have reached a dead end in their careers and are looking for new opportunities. To receive funding for such projects from the local government, one has to convince them through government representatives that theirs are the best ideas of all.

Maya swoops in with her idea, with a new name for an otherwise unfamiliar concept of meditation – she calls it *body and mind exercises*. This sounds less intimidating and more familiar! Lenny once told her that if she wanted to be successful in teaching yoga and meditation, she had better choose attention-grabbing words for the practices. Lenny called his course *Summer-Meadow Yoga and Meditation* before he simply called it Yoga and Meditation.

'How did it differ from what you're teaching us now?' Maya asked.

'Not much. At that time, I slightly raised the room temperature and played nature sounds for background music,' Lenny then started whistling the tune of a song from Mary Poppins:

A spoonful of sugar helps the medicine go down, the medicine go down!

☼

Gemma attends an art exhibition in a school for children with special needs; she is impressed by a piece of artwork by eight-year old Martin - a boy with autism. He has painted a symmetrical picture of people collectively engaged in various activities.

'What is this picture of, Martin?' Gemma asks.

'A new world,' he replies inaudibly.

A spectator catches the boy's remark and asks him to describe his picture. Martin fidgets and mumbles.

'Martin ain't talkative, but his picture speaks volumes,' the man comments.

'Do you know Martin?' Gemma asks him.

He just smiles and says that children with such conditions often possess unique talents and skills. He thinks their abilities rather than their disabilities should be brought to the attention of the rest of the world. This gives Gemma a point to ponder and act upon.

'What's your name, Sir?'

'Ruben.'

✿

Gemma and Phillip have organized a trip for a group of children with special needs to visit the Mayor of London and show him their artwork. They will be accompanied by their teachers, Gemma and Phillip. Gemma is also going to discuss with him the possibility of having their artwork exhibited for the general public so that they are informed about these children's talents and achievements. This may mitigate the stigma people tend to attach to children with special needs.

Gemma's prior experience of dealing with the hierarchy of personnel made her realize that if she wanted something done quicker, she had better start from the top. The Mayor, in her opinion, was on the top rung of the ladder. Phillip shared the same view. Together they wrote a letter to the Mayor. They received a positive response from his secretary. The second paragraph of the letter said:

The Mayor would be delighted to meet these special children. He would also like to discuss ways of removing the social stigma attached to them and collaborate with any ideas or suggestions that you and their teachers may have regarding the matter.

A small wave of positivity has surely emerged from this part of the world.

Chapter 31

THE IDEAS FAIR STARTED IN THE MORNING. IT WILL continue until the early part of the evening. People can join the fair at any time during this period. Maya goes to the fair in the drizzly afternoon. She settles down on a seat near the entrance door of a fairly large room. Everybody is cheerfully welcoming each other's ideas about doing something new and innovative for the community. There is a big poster of a tree on the wall behind her with branches, devoid of leaves; the colourful post-it stickers that have already been filled in with ideas are stuck on the picture. They clothe the tree!

Sunanda Mitra, leading the fair, invites Maya to say something about her ideas. Maya talks about meditation and its manifold benefits; she says that a shorter version of this could be piloted in schools, adding that some schools have already incorporated this into their curricula. When children's minds are calm and settled, they will be able to focus more on their studies and other curricular and extra-curricular activities. Everyone receives her idea well and from Sunanda's keen interest, it seems that there is a chance that this will see the light of day. Maya quickly writes down her proposal on a pale green sticker and sticks it on the poster.

Participants gather around the poster after the meeting and eagerly read each other's ideas. Maya chats with some over a drink and a sandwich. Nathan, one of the participants, tells her about his idea. In partnership with Wildlife Trust, he can set up a project with incredible opportunities for youths aged 12 to 15. This will enable them to explore the secluded landscape and its conservation through many outdoor activities. They can do this during their long school holidays in July and August to keep themselves engaged in something new, positive and productive.

At the end of the fair, all the idea-stickers are collected from the poster and put in a box.

☼

Maya does not know the outcome of others' ideas, but hers have remained locked in the box. She has an inkling that most of the ideas at the Ideas Fair, if not all, have suffered the same fate. The participants came up with interesting ideas in the fair with great enthusiasm, but their initial drive fizzled out for varied reasons. On the one hand, they needed to pursue the matter and find ways to persevere in the event of things not working out as expected; on the other hand, the organisers had to deal with the lack of resources or other limitations. In the process, it was normal for both parties to fall into despair and abandon the projects altogether. When something like this happens to Maya, a few encouraging words on wayside posters, lines from a song or a book act as restoring driving forces for her.

In the absence of the desired response from Eleanor Hatfield or Sunanda Mitra, Maya nurtures the hope that opportunities will knock again on the door.

One day while walking past a church, she finds a message on the church door that says:

When the flow of a river is stalled, it takes another route.

This inspires her to continue with her meditative journey along with her own small meditation group at her workplace. Also, her belief that there is a spark within everyone keeps her going. This goes way back to when she read a story about a man in a book written by her favourite author Mark Twain.

She did not see much of her father but one day he gave her the book in a Hindi version. This was during one of his rare visits. He said, 'Maya darling. Come here. This is for you.'

The man in the story was very poor. He wore donated clothes and shoes. By a strange twist of fate, he received a pair of old shoes. Two priceless stolen diamonds were cleverly plugged in inside the shoe heels. The man had no idea about their existence and kept roaming about in the streets like a destitute man! Maya believed in a hidden diamond embedded inside everyone although she did not have a clearer picture of it.

✿

Maya experiences incoherent visions of a reformed world sometimes in her dreams and sometimes during meditation. The images are somewhat hazy. In one such sitting, she is able to hold the image of the world a bit longer in her mind. She decides to use the opportunity to meditate for world peace.

The image of the world is surrounded by light – the light of mass human consciousness. A faint soothing Chinese music is coming from nowhere! Maya is not particularly fond of this type of music, yet she savours its calming effect and sends out love and light to the beautiful, radiant blue-green Earth, swathed in swirling silver clouds. She becomes her own guide and follows her own words. She intuitively knows exactly what to say:

Imagine you are a speck of light in the mass human consciousness.

Be still...and breathe deeply...allow your light to flow smoothly through other sources of light that belong to other individuals.

You notice that there are some sparks within the pool of light that are rather faint. These are situations or minds of people that dim the brightness.

The silver clouds in her vision now grow darker and darker and the light around the world gets dimmer and dimmer. The image of the earth slowly alters into a human head that belongs neither to a woman nor to a man, neither to the west nor to the east. It is a neutral embodiment in a backdrop of purplish blue colour. Its pain is masked by a forced smile.

The head rotates to exhibit all its angles until the focus rests on the crown and finally on the intricate layers of the brain inside the crown. Dispersed blood clots are visible on the surface of the brain. The scene zooms further into the microscopic features of the brain cells to reveal more diverse images. The cells now become alive as roving humans, occupying the left-hand and right-hand sides of the cavity with distinct barriers. These zones represent the left and right hemispheres of the brain. People within their respective zones move about in small, isolated groups, creating divisions among themselves, occasionally mingling with each other at a very slow pace. The blood clots in the brain represent wars, conflict and unrest. The clots grow bigger and bigger until they appallingly cover the whole expanse of the brain and burst into an ugly flame.

Maya continues:

Breathe in deeply; breathe out fully.

Along with other radiant specks of light, cover the flame with love and light.

At this very moment, a faint dot of light mystically appears. It gets bigger and bigger – the centre of it is radiant green with a glowing pink border. The light cascades its calming rays over the flame. The flame subsides and the face starts to smile again!

This time, it is a spontaneous smile.

Maya concludes:

Along with others, you have established peace in the world!

✿

The vision itself has unravelled a story: the left hemisphere of the brain is responsible for logical and analytical thinking and the right hemisphere, creativity and mysticism. Meditation harmonises both hemispheres and brings about relaxed and calm sensations in the body, mind and soul.

The words *West* and *East* spring to Maya's mind. If the globe represents the brain, then people in the West represent the cells in the left hemisphere of the brain likewise people in the East represent the cells in the right hemisphere of the brain. If these people come together in brotherhood and rise to the next level of consciousness through mass awakening, they will be able to establish peace and harmony in the world that is akin to the harmonization of the left and right hemispheres in the brain.

For Maya, this solves the mystery of the harmonisation of the left and right hemispheres Baba Sattyaram in Delhi had mentioned.

✿

At the height of vacillation between peace and discord in the physical world, a group of refugee children gather together with their adult guides: Ramola, her husband Mosein and their team. They form a peaceful rally in a safety zone, not too far from a warring country. Children at the front of the procession are holding posters with a question on each poster:

Is hunger necessary?

Is hatred necessary?
Is killing necessary?
Can anyone say 'yes' to these questions?
If no, then why are we still having them?
Who can put an end to them?
We, the children of the world, are asking
YOU.

These young people are motivated by Ramola and Mosein who are peace activists from an allegedly antagonistic country.

✺

Mosein and Ramola saw a documentary film about the after-effect of a war especially on children. Anne Wilson went to a refugee camp with a local interpreter who would instantly interpret English into the native language and vice versa.

Refugees in the camp were eagerly waiting for food. A few of them came out to see if Anne had brought some food for them. First, the adults came out, and then the children walked in their shadows. There was no food. They were about to slip back into their camp in despair when Anne called out,

'Hello there, how are you today?'

There was no reply. She stepped forward towards the children.

'How are you?'

'I miss my home and I...I miss my school,' said a girl, aged ten.

'I want to play with my friends again,' a boy of seven exclaimed. Half of his right leg was missing.

A girl of about nine began to cry uncontrollably. She said between her sobs, 'We have no bread.'

Ramola and Mosein thought enough was enough; they felt the urge to do something about it. Together they began to post thought-provoking texts to their online blog about sadness and happiness, about love and hatred and, above all, about restoring peace in the world.

Ramola attached a video presentation to the blog showing children from various backgrounds with accompanying flashing slogans that said:

I want food,
I want clean water,
I want my mum,
I want my dad,
I want to go to school,
I want to play with my friends,
I want to laugh again,
I want to live a joyful life.

Then a script flew in from the left and moved along to the right saying:

These are the voices of our future generation, our successors. What can we do to help them to have a decent and a joyful life?

Surprisingly, encouraging responses worldwide started to pour in with pictures and messages saying:

We love you; go ahead, we are with you.

✿

Charitable donations of money begin to pour forth.

Mosein, Ramola and their team visit the refugee children in an unwelcoming neighbouring country against all odds. Together they form a peaceful procession. Mosein organises art, music and sports events to appease the traumatised minds of these young people. Citizens of that country come across as more friendly and helpful than expected.

Ramola, Mosein and their supporters momentarily cross the barriers of resistance and hatred.

A slow process of harmonisation begins.

✿✿✿

Chapter 32

FIND THAT HIDDEN DIAMOND DEEP INSIDE YOU. IT HAS *always been there and it always will be!* Maya often chants this slogan to herself.

As Maya sails through her meditative journey, the cosmos reveals a new world on a different level of consciousness; the one that exists beyond her perception. Random and vague images of the new world in her dreams and meditation become vibrant and alive in a realm that is turned away from her! Only the cosmos can see this vibrant new world - there, everything is brighter, everything is more colourful with a crisp freshness. Everything is bluer, greener, redder – joie de vivre exists in evolved human consciousness. The intricate structure of this world, from the composition of the coral reef under the sea to the flora and fauna on the landscape with the canopy of the blue sky, is phenomenal. This is a radiant reflection of the old world. The seekers have become active doers in this world!

✿

Move forward many years into the future, the cosmos will reveal that the new era did not begin one fine morning; it took many fine mornings when one tiny positive move was followed by another. Committed socialists and activists held several peace talks and debates that happened simultaneously in many parts of the world with no immediate positive outcomes – their efforts were just strings of initial steps, they were the first zephyr of collective consciousness.

As a result, wars in some places in the world ceased and then started again. Then they were off again and then, on again. Debates and peace talks went on and on and on; and when talks were still going and the hopes were almost fading, two combatant tribes in an obscure area decided to resort to an armistice. One of the tribes initiated this by adopting the historic *White-call* strategy. They asked their captives three questions before releasing them and the captives gave similar replies to the ones the prisoners in the *White Call* story gave ages ago. The questions and answers were:

Do you know why we are fighting? No. Our forefathers started it.

Do you personally have anything against us, our families or friends? No, but we still hate you because our ancestors hated you.

Have we gained any good from this? Um...no.

The prisoners, who were set free, saw the triviality of fighting through their own answers.

The truce was for 12 hours, then for a week, a week turned into a month, followed by three more months; then six months, then for a year, and then, beyond anyone's belief, for a longer period of time until the compulsion for battle phased out. The news spread across other parts of the world where obliged soldiers and rebels grew weary of fighting and killing, in many cases, killing their own people. This prompted them to think about their own defenceless parents, spouses, children, brothers and sisters - ceasing fighting seemed the only remaining option.

Was it that simple? What was the aftermath like? Who owned the lands and in what proportion? Who ruled them, the ethnic majority or minority? More questions emerged than answers. The bottom line was that while everyone on both sides of the troops wanted an armistice they were not sure about realistic solutions to conflicts.

Finally, they picked one simple solution:

Stop the war, the rest will fall in place.

Others slowly but surely followed suit as if the world was coming out of its slumber by the power of the morphic resonance - the earthly effect that worked on glycerine and many other things - and by the power of the eventual realization of the fact that there were far more important issues to solve like natural disasters, diseases and poverty.

As peace was restored on an individual level between a mother and a daughter or a sister and a brother, peace was regained on a global level based on one simple principle:

The ripples of positivity have positive outcomes and the ripples of negativity have the power to destroy.

A series of organised public rallies were held to deal with other persistent matters involving territorial boundaries and rivers that ran across countries; so many lives were needlessly lost, so much of the landscape was destroyed or left barren. People finally realised that the notion - *this is mine and that is yours* - created divisions and distance; the notion - *these are ours* – connected all and established peace.

When the silent majority woke up from their coma-like state and began to recognise the power of their true selves, a new Renaissance of human creativity and love began to flow with new hopes and a new poem:

The voice of people now has power,
The ones high in number are high in spirit.
Lord Vishnu's world sees them awakened
And that is better for the rise of nations.

Human discernment flourished. A plethora of positive ideas and actions began to pour forth. Negativity lost its power as mass consciousness gathered momentum to move towards the light.

Like the Renaissance that began in leaps and bounds in all aspects of human creativity in the 14th century across Europe, a renaissance that faintly began in the 20th and 21st centuries got off the ground. Positive activities and events swept across the world like outreaching waves on the shore of life. Individuals and groups of people began to explore how they could work together to help their communities *'for the rise'* with officials lending an ear to innovative ideas that emerged from Ideas Fairs and similar seminars held everywhere!

This-is-our-world was the motto behind actively going green at home and outdoors. Reusing, reducing, recycling resources and growing one's own plants and herbs; implementing comprehensive curricula in schools that incorporated components of teaching and learning for children's emotional, spiritual and physical growth; introducing breathing and mindfulness exercises with contemporary physical workout in educational institutions and also in neglected institutions like prisons, were some of the features in the massive awakening (the need for prisons gradually phased out as the beauty and brilliance of the new world phased in).

Contrary to popular belief, the media played a key role, online and offline, to spread the good news of the awakening across the world. The excellence of mind power of humanity stretched to an extent where one recognized the adverse or happy state of others like dolphins. The thin layer of vainglory gradually wore off and harmony set in. This was the beginning of the era that everyone was dreaming about. It took humanity years to achieve this at the expense of needless bloodshed, friction and destruction. The leaders, inventors, scholars and entrepreneurs congregated in world summits; their collaboration gave birth to three simple but effective ways to make the world a better place.

Firstly, exchanging and working on ideas that worked and discarding the ones that did not, truly embracing love and concern for others in the process. They recognised that this single strategy strengthened bonds and improved everyone's life across the world. The dream once dreamt by Martin Luther King, the song once sung by Tagore, the love and peace wished by many became a reality.

The second strategy was about finding similarities in ways of life, acknowledging and accepting differences and consolidating bonds among people, among nations.

The third and final strategy involved little people. This brought a radical change to the whole world!

In the old world, power lay in the hands of a few, in the emerging new world, the song, *we are all sovereigns of this land*, became an inspiration to many. Most importantly, after thousands of years of wars and violence, dwellers across the world finally realized one…universal…truth:

EVERYONE'S LIFE ON EARTH IS PRECIOUS!
✪
Back on the flip side of Maya's perception, the cosmos unfolds a string of snapshots:

The massive arched entrance of a train station is less crowded; there is no rushing or pushing. So huge a station, not many passengers are around! Fewer people that are out and about are moving in all directions; they are talking less and connecting more by conveying their best wishes and smiles.

People of this world are of varied heights and complexions - black, brown, white, pink, beige and yellow - wearing glossy, colourful clothes.

On the span of the open space in front of the station, some people appear. They smile and nod at each other. Within a blink, a few more spring up and form a group of flash dancers. They give their best performance with mellow music apparently coming from nowhere. Lookers-on gather around them, cheer them and some even participate with them. When they finish, everyone disperses and goes about their daily lives as if nothing much has happened, but the sweetness of the act lingers on.

Inside the station, commuters are tickled pink by a holographic projection of them in the shapes of animated cartoon animals. Scripts float along with the images saying: *we are outrageously funny, we are mind-numbingly lazy, we are menacingly daring, we are annoyingly boring ... just kidding...we are charmingly dynamic, we are fascinatingly creative, we are eternally grateful, we are forever joyful!*

Small groups of instant party-makers assemble outside shopping areas with folded tables, chairs, food baskets and big grins. Some shoppers step towards them to share food and have a good laugh; afterwards, the party-makers and the shoppers clear up and tidy up the place, and they disappear in a flash. More flash party-makers appear in another place, another time, with their collection of flavoursome food. Such drills are not charitable practices, they are for sharing and connecting with one another!

A tall and slender, cheerful man is often seen in these parties, smiling from ear to ear and spinning on his toes. He collects food from the food baskets with a countenance that says he is spoilt for choice. He does silly acts before vanishing into the crowd, leaving everyone amused!

📷 Large passenger carriers slide on metal rails over the bridge nearby; these carriers are eco-friendly, safe, comfortable and move fast, a little above the rails. Interior electro-magnetic devices help them to defy gravity and stay off the rails. The principle of this mechanism originated from an ancient discovery. These carriers are really not used much as there is another sensational way of travelling that is far more popular! The space below the bridge is used by foot-travellers and bikers.

On a nice, sunny day, three burly men ride their bikes. These bikes are just the right size for them contrary to the hilarious child-sized bikes they once rode at another time, in another place. Three jolly women race along with them, they go up the meadow, down the valley, giggling away.

📷 Neighbours come together in an expansive, communal garden where they grow plants, trees and groves, flowers and herbs. Subtle fragrances of orange and lemon blossoms, intersecting rapturously in the wind, bring to mind the assorted scent of honeysuckle, jasmine and tuberose. Girls and boys fill their baskets with apples and pears. They dance merrily cheered by the fact that they will be feasting on fruit pies in the evening. It is all about merrymaking, about sharing the fruits of their labour. A graceful, petite lady in golden attire has organised the pie-making activity to promote the merriment. Today is the pie-making day in their neighbourhood.

For the inhabitants, food and drink are not only for consumption, they are also for aesthetic pleasure through all five senses. They think about the land where crops are grown beside the waterways under the bright sun. They think about the fact that the crops have travelled all the way with the nutrients absorbed through the soil of the land.

Smelling, swirling and tasting a sip of drink take the dwellers to the garden or orchard where every inch of the roots of the fruit trees or plants drank the sap of the earth to make the fruit juicy, ripe and right for the drink. Their preparation and consumption of food and drink are inspired by the thought of the chain of events behind the scenes.

📷 In a warm afternoon when the pleasant wind blows, neighbours gather together in the nearest green space to fly kites and do ground sports. In the green space, children hop, skip and jump and adults sing away at the top of their voices. This is not out of compulsion, this is for joy, laughter and a bit of fresh air! They can also do sky sports if they so wish - there are sky-arenas for doing and viewing the sports.

Groups of valleys and meadows, uninhabited in the past, are now nature reserves on the land; they are used for shared joy and merriment. Instantaneous joy and fun are normal occurrences here. Maya's words in her script become alive in this world:

If we return to nature, nature will return to us.

We can find the door of love and gratitude that will lead us to a life we so desire – a life of love and compassion for all and gratitude for all. This is the world we want to live in.

📷 In the distance, well-paced high buildings with hanging gardens are visible. The rooftops and side panels absorb sunlight and heat to provide light and heat to the residents in the winter and to dispense converted cooler air in the summer. Simple eco-friendly mechanisms, used for this purpose, can store the solar energy even if the weather is gloomy and cloudy. The wind power is also harnessed to operate scores of day-to-day appliances that simply appear magical and innovative. In most cases, human power is combined with the procedures to produce the desired energies: when ballet dancers dance on the slow, revolving stage, their soft graceful movements on it activate mechanisms that produce light and heat in the auditorium.

Water is one of the notable features in many global villages. There are water cities with waterways, lakes and ponds. Fountains on diminutive isles and on lakes gush out in sprightly vigour. Big reservoirs of rainwater are deployed in selected areas for a variety of uses in towns and cities, and in the fields. The inside of each reservoir is specifically designed for twofold purposes - to hold tonnes of water in a finite space and to keep the water purified.

From time to time, the inhabitants perform a strange ritual of looking at their reflection in the water as if they are checking their appearance in the mirror. From the reflection of themselves and the surroundings, they have a full view of the scene; they can see if all is going well. They also look for something else in it!

Who would have thought of making full uses of all of nature's free gifts that have been hanging around since the creation of the world?

People just walk in to join or view a range of events in colossal auditoriums. Food stalls outside the auditoriums are lined up with displays of freshly baked bread; fleshy walnuts and raisins in a bed of fresh leafy salad, sun-dried tomatoes, green and kalamata olives; honey, cinnamon, almond, chocolate and hazelnut cupcakes; dried fruit and nut mixes and fruit and seed flapjacks. They are all full of flavour and nature's favour and are served in handy punnets. Various types of luscious, juicy fruit are exhibited invitingly in the stalls; one cannot help but have a crunch on them, and there is a lot more wholesome produce of the soil.

The new world inhabitants use natural resources wisely and innovatively. They have also learned to quieten their never-ending, chattering minds.

The behind-the-scene images now reveal a snow city.

✿ ✿ ✿

Chapter 33

IN A WINTRY CONURBATION IN THE NEW WORLD, AN ice-and-snow festival goes on. A massive ice sculpture of the bust of a goddess, emerging out of a snow mountain, covers a big segment of the sky. Her untamed icy curls are neatly sculpted sideways. Her white shimmering icy hands stretch outwards along the long panel of ice underneath. The white radiant sun deluges her half-closed eyes, her numinous smiling mouth and the surrounding area. It is the largest ice sculpture ever produced on Earth. It emits:

magnificence and grace,
awe and beauty.

Its enormous shadow is cast on the snow below. There are high-rising ice segments behind the sculpture that replicate ancient buildings with domes and towers. At the base of the sculpture, there is a small cave-like opening to a food hall and other amusement areas. In the food hall, plates and cups are made of ice; tables are blocks of ice and the stools are made of water pipes with circular rubber tops - these are recycled materials used in the low-carbon eatery.

The joy-makers are jovial; they are drinking sweet nectars of fruit that come in different colours: red, blue, green, yellow and orange. They are wearing fleecy fashion clothes, gloves, hats and flat snow boots; some are smiling and waving, others are speaking softly; they form a harmonious community in the snow village. Some of the others are merrily dancing and singing enchanting songs; some are just absorbing the beauty of the pleasant setting around them. Waves of pleasure and equanimity sip through the cavern and the thriving life inside it. This resonates with what someone had once commented in an open-air event:

It's really nice out here – it feels as if everybody knows everybody.

A group of painters and artists appear in the cave, wearing old-fashioned garments; they were tipped off by someone that it was going to be a fancy dress party. Realising that they were tricked, they get down to business; with their mischievous brush strokes, they squirt magical paints on others to transform their clothes into fanciful and archaic ones. Those who try to escape from the deluge get sprays of dancing spree that make them float in dancing poses in reverse order in their newly acquired primeval outfits. Musicians appear from nowhere to match the painters' playful act. Musical notes pop out of their ancient musical instruments in rainbow colours and whirl around everywhere, around everyone, creating an amusing milieu.

At night, the dazzling city rejuvenates once more. The neon-coloured criss-cross laser beams and street lanterns compose an enchanting aura in the place. Sledge-like transporters carry commuters from one place to another. The snow and ice here are harnessed for pleasure!

People enter into the city's night garden holding flashing light gadgets. Tall trees with hanging icicles dazzle in the beams of northern lights; the surreal scene merges blissfully with pleasant cool nature. The garden is laid in terraces – each terrace represents the diverse beauty of nature in winter and in the bottom layer, there is a basin with crystal clear water that reflects the wavy contours of all things around it. The dwellers in Maya's new world frequently check their collective reflection in water not only to see if everything is going well around them but also to remind themselves that their shared joy brings more joy, their shared prosperity gives rise to more prosperity.

The physical, emotional and spiritual landscapes have been transformed for the better through everyone's concerted effort! The seed to success lay dormant in the time-honoured myth:

When the gods identified and settled their own differences after a thousand years, they won the wars with the demons, and a blissful era began!

✿

In the middle of another garden in a much warmer place, a cheerful man is reading extracts from a book. Children are sitting around him, cross-legged, on firm cushions with their spines straight. They are still but alert, listening to him intently. Nature's beauty in the garden has been preserved for many years. The garden emits wisdom and intelligence amassed in it throughout those years!

✿

Connecting to one's own inner self, in other words, practising mindfulness is a common practice here, both in designated public places, teaching and learning institutions and in one's own home.

On a golden beach, some people are meditating, sitting in a circle. In their collective awareness, a scene of a primeval city emerges with a pastel green dome and the rest of the building. Strange people are moving about inside and outside the building. The sound of their footsteps indicates that they are rushing in and out of it and going past each other in a daze, oblivious of the world around them.

The meditators listen to a leisurely voice:

What did the people in the ancient city do to bring about changes to our world?

In their shared vision, they can see a vague outline; it gradually becomes distinct and takes the shape of a woman who once foresaw her own city as an ancient city during meditation. Her city is indeed an ancient city now to new world meditators; their collective vision then discloses images of two people: the woman herself and her kindred spirit – her companion. Then come the images of the woman, her companion and a few others, sitting in a circle, doing meditation; simultaneously, in different parts of the world, millions of people are doing trillions of joyful things, creating ripples of inspiration and triumph.

The images surface as the answer to the question:

What did the people in the ancient city do to bring about changes to our world?

The meditators in the new world are encircled by a ring of light and then they are gone!

The time stands still. Maya's mind is now hovering at the portal of the next level of consciousness that still exists in obscurity.

✿✿✿

Chapter 34

HELLO THERE! WE WOULD LIKE TO INVITE YOU TO A *glimpse of the 40th century on our planet Earth. We are your successors, your descendants!*

This is the new world some of you have been talking and dreaming about. This is the world where we live in peace and harmony, where conflict and chaos are but history, where abundance, affluence, beauty and brilliance are normal occurrences. Since when has this all begun? When our forerunners embraced the truth and began to apply this in their lives, good things followed! We will surely tell you what that truth is before we leave.

For us, science and spirituality are like two harmonizing musical notes on the same line. This was unthinkable in your time; for you, they appeared to be two different things and some of you were governed by the notion that the laws of nature were fixed as far as science was concerned. However, before the rise of western civilization, science and spirituality were seen as one and the same. It was evident in the lost civilizations like Greek, Egyptian, Mayan and other ancient traditions. By delving deep into these traditions, we realised that body, mind and soul could not be explained through physical sciences alone!

Your physicists were just beginning to study the world from the quantum level; the more they probed deep into this level the more they became aware of bizarre behaviours of subatomic particles. They realised that this could be harnessed to create a peaceful, new world, but this was as far as they could get.

Broadly speaking, science in your time revolved around mechanistic views, around what could be touched, observed and felt. The focus was on this premise for a long, long time. Science did bring about radical changes to your world and you did take account of the invisible ranges of light and sound, but it required a leap of faith on your part to go beyond the usual understanding of the relationship between matter and energy. Having said that, you had a handful of scientists who challenged the dogmatic worldviews. We are glad they did as most of our researches are based on their findings! They made it easier for us! We can't thank them enough.

Teleportation or travelling across space and time is part of our day to day lives just as driving a car or flying an airplane was a norm in the 20th and 21st centuries. We do this by transforming our physical bodies into light bodies (not the light as in light weight but the light as in a ray of light. Well, to be honest, light bodies eventually become very light in weight) and then changing back into the dense physical forms.

Does that sound crazy or maybe scary? How would you like your body particles to reach the highest level of vibrations in order for teleportation to happen? There is no need to panic. The highest vibrations of all particles are akin to stillness, total stillness, so whilst teleporting, you don't feel a thing, and, BANG! There you are – in another place or time! And how do you change back to the dense body? Easy...when you reach the desired destination, just think about any worldly pleasures, like, craving for an ice cream, or, wanting to hop on one leg; there you are – back to your own fleshy self!

As you know, everything in the universe is made of energy that vibrates at various frequencies. Matter can be transformed into energy, likewise energy can be transformed back into matter (you already know this) – we have successfully used this principle in teleportation. For us, transforming into light bodies is much easier than learning to manoeuvre express trains or spacecraft though some dwellers here are lazy – they want to use the ancient means of transportation. Well, they are not exactly lazy; they just want to use them as much as people in the 21st century wanted to use horse carriages for fun rides so we have travellers' trains and passenger carriers for pleasure trips. We also have spacecraft, but we only use them for special voyages.

As long as we stay focused and fulfil certain criteria, teleportation is not a problem! Because of this, you will never find our transport stations crowded! Well then, what has become of those vehicles that congested your roads? Some people in your era cleverly thought that there would be better use for them in the future so they stored them in a compressed form! Remember? We then reprocessed some to build carriers, space elevators and spaceships, and we used the rest to build large auditoriums for special events.

You are probably thinking that evil people can easily get away by turning themselves into light bodies and disappearing from captivity or reappearing in forbidden places. There is a CATCH here. The light body can only be achieved through purity of mind – no purity of mind, no light body! This is where science and spirituality meet!

Our forefathers did experiments with teleportation using mechanical procedures. They did this by getting the subatomic body particles transfer from the regulatory room to the desired destination where they could be reassembled into their single dense form like Captain Kirk and his crew members did in the 1960s' TV serial 'Star Trek' but there were some problems; not that they couldn't be solved. As with all experiments, scientists started off with teleporting animals. However, these animals ended up having their ears, nose and legs misplaced. That being rectified and tried out on people, other issues cropped up – a Mr Jackdaw ended up in a queen's study room and it was tough for the palace staff to remove him from the palace. We don't blame him – who would like to leave the comfort of a palace? We wouldn't!

In another part of the world, the head of a state mistakenly landed in the middle of a desert island and because of the interference in the sound transmission, his frantic call, 'Beam me up, buddy' (the way Captain Kirk commanded his chief engineer in 'Star Trek') sounded like 'Beat me up, buddy' to the confused controllers in the regulatory room. All sorts of mishaps began to take place thereafter. Rather than fixing myriads of problems, we realized that using the subtle energy system was an extremely reliable and easy solution! We will tell you more about this system in a minute.

We returned to nature. We relearned to conserve nature and use its natural processes and resources without exhausting or taking away any part of it. Everything in nature is recycled and reused which, in effect, maintains a balance; think about the carbon and oxygen cycle in the atmosphere that has existed as long as plants and animals have existed. Everything in nature has a role to play, nothing in it is wasted until it is interfered with. We opened our eyes, looked around and learned from nature!

We have also decoded messages in nature. We have made use of a process based on repetitive patterns practically in everything around us; we have rediscovered that there is a fascinating repetitive ratio that exists:

in our own bodies, in DNA molecules, in plants and trees,
in the spiral pattern of sunflower seeds,
in the arrangement of its petals,
in fish, in bees, in butterflies, in sea shells,
in spiral wind formation and in all parts of creation.

Through this process, an awesome amount of data can be stored in and retrieved from a tiny energy unit. We can send a large amount of information through space and time in a nanosecond, using the procedure powered by mind technology. Technology reached a point where the work of mind began. This finding remained unexplored for a long time and then it was only used by a few. It was later modified and shared in our global summit.

Within the pattern of creation, there is repetition filled with love, gratitude, intelligence and harmony, continually evolving and changing. Alfred Tennyson's line in one of his poems explains this well - nothing was born, nothing will die, all things will change.

The layout of our towns and cities portrays architectural brilliance with fine and well-paced patterns found in nature. We were especially intrigued by how ants angled their side streets inside their colonies at 120 degrees to avoid congestion and collisions as opposed to our ancestors who positioned their side streets at 90 degrees, causing congestion and numerous collisions. We simply learned from their mistakes and copied the ants' town planning strategies!!

You are perhaps wondering whether we still go hiking, running, swimming or biking. Yes, we do. We know that these exercises are good for the physical body; the energy body uses the subtle energy system for teleportation and telepathy. As you know, telepathy was a term coined by an analyst in the 19th century. See, we base our findings on past discoveries. However, we fine-tune them through integrated studies of science and spirituality.

Coming back to the topic of subtle energy system, this existed as far back as five thousand years before your time during what you call the ancient civilization. The system consisted of yoga, Qigong (chi-gong), Tai-chi, meditation and other forms of energy exercises but the reliance on modern technology soon caused people to forget about the enormous benefit of such techniques and, in your years, the majority did not pay attention to them or did not consider them worth doing! Once you get to know and use them effectively, you will not be far away from where we are! No pressure!

We are forever grateful to our Source Creator for our wonderful collective existence in our world that thrives in love, peace and harmony. This has been possible through connecting truly to our Source energy where all things begin from and end in. In the past, we were disconnected from our Source; this caused a huge problem – we felt isolated and miserable! So we got ourselves immersed again into what we were a part of. Here is a single analogy to explain what we mean by this. If you ask a fish, 'What is water?' What reply do you expect from it? It is submerged in water all its life so water is its life, its life is water. It does not perceive water as something separate from it so it might ask you back, 'What do you mean?' Similarly, we perceive ourselves as little sparks of light within the Greater light!

Why did we select the 21st century and why not any other centuries? You see, the dawn of the 21st century was the commencement of the new golden age, the period of awakening. People were j-u-s-t beginning to be aware of what was going on around them. The world, at that juncture, was in need of right people and events so as to initiate and build a strong platform for our world but there were more quarrelsome and warring individuals and nations that constantly put a hold on the emergence of the golden age so we decided to appoint and send a delegation of initiators from here. The world in your time indeed had its own initiators, but these people were few and far between.

Why do we care about what happened in the past? As far as we are concerned, we are fine, we are having a great time, but what went before our time does have an impact on what's happening now. The field of collective consciousness extends across space and time!

For you, time is linear; for us, time is spiral. We will elaborate more on this.

Are you thinking that we could have influenced your world leaders in order for us to achieve our goals sooner? Good thinking! But we decided to empower YOU instead. Remember, Baba's poem?

The voice of people seldom has power,
The ones high in number are low in spirit.
Lord Vishnu's world will one day see them awakened.
And that is better for the rise of nations.

Having that in mind, we sent Kind Kiran from our 3rd group to Maya's garden to get her attention and inspire her to meditate. Maya was so sweet and thoughtful. However, we knew that she would come up with many questions and resistance regarding her newly acquired spiritual knowledge so we requested Baba Sattyaram and his assistant Nimu, living in the 17th century, to deal with her queries. The transitory indoor passage in the hut in Delhi was created to prepare her and her companions for a journey to their inner selves and to another time zone.

As for Baba and Nimu, they had been shifting between two eras to get the job done. There was a bit of a problem though afterwards with Nimu. He did not want to go back to the 17th century when Baba suggested they needed to return. Nimu found the 21st century so fascinating that he wanted to stay in that century. However, Baba told him that going back to his own time zone would be far more beneficial for his spiritual growth. Nimu was half-convinced, but he zoomed back gleefully to his century when he saw the image of his beautiful future wife!

The Chinese musician and dream expert, Mr Bingwen, volunteered thought projection and dream visits to Maya from time to time so that she could probe for more. However, we noticed that she was not being attentive to the signs bestowed upon her. She needed encouragement and assurance from her loved ones and from her own community; this was quite normal for someone who underwent a sweeping change, spiritually and emotionally, in a short space of time! In the end, she achieved far more than we had expected of her!

We also sent Ruben from the 25th century to inspire people into new age thinking (unlike Nimu, Ruben was understandably not interested in going back to the 21st century but he did this by virtue of his obligations towards creating a new world); not to mention infinite numbers of flies, pigeons and butterflies that we diverted from a nearby woodland to an English writer's house to motivate him to write books of inspiration!

We persuaded Cheerful Charles from our 5th group to visit a young man who thought he dozed off at the airport, well, he kind of did. Actually, Cheerful Charles did not visit the man, the man, in his drowsy state, was rather teleported to him for a short while. Charles was far more concerned about his lunch that he left at home than meeting this serious looking guy. What was his name? Yes, Leon. He was good-hearted but was a hard nut to crack so we conjured up dramatic events to get his attention. When Mr Yoda's boss told him off for agreeing to see a total stranger, we moderately influenced him to leave a message for Leon. In a manner of speaking, it worked well - Leon spent the time in Siem Reap in self-reflection.

The car chase in Tokyo was due to inconsistencies of energy frequencies between the two men in the car, in other words, their minds were playing tricks on them. Well, the taxi-driver was quite tired and the chase was pretty much a mirage-effect of something he had experienced in his recent past. On the other hand, Leon couldn't see any cars behind them at all as he was lost in his own world. Although he was a down-to-earth man, he often engaged in daydreaming – a prerequisite for teleportation. Ha, ha. We have given away a secret!

Our 9th group of artists and painters did a great job too. We will name a few of them; mind you, they are not the ones that you know (they want you to use a mirror to read their names. Why? They are fun-loving and jovial people ☺☺☺, or you can read the names without a mirror, if you so wish):

. ʜǫoⴹ nɒꓦ bnɒ ɈɘnoM ɈɘnɒM ɭɘɒʜqɒꓤ iɔniⱱ ɒb obɿɒnoɘ⅃

With their brush strokes, they skilfully inspired thoughts among the strollers in the gardens in Coombe Wood to the extent where they linked each beautiful section of the gardens with their poems and ideas. How cool was that?

Did we only choose to inspire the garden strollers and a few others? No, we inspired others too. We're talking about those who you are familiar with! You know their stories!

The three giant honeybees on the bikes in the Croydon event were thought to be hired by the organizers themselves. Well, they were actually our jolly old Temperate Tom, Willing Wong and Jovial Jitu in disguise. They are in high demand for their fun acts. They often travel to parallel planets like Stella Magna and Stellulam every now and again. These visits are supervised by our cheery group of ladies who are known as Positive Pam, Mindful Melanie and Spirited Sohini.

Yes, we do visit distant planets from time to time, especially the ones that match our own planet's vibrational frequencies and density but we also visit lower frequency/density zones if we regard this as worthwhile. Our star-seekers are constantly working on such projects. That said, we will now tell you about the little people in our world.

Chapter 35

CHILDREN ARE SIGNIFICANT LITTLE PEOPLE IN OUR world; they are our future leaders, inventors and our future workforce. We took heed of Confucius, a Chinese teacher, politician and philosopher of bygone years. He said:

If your plan is for one year, plant rice. If your plan is for 10 years, plant trees. If your plan is for 100 years, educate children.

Educating children does not only involve imparting knowledge to them which is indeed important, it also entails a continuous bonding with them, especially when they are very young, and it does not stop there. Notice we used the word 'continuous'. As you know babies are in their mothers' wombs for approximately nine months. During this period, they get an unlimited supply of warmth, closeness, food and oxygen. In your time, as babies came out of their mothers' wombs, they were generally expected to do the business of growing up in their cribs. Frequently picking them up or carrying them around was seen as spoiling them!

We realized that these little people needed a continuation of the womb environment - a womb outside the womb, if you like, for, at least, the first twelve months. They are in transition during this period when their emotional, mental and physical growth takes place. With this in mind, we closely observed our ancestors and found that in some cultures, mothers or caregivers carried their babies in slings close to their chests or on their backs for the better part of the day. These people did not experiment on bonding, they simply responded to the necessity of looking after their babies while working in the fields or gardens. They were just in tune with Nature's way. Their babies didn't get to play with toys or any other technological wonders for that matter; they simply received love and warmth by being snuggled up to their mothers, and they also had breast milk on demand.

Mothers and caregivers in our communities shadowed these people. As a result, a whole new generation emerged! Contrary to popular belief, these children grew up into fearless, well-adjusted, independent adults. By nurturing our children, we nurtured the whole world. How simple was that?

We also looked at the proverb relating to children that was originated in the 15th century. It went like this:

Children should be seen and not heard.

Our group of performers introduced an amusing proverb:

Children should be heard and not seen.

Joking apart, we actually made a slight but significant change to the original saying and that is:

Children should be seen <u>and</u> heard.

We organized a satirical presentation of all three sayings. The show was staged by the Red-and-Yellow-and-Pink-and-Green group along with the Purple-and-Orange-and-Blue group.
The first saying was enacted by children looking serious, wearing adult clothes, lying, sitting, standing and communicating only by gestures; not making any sound whatsoever.
For the second fun proverb, no children were visible, only their deafening screaming, yelling and stomping could be heard from behind the scene.
The final act showed the talents of these little people in singing, dancing, playing musical instruments and voicing their opinions thereby portraying the third and final saying – children should be seen and heard.
That was really amusing and entertaining!

And then came the necessity of scaffolding - helping children to develop their skills and knowledge on the podium of love and curiosity. What Maya had once said to Ranjit perfectly fit in with our programme: ...everyone starts off their life journey with a heart full of love and a mind that is forever curious.

Scholars and decision-makers have unanimously agreed that children are our future so they began to educate them with revised, user-friendly and more comprehensive studies that embraced intellectual, physical, moral and spiritual wellbeing.

The conscious mind is like the tip of the iceberg, as you know, and the subconscious, the rest of the large chunk of the iceberg - this is the limitless part where a great amount of knowledge can be stored in and retrieved from. Imagine that the conscious mind is the door-keeper; it may not be easy to dodge its eyes and access the subconscious. This can be done through the meditative state or the Alpha state of the mind. However, the conscious mind is also useful because it has the ability to ask questions, to explore and to discover so we encourage our children to use both the conscious and subconscious minds,

...and voilà, education is so much more fun!

Children sit comfortably with their legs crossed and eyes closed; they focus on breathing. When they reach the desired Alpha state, they slowly open their eyes. Concepts are then presented to them by a facilitator together with audio-visual aids. Through this method, children acquire a great amount of knowledge in a flash. Consolidation of learning is attained through student-led practical tasks during children's waking hours when their conscious minds are at their best. Children's queries are addressed by the facilitators during this time. Teachers are known as facilitators as they facilitate and encourage learning. It is important for parents and carers to work in partnership with facilitators. A great many lessons take place outside, weather permitting, close to nature! The procedure is continued throughout their adulthood.

Learners accomplish reading either by using the old-fashioned books or shimcus – the abbreviated form of shimmering curtains. Shimcus are holographic, drop-down, shimmering quantum curtains, powered by mind technology, that catch floating texts from space. All you need to do is clearly say the name of the author and the title of the text to the activated shimcus and they collect and store the chosen text into their memory location. Readers can then retrieve the text and physically walk and read through it in their own time. The other day a granny was trying to catch a novel in her shimcus. The novel was called Elephants Fly by Prompt Pamela, instead, she caught a wrong one called Elephants Lie by Chrome Camilla. Not to worry, she just uttered the word, 'Delete', and the text was deleted.

The teaching and learning programme is carefully planned and agreed universally. The programme begins at home. Here is the programme used at home and at teaching and learning institutions including cross-curricular elements; mind you, this is not all-inclusive; this is just to give you a taste of what the programme is like.

From age 0-3: *(At home and playgroup) Love and Compassion; Warmth and Bonding; Nutrition, Cleanliness and Tidiness; Learning about Self; Colours and Movement; Songs and Music; Stories and Poems; Quality Time and Playmanship.*

From age 3-7 *(At home and primary institution): Love and Compassion; Pet Care; Shapes and Colours, Counting Pebbles and Flowers; Growing and Nurturing Plants; Cleanliness and Tidiness; Caring and Sharing; Learning about Self; Respecting Self and Others; Nutrition; Songs and Music; Reading Books and Shimcus; Breathing Exercises; Quality Time and Playmanship.*

From age 7 -14 *(At home and higher institution):*

Mind, Matter and Environment: Physiology and Mind Technology; Quantum Physics: influences of thoughts and emotions on matters; Hygiene; Growing and Nurturing Plants; Sharing Fruits of Labour; Pet Care; Science of Numbers and Shapes with 4D component; Revised New Economics and Resource Exchange Studies; The Three Rs - Reducing, Reusing and Recycling.

Empathyology: Empathy; Loving, Giving and Sharing.

Sociology: Becoming a good citizen; A Comprehensive Study of: friendship, companionship, relationship, leadership, workmanship (a basic study of fixing things at home), working individually and in a team; World Cultures: understanding cultural similarities and differences, and exchanging ideas; Childcare: caregiver and infant bonding; Giving and Receiving praises; Learning from Elders.

History & Geography: Ancestors' Ways of Life: learning from their successes and failures; Travel and Planeterism (formerly Travel and Tourism) and Physical Geography: then and now.

Hospitality and Food: Feel-at-home Study; Food: nutrition and nutritional balance; Cooking and Chemistry.

Sight and Sound with elements of Arts: History of Art and Music, Creative Art and Music (with magical components); Drama: understanding people and situations through role-plays; Literature and languages: ancient and modern literature, transcoding ancient to modern languages and vice versa; Quantum and Holographic Film making.

Sports and Well-being: Physical Study: postures, fitness, stamina and body flexibility; Relaxation and Mindfulness Exercises; Contemporary Workout and Dancing; Sports (Indoor and Outdoor): multi-level sky sports and ground sports; Sportsmanship: dealing merrily with winning and losing.

Triology with Metaphysics: Telepathyology, Teleportation Technology and Theology: the purpose of life – why we are here.

From age 14-17: Further studies and apprenticeship in chosen fields.

From age 17-21: Higher comprehensive studies leading to successful and fulfilling careers and interests.

What is more, children and adults are encouraged to pursue multiple passions so a politician can also be a musician, a chef or a puppeteer; a sportsperson can also be an actor, a stand-up comedian or a synchronous dancer!

We know that some of the above studies may seem strange to you; you may even think they are mumbo-jumbos. Where are all the usual studies? How come institutional education is completed by the age of 21? (We're pretty sure that Jamie, the boy in wheelchair, would have loved the programme). We remained stuck to the usual studies for so long; not that they didn't work, but it was time for a radical education reform.

As for the duration of institutional education, we felt that there was no need for this to drag on for as long as 30 to 40 years although there is no end to learning. As we make an extensive use of the subconscious, institutional education does not need to be longer than necessary.

By using the subtle energy system and mind technology, we get things done in a short space of time; therefore, we are left with a great deal of spare time. We use this time productively for threefold purposes - to learn, to enjoy and to share. To this end, we have Pie-making Day, Cake-baking Day, Fruit and Veg picking Day; Sky Sports Day, Ground Sports Day, Flying-boat Racing Day, Skills-exchange Day, Kite-flying Day, Fun-skiing Day, Language and Cultural Day, Yoga-mindfulness Day and many more! And, of course, all the usual ones that you have. We have these occurrences every day; every day is 'something' day. Some of the ground activities take place inside the auditoriums, some outside them, and sky sports in sky-arenas. Holographic images of the latter are projected on designated receptive fields for all to see and enjoy.

It is not essential to go through channels of authorities to have these events organised. Enthusiasts can just appear and participate in these events; some of them can choose to be spectators. No one's hands are tied. Everyone is free to ride on the crest of their creativity.

We get a great deal accomplished in one lifetime! It may seem to you that all we do is have fun. That's true! Through fun, we learn and share joy. Through sharing joy, we stay connected with the inner and outer worlds. We have come to this plain to have fun, laughter and joy. It is so much better than living in misery! We also acknowledge the need for space and privacy and, at the same time, we focus on teamwork. It is kind of what Leon had perceived about Japanese people. In fact, we borrowed your ideas. You gave birth to ideas and shelved them away; we unshelved and used them. Remember, you started the saying 'united we stand, divided we fall'?

We were fascinated by Maya's illusory bubbled worlds in which people were unmindful and separated from each other. We have found that big, imaginary needle that she was in search of; we named the needle 'connect-all' and it lovingly pierced all the bubbles until they dissolved and merged happily into each other, leaving everyone enriched, connected and jubilant! As a result, territorial boundaries do not exist in our world. Think of the whole world as URW - the United Regions of the World. We do have named wards for administrative purposes.

Our scholars acknowledge that the mind and body are interconnected. Together they can lead to wellness or illness so we have combined the study of mind with the study of Physiology. We learned from our ancestors that the application of knowledge acquired through studying a single subject can lead to solving fractions of the problems. You may find this odd but when you get here, you will see that our healing-facilitators (who you call doctors or medical practitioners; we don't refer to them as healers as no one can heal you unless you are willing to heal yourself; they can only facilitate healing) are great believers in all components of study. This helps to accelerate the process of healing in healing-enthusiasts (patients).

There are, however, women and men who prefer to specialise in a single subject, but when it comes to facilitating healing, they consult other colleagues who have specialised in other fields of study. You may have noticed that we are not using the term 'treatment', as for us, it implies a one-directional approach. Treatment comes from a source outside us whereas healing occurs within ourselves; the process of which is set in motion by healing-facilitators through holistic approaches and healing-enthusiasts' own effort and willingness. Anyway, we don't have very many of healing-enthusiasts as we tend to nip the issues while they are at the bud stage. If you go back to the teaching and learning programme, you will see that it incorporates all aspects of well-being.

As food provides nutrition to the body, we ask ourselves and deal with these simple questions:

What food are we giving to our children?
What food are we giving to our nations?
Is it laden with hidden piles of salt, sugar and saturated fat?
Or balanced nutrients?

At the core of matters, there is a single issue, and that is 'fear'. You deal with fear, you deal with everything and we do that by focusing on love (we are aware that the word 'love' may not be instantly palatable to all. If some of you want to trade the word with another word, go ahead, do it; choose 'compassion' or 'empathy', or a similar word for that matter).

The study of Child Development in your time claimed that babies were born with two types of fears - fear of falling and fear of loud noise. Such claims were debatable, but what about other hundred types of fears and inhibitions that were later instilled in them? We have taken care of that too. As a result, most babies in our time grow into confident, fearless and healthy adults. Therefore, we don't have very many wellness-regain centres (we mean hospitals) except a few for the odd few!

We know that we're treading on controversial issues here! We can see raised eyebrows! That's normal! You can rest assured that you are not going out of business because of these new age ideas and applications. You are moving at a snail's pace so it will take you ages to experience or bring about such changes ☺!

Oh yes, and you are right in thinking that people in our global village live longer! You may now be speculating on the issue of the increased world population.

211

Chapter 36

NATURE HAS MAINTAINED THE BALANCE; WITH THE increase of people's longevity, the birth rate has fallen. Besides, quite a number of us have mastered teleporting to other incredibly beautiful, user-friendly planets. Picture the world as it is now to you in your mind. Now, magnify its beauty, colour and magnificence – that is what these planets are like (not to mention our own beautiful planet as it is now to us).

Teleporting may sound absurd to you but think about those sketches of flying objects drawn by Leonardo da Vinci in the 15thcentury. Those extraordinary drawings appeared bizarre to people of that era. Imagine talking about airplanes or rockets to them who may not have a clue as to what you are talking about unless they are teleported to your time.

Most importantly, know that this is an abundant universe and an abundant thinking mind gives birth to abundant reality.

Let's now examine the popular concept of money or the monetary system. You want to know what has happened to the system in our world! Well, inflation went so rocket-high during and after your time that it did not only hit the roof, it went through the roof! Imagine buying a small loaf of bread for fifty thousand and one and a quarter Rupees or a portion of Nan bread and Tandoori chicken for three thousand British Pounds and point zero, zero and one pence or a can of soda for one thousand American Dollars and ninety-nine point nine cents. So the whole system irreversibly collapsed one day!

The world leaders realised that something radical needed to be done, so they invented a system that was similar to what some people in a village in India were following during your time. The makers of the new system furthermore devised a workable tracking system called New Economics and Resource Exchange to keep track of services given and received. It was not that they did not trust each other, it was because there could have been human errors!

Nonetheless, the whole system was not well received at first, and it created a lot of hoo-ha as we, humans, always do but eventually it got off the ground. Our Resource Exchange experts revised and improved the system further in our time.

Do we hear you say, 'Why should anyone work without a financial reward?' Well, we are already rewarded in kind with whatever we need to live a meaningful life. Does that mean we only have our basic needs met? Yes, it does, but we get more than what we seek minus greed and wastage and this is possible by shadowing honeybees.

Incidentally, in your era, these bees were mysteriously disappearing each year; they were on the verge of becoming extinct. You could say that artificial pollination could have been the solution. Many farmers did that on a small scale anyway, and succeeded, well, on a small scale. A farmer called John, tried this out on strawberries. What did he get? A few puny looking red-green strawberries as opposed to luscious, juicy red ones produced by natural processes. Moreover, artificial pollination on a larger scale would have cost you billions of dollars. When the ammunition industry worldwide was flourishing at rocket speed, where was the surplus money to take care of the food industry?

In the end, you could have been left without any honeybees. Imagine no bees, no pollination, no plants, no life on Earth (they say that when one door closes, another opens, this is also nature's law, but you seemed to have remained focused on the closed door for so long that you were unmindful of the one that was open). Something came to humanity's rescue at the last moment. More on that in a minute!

Coming back to the money issue, during your time, money gave rise to prosperity, affluence and wealth and the lack of it created poverty and hardship. The on-going money issues gave birth to proverbs like 'money does not grow on trees', 'money can't buy happiness', 'money is the root of all evil', 'bad money drives out good' and so forth, yet you could not do without money. Your concept of give-and-take naturally had an attachment with money so no matter how absurd it may sound, we removed money from the equation and just kept the elements of give-and-take.

Lo and behold!

The problem was solved.

Our experts know that the system may collapse again if the cycle is broken, that is, if more is taken away than given. However, the focus is more on giving so we end up having more than we ask for – the material surplus goes back to the cycle of giving. This is inspired by the fact that a honeybee gives a great deal more to the flower than it takes. What it gives - the pollen - makes the life of the flower better and what it takes from it - the sweet nectar - doesn't cause any harm to the flower and it takes only a little. It does not visit the flower another bee has visited. The world is full of abundance so the bee looks elsewhere and if it finds a wonderful domain of flowers, it informs other bees. By helping others, they help themselves. They know this and put this into practice, humans don't. Well, they didn't.

While we are on the subject of bees, we actually shudder to think that these bees were on the verge of becoming non-existent. The crisis was reaching a point of grave repercussions for life on Earth. However, your government and your people became aware of this peril along with other green issues and ultimately took prompt actions.

Remember, the thing we mentioned earlier that came to the rescue at the last minute? It's called the mason bee. The solitary mason bee, unlike the social honeybee, lived in a reed, a hollow wood or an empty snail shell. It didn't make honey, but it was a much more efficient pollinator than a honeybee. Just 250-300 female mason bees could pollinate a whole acre of a cherry or apple orchard. Nature provided a means for its own speedy recovery with these speedy bees. You made use of this provision effectively and cultivated a whole population of mason bees that saved life on Earth from being annihilated. Good job! Well done! And thanks!

Did people from our time and space visit yours who just appeared, disappeared and reappeared as and when they wished? Well, most of the time, yes, but Tranquil Trevor from our era decided to go to your time to live, have family and cross over from there even though he knew he would have to deal with a plague of adversity. Overall, he had a happy life there and his daughter, Radiant Rosie, was kind and caring, and she helped many people during her lifetime.

We didn't send people to you from beyond the 40th century as you, being in the 21st century, would not have been able to cope with them. We seldom go there ourselves as we are happy the way we are and we know that our happiness will have a positive impact on theirs. Having said that, someone from the 42nd century insisted he teleported to the 21st century. Guess who? You got it. It was Nhean, the temple guy!

The truth we referred to at the beginning, was familiar to awakened pioneers, scholars and enthusiasts. It posed rhetorical questions to humanity with obvious answers: Would you consciously invite something into your experience that is potentially harmful to you? Would you rather gravitate towards that which is good for you? Where do you think these questions are leading to? To karma. Your karma, good or bad, returns to you in like measures! That is the truth!

How would you define 'good'? You may ask; what is good for one may not be good for the other. Well, we can say that your inner self, your 'l'uomo saggio' knows what is good for you, especially when you can freely move along the emotional scale, you just know it!

✿ ✿ ✿

Chapter 37

IN THE WAKE OF HUMAN AWARENESS, THERE WAS A national electronic poll in a country based on the true meaning of democracy. A single question was asked to inhabitants of that country. The question was: Should citizens be actively involved in making decisions about matters that affect their lives? The result was a whopping 90% 'yes' with 9.99% 'can't be bothered' and 0.01% 'no'. This was followed by a massive awakening in this country that had previously remained detached and unconcerned. All it took was one country to change, the rest eventually followed suit.

The gradual process of practising doing-good-to-self-and-others (like honeybees) was initiated by each individual, each home, each neighbourhood and each country. They restored peace within themselves and in their households. They settled differences among themselves and others. Each person's small step was a giant leap for the whole humanity. You can do the same. Yes, we are talking to YOU (plus billions more). You can be at peace with yourself and with the world around you. You can team up with Maya or Ramola and Mosein or others, or you can form your own group and light up the world. Oh, we're getting so excited about this, allow us to be a tad expressive:

If all the drops in the ocean went with the flow
Oh, what an ocean that would be.
If all the sparks in the world were aglow
Oh, what a world that would be.

We know that there are unsung volunteers out there, but we need more! Take it as A WHITE CALL from us to you from across space and time - a call for you to return to peace, love and harmony. You don't have to move mountains (we would appreciate it if you could do that ☺). Take that small step - TODAY is a good day to begin! Just one good thought, one good word and one good deed from one person – that's all we need. One single ripple of good work will expand and merge with another ripple, and another, and another until the whole world becomes an ocean of your good deeds!

We live in peace and harmony in our world; simultaneously, we aim to have our hopes and dreams come true! How do we do that? In order for our dreams to come true, we need to dream first! And then...well, just imagine there is a block of flats and there are ten floors or levels in the block. Each level represents an emotional attribute that has its own vibrational frequency. Actually, there are more than ten, however, to keep it simple, we have chosen ten.

Before you look at the format of the emotional attributes, let's give you brief examples of the polarity of all that we experience. These are the opposites, for example, light and darkness, joy and sorrow and so on. Because of the presence of one, we know that the other exists, that is, because of darkness, we know that light exists, because of sorrow, we know that joy exists, and vice versa. By the same token, if we want to appreciate light, we acknowledge darkness. If we want to appreciate joy, we acknowledge sorrow. By acknowledging the polarity of emotions, we have learned to freely move up and down the levels and attain a good-feeling state of mind. Before talking about what we do next to achieve our goals, let's take a peek at ten levels of emotions:

Love and gratitude
Joy
Enthusiasm
Satisfaction
Optimism
Monotony
Dissatisfaction
Anger
Hatred
Fear

We need to identify where we are on the scale at any given moment, we acknowledge that attribute of emotion, we go with the flow, move on to the next level and gradually achieve that good-

feeling state of mind. Which level do we need to be on in order to achieve that state of mind? Well, the idea is not to suppress the emotions but to acknowledge them and to attain that ease of movement along the scale to reach that state (it is like adjusting the tuning device on the radio to the right frequency of the radio station you are after); and when we reach that state, we contemplate on things we desire in a way as if they already exist; we visualize them, we feel excited and grateful for them, and we see their holographic images in our minds; they then show up in reality with ease, joy and glory!

You can do the same, but if your desires are attached to doubts or negativity, you will push them away. Say, you want a new car, a new house or a raise in your salary, or maybe you want to become very, very rich and, at the same time, you may also be thinking: I don't have enough money or I'll kick his butt when I get very rich. Can you expect a positive output from a negative input?

How do you move freely along the emotional scale and reach that good-feeling state? If you are used to certain ways all your life, how do you do this? How do you take that initial step?

Do something NEW (yes, we know who said that), let your mind get used to doing something new, something that feels good. L'uomo saggio, the wise being in your heart, knows what feels good; it is always right.

You may already have been doing some or all of the following but here is a list of things you can do to begin to feel good and you can add more to it, if you like:

Love yourself. Accept yourself. Forgive yourself. Bless yourself. Appreciate yourself. Praise yourself.

Help someone. Love someone. Forgive someone. Bless someone. Appreciate someone. Praise someone.

Above all, praise and thank the Lord or nature - whatever you believe in. Stay connected.

Count your blessings. Smile. Laugh.

Live in the 'now' moment. Appreciate things around you as if you are seeing them for the first time! See wonder in that child's eyes and keep it alive in your eyes.

Go for a walk. Stop by the woods. Smell a flower. Taste a sweetcorn. Watch the birds. Listen to the waterfall.

Do exercise. Do sports. Do yoga. Do meditation. Dance. Sing. Listen to music. Eat a healthy, balanced diet.

Learn that new skill you always wanted to learn. Take up a new hobby.

Play with your little ones. Play with your pets.

Make that important phone call. Respond to opportunities that present themselves. Be at the right place at the right time. Finish that project.

Take your pick and do them on a regular basis. Take a small step at a time. Don't despair if you seem to remain stuck in a rut. Your mind is used to certain ways; it will take some time to change, but change, it will.

To convey our messages to you, we are using the past and the present forms of tenses that are conceivable to you but in our world, at any point in time, it is always 'now'. This was quite confusing for people of yesteryears because they perceived time as linear. They just about understood the concept of the probable future but it was difficult for them to grasp the concept of the probable past because moving freely across time and space was something that did not occur in their reality. It occurs in ours; this does not mean that we dwell on the miseries of the past; instead we endeavour to make some changes in the past for a better present.
And one more thing, we're actually using a language transcoder to speak to you because in our world, along with other things, languages have also evolved. Our current forms of languages consist mostly of one-syllable words; a phrase can be expressed in a

single word! This is very useful, especially for telepathic communication.

Coming back to the topic of time, we exist in the fourth density and we now know that time is spiral, therefore, it is possible for us to visit any point on the time scale but mind you, we do not and cannot change the past altogether. We do have limitations! We repeat, we do have limitations! We cannot bring back the lost and oppressed child; we cannot rescue the tortured innocent; we cannot wipe off tears from a lamenting mother; we cannot totally right the wrong in the bygone times; we cannot becalm the wild and savage elements in the past but we can make minor adjustments there to improve the here and now so we need your help for our and, of course, your own good. However, we only do this if we think this is essential as we do know that there are kind, loving, caring and wonderful individuals among you to whom we owe what we are today; otherwise, as we always say, we are happy as we are, so be happy and pave the way for our happiness or rather, your own future happiness!

Have a nice day!

✿

Maya opens her eyes at the end of her meditation session. The dim imageries in her mind are quickly fading away, but their sweetness remains. She tries to recall more from the shadowy images; she searches knolls and dells of her memory for any messages from the new world dwellers!

✿

The phone rings in the morning.

'Hello, Maya.'

'Oh, hi Antonios. How's it going?'

'Great, thanks…I'm back in London. Got my own yoga and fitness studio in Norbury.'

'That's great.'

'Listen, some people are interested in doing body and mind exercises. Will you be interested in leading the session?'

'Really? When?'

'TODAY, if possible.'

✿ ✿ ✿